# The
# Merry-Go-Round Man

## JOHN B. ROSENMAN

# Author's
# Introduction

## Three Kids on a Merry-Go-Round:
## Why I Wrote This Book

Thirty-four years or nearly half a lifetime ago, I wrote the opening scene of *The Merry-Go-Round Man*. On a spring day in 1954, three sixth graders ride a small green merry-go-ground outside an elementary school. I was one of those kids, and in some ways it was a much simpler and more innocent time than today. I remember that day well. Like Johnny, I didn't really know what "bra" and "laying a girl" meant. Soon I did, but at the age of twelve or nearly so, they were a mystery to me, as they were to a lot of young kids. Today, in 2014, with cable TV and everything else, even five-year-olds know these terms.

*The Merry-Go-Round Man* is a *bildungsroman* or a coming-of-age novel, and the rites of passage for the three boys take place in a society which at first glance seems so much more benign and G or PG rated than the dangerous R or NC-17 rated one we live in today. How "safe" was America in the straitlaced Eisenhower 1950's, which is when two of the novel's three sections take place? Just consider: on TV, programs couldn't even use the word "pregnant" or show a married couple in the same bed. Elvis Presley's sexy gyrations provoked angry controversy across America and made CBS censors demand (unsuccessfully) the emerging King of Rock 'n' Roll be shot only from the waist up. As for edgy, spiky series, forget about *Dexter* or *Breaking Bad. I Love Lucy* and *The Adventures of Ozzie & Harriet* ruled.

But for my three boys, Johnny Roth, Jimmy Wiggins, and Lee Esner, snakes crawled in the Garden even then. While Johnny Roth seems blessed by two transcendent talents (he might become both an unbeatable heavyweight boxer and a revolutionary expressionist painter), his path is rendered unbelievably painful by a rigid, unsympathetic father who insists he renounce both gifts and study to become an Orthodox rabbi. As if he isn't tormented enough, one night a demented gang leader tries to castrate him.

Jimmy Wiggins, based upon a black friend of mine, encounters cruel and frequent racism. Back in the fifties, it was worse than it is today, especially in the segregated South. This was before Martin Luther King, Malcolm X, the Civil Rights Movement, and all that came after. We attended an upper-class, primarily white school in Shaker Heights, Ohio with high educational standards. Johnny and Lee did all right but Jimmy struggled, getting D's. The Jimmy I knew, now long deceased, often said to me, "John, you don't know what it's like to be colored." Like the boy in the novel, Jimmy lived in a largely black section of downtown Cleveland. His father was an even more successful boxer than the one in the novel, though he was also cursed, for he never quite succeeded in winning the heavyweight crown.

Lee Esner, the third boy, is also modeled after a friend. Like him, he's a lady killer, irresistible to girls. In Lee's case, though, I take liberties. I don't believe the boy I remember was ever "collected" by a salacious cougar three or more times his age or that he became addicted to women. On the other hand, it could have happened. The Lee I know sure had a knack. It's dangerous to be too handsome, charming, and athletically gifted, and to have everything come too easily to you. Anyway, I wrote him this way. Please be advised: all three characters, including their names, are creatures of fiction, inspired by people I knew but changed in various ways.

There were some scary, ominous changes in American life during the fifties. I remember the Cold War and the Red Scare, the terrible fear of invasive communism aided and abetted by Joseph McCarthy. Also, Johnny's generation and mine was the first to grow up under the threat of nuclear war and the mushroom cloud of atomic and hydrogen bombs which COULD END LIFE AS WE KNOW IT. In school we regularly practiced 'duck and cover' safety drills in order to be ready for a Russian attack. The ability of nations to attack each other is suggested in the novel when Johnny knocks out Sammy Duckett and is called "H-Bomb Johnny!"

Why did I write *TMGRM*? Besides wanting to write, create, and express myself, I can think of three intertwined reasons: wish fulfillment, a desire not to let my childhood slip away, and a need to make sense of my past. I always wanted to be a boxer but couldn't. Johnny fulfills my dream and does it magnificently. Also, he's a brilliant artist, and I'm a writer. Second, while my past and the people and places in it have undergone a sea change in this book, I've somehow managed to preserve the essence and spirit of much of my childhood. Third, by recovering the past, I've been able to understand it and see how it has contributed to the man I am today. It all waits for you, dear reader, within these pages. I hope you enjoy your ride on the merry-go-round as much as I enjoyed spinning it for you.

John B. Rosenman
February 2014

# Part
## One
### 1954

"Round and round she goes,
And where she stops, nobody knows!"

# Chapter
# One

## The Merry-Go-Round Man

**S**itting on the spinning green merry-go-round, Johnny saw the elementary school door open and a pretty red-haired girl come out into the May sun. Shyly, he glanced at Lee Esner and Jimmy Wiggins. Lee, handsome and lanky, pretended disinterest while Jimmy, small and black, continued to push the merry-go-round as fast as he could against the concrete of the playground.

> "Round and round she goes,
> And where she stops, *no*body knows!"

"Hi, boys."

Like an evocation of spring she stood there, her budding body no longer a child's, which it had been just a few months before, but astir with new currents and desires. Her violet eyes sought out Lee, who blushed and looked away. Of the three, only Jimmy had the courage to answer.

"Hi, Rosemary," he said, hopping back on the merry-go-round. "Whatcha doing?"

"What are *you* doing?"

"Nuttin.'"

"Oh. I thought you were trying to make them dizzy."

"Naw. Say, what you been up to, Rosemary?"

"Taking a shower."

"What for?"

"Gymnasium." Gracefully, she executed a pirouette while they watched her skirt swirl up around her panties.

"You boys. You know, it's just terrible what you say when we shower. We're right next to you, you know."

"No kidding."

"Right through the walls. Clear as—"

"So what you hear?"

"Not telling."

"Come on, Rosemary. What you hear?"

"I'm not telling." Stopping, she looked haughtily at Jimmy while stealing a glance at Lee. "Besides, it's not nice," she said. "You boys!"

Jimmy grinned while she did another spin. "That's nothing," he said.

"What?"

"I said that's nothing. You oughta hear what we do."

"What's that?"

"About you."

She stopped, wide-eyed and no longer quite so coy. *"Oh, jump.* You haven't heard anything."

"Yes, we have."

"No, you haven't." She started another spin and then stopped. *"What,* for instance?"

"None of your beeswax."

"Please?"

"Aw, it's just about that thing you wear."

*"What* thing?"

At this point Lee laughed and Jimmy snickered. Johnny, who had climbed to the rounded top of the merry-go-round, flushed with embarrassment and avoided looking at her directly.

"Oh *that,"* said Rosemary. She did an embarrassed spin while glancing furtively at Lee. "It's nothing; half the girls wear them now and don't have *any* modesty. You know Barbara? She . . ."

"Yaa-hoo!"

"Whoop-de-do!"

This came from Jimmy and Lee. Another spin had coaxed her skirt up around her waist, revealing more of her tight pink panties. She pretended not to notice.

". . . stands naked before the locker room door and says, 'Come in boys, come right in and see my bra!'"

Bra. To Johnny, the word sounded exotic and mysterious, like others he had heard lately. Maybe it had something to do with "laying a girl," a phrase which didn't mean much to him either. Watching Rosemary spin, it seemed to him she embodied all the new questions and secrets which had begun troubling him just a month before.

Suddenly he had a feeling. It came unexpectedly, yet with a certainty he could not deny. Something was going to happen. Any moment now—any moment!—something was going to happen to him that had never happened before. He didn't know what it was, but the fact it was completely new and undefined did not make it any less real. If anything, he knew for sure it was about to happen because it *was* just a feeling.

He was so stunned he almost fell off the top of the merry-go-round. Snapping out of it, he found that Jimmy had jumped up and was actually trying to get Rosemary to give them a look at her bra.

"C'mon, Rosemary, lemme see. I won't tell nobody."

"Let go, Jimmy!"

"Just one look and I'll—"

"You're awful! Let go!"

Jimmy broke into laughter. Holding her hand, he pulled at her blouse to get a peek. She screamed and tried to escape just as an ice cream wagon stopped by the curb, bell ringing.

"Hey, Rosemary, how 'bout buying me a Popsicle?"

"I'll buy you a black eye, Jimmy!"

"Only costs a nickel. Bet you'd buy *Lee* one if he asked you."

"Would not!"

"Would too! Bet you'd like to eat 'im up yourself just like an Eskimo Pie and throw away the stick!"

Rosemary blushed a deeper red and screamed as Jimmy pulled at her blouse again.

"Aw, c'mon. We won't tell nobody."

"I'll tell my big brother!"

"Shoot, I'm not scared of no big brother."

"Well, you'd better be. Brad's in the tenth grade and he can stamp any ten of you!"

"Yeah? Well, you can tell him—"

"He's got a gang too," she said, looking imploringly at Lee. "They'll beat your friends up!"

"Aw, I can protect them any day."

"Hear that, Johnny?" Lee winked. "Jimmy's gonna protect us."

"Yeah? How's he going to do that?"

"Simple, he's going to use his good looks."

"His good looks? Boy, are we in trouble!"

"C'mon, Rosemary," Jimmy persisted. "Bet you'd show me if I was Lee. I've seen how you been sweet-eyein' him. Shoot, bet if I was Lee you'd show me *everything!*"

Rosemary blushed and glanced at Lee in embarrassment. Johnny watched Lee laugh and get up to join in. Rosemary screamed. Then with a superhuman effort she pulled free and ran off, followed by Jimmy's buttery run of laughter.

"Bird flew the coop. Go get her, Jimmy!" Lee cried.

"Aw, she's in the next county by now," Jimmy said. "Let her go."

Sitting on the merry-go-round, Johnny became aware of the fragrance of blossoms and steadied himself, not wanting to fall. Yes, the feeling was back, and this time he was even more certain. Something was going to happen to him that had never happened before, and it was going to happen any minute. All he had to do was wait.

# Chapter
## Two

## The Awakening

**M**inutes later, as they walked through the woods, Johnny had forgotten about the feeling and found himself wondering again what a bra was. If only he could come right out and ask. But he couldn't. They'd just laugh and call him a little boy and tell him he didn't know anything. And the last thing he wanted was to have his ignorance exposed and hear them laugh. At the moment, they were making their way through a particularly rugged part of the woods where he had to struggle to keep up. Lee's long legs were built for climbing, and Jimmy, the fastest runner he knew, climbed hills like a mountain goat. As usual, they were walking Jimmy all the way to the station, where he caught the Rapid Transit to downtown Cleveland. Unlike them, he did not live in Shaker Heights but somewhere his father called a "ghetto."

At the top of a knoll Jimmy stopped and produced a pack of Camels, which he passed around with an air of adult importance. Johnny took one and waited as Lee lit it, trying not to cough. The ritual completed, they all sat down. Lee lay back against a rock, a cigarette jutting jauntily up from between his even white teeth and smiled in a way that was already proving irresistible to girls.

"Boy, ain't life grand?"

"Sure is," said Johnny, glad to rest. Aware of their superiority to others, he set his cigarette down and wiped his glasses, grateful for the shade and the buttercups a few feet away. The feeling he'd had on the merry-go-round returned, and this time it was definite and overpowering. Sunlight bathed his body, and he felt the breeze blow through his veins and wash his hair in flame. Buttercups! How lovely they were, rich golden cups, how they had flourished in the field beside his home when he was only three. And how he had searched for the pods of peas beneath the secret leaves, for the peas that crunched so sweetly between his teeth. . . . Dazed, he fumbled his handkerchief away and reached for his cigarette, but as he did, the whole world shifted. An instant before, everything was one thing. Then—*blink!* and it was as if an enormous light had been turned on. He saw new dimensions and tonalities of color. Leaves exploded into a million different greens, luminous and composed of contours containing shapes within shapes. He felt his eyes move out, touch them like a hand.

"Hey, John."

"Wake up!"

He did not hear them. A cardinal lit on a branch, and he felt his eyes touch it like a hand and shape its wings. It was as if his eyes and hand were—painting. And it was not just the nice, correct drawings he had been taught to color in Miss Benson's art class but something so new he could not understand it.

"Hey, John, snap out of it!"

Lee's voice broke through this time and he almost came back, but the cardinal's brightness changed into Rosemary's red hair, and she was spinning in graceful pirouettes before him. With each turn another piece of her clothing dissolved, and he moved his hand to mold and shape her flesh. At some point in her turning, the mysterious thing called a "bra" stripped away, and he could see the profound subtleties of her form. She kept turning and turning, smiling for him alone as she revealed more and more of the beautiful subtleties and shadings of her body. He could not believe the pink buds of her nipples, the delicate softness of her thighs, the secret hidden places she revealed to him. Then she was naked, better than peas waiting to be tasted, and his whole body became alive in a way he had never known. Aching, he reached out to touch her—

His face stung. He blinked. Then his face stung again. Abruptly he found they were pelting him with handfuls of dirt.

"Crimmey, stop dreamin'. What's wrong with you?"

"Just thinking," he managed to say. "Where—where's my cigarette?"

"Right by your hand, dummy," said Jimmy.

"Oh."

Still dazed, he picked it up. Jim had introduced him to smoking just a few weeks ago, and the first time he had tried it, he had coughed and gotten sick. Well, Jimmy wouldn't laugh again. Carefully, remnants of his vision still clinging to him, he took a respectable puff, trying to capture Lee's casual flair without getting dizzy.

"Hey, lover boy," said Jimmy, "don't look now but I think ya got company."

"What ya mean?"

Jimmy poked his cigarette at a rise in the distance. "Got a skirt after ya, champ. Shee-it, they just can't stay away from you, can they?"

Lee turned and shaded his eyes in the sun. "Who is it?"

"Rosemary. She must a been following us ever since we left the merry-go-round." Johnny watched him get up and cup his hands around his mouth. "Hey, Rosemary!"

"She didn't hear you," Lee said.

"Shit she didn't." He winked at them both. "If we can just get her to come down, man, we can have ourselves a hot ole time." He cupped his hands and shouted again. "Come down here in the woods, Rosemary, I wanna talk to ya!"

Rosemary stood still in the distance. Johnny swallowed nervously, thinking of how her clothes had dissolved and of the secret places he had glimpsed. Now, Jimmy was shouting again. "Hey Rosemary, Lee's got somethin' to show ya!"

"Yeah!" laughed Lee. "It's right here in my pants!"

"Aw, come down, Rosemary," Jimmy shouted, his voice syrupy and dangerous. "Don't be scared."

He laughed in that throaty way of his and started playing with his crotch. Stunned, Johnny watched his brown fingers flaunt his invisible manhood.

"Well, I'll be a monkey's—"

"What?"

"She's comin' down!"

"Aw, stuff it," said Lee, getting up.

"Yeah, well just look at her hustle. She must want somethin' *awful bad*."

"I don't get it. Why's—"

Jimmy laughed and poked him. "'Cause you're here, pretty boy. Ain't I been tellin' you girls are nuts about you?"

Johnny watched Rosemary slip and slide down the hill in a shower of stones and approach through the heavy brush. Once she fell. Even before he could see the look on her face, he sensed what it was costing her. Imagine! Risking scratched legs and a torn dress, not to mention her reputation by going alone into the woods where three boys were. He could guess what they'd say at school if the word got out. Why was she doing it? Then he saw her face as she looked at Lee and knew Jimmy was right.

"Hi there, Rosemary," Jimmy said. "Glad to see—"

"I want to talk to you," she said, out of breath.

"Sure," Lee said. "What—"

"Come here!" She snatched his hand.

Johnny watched her lead Lee into a six foot high stone drainage tunnel nearby which he and Jimmy had walked through lots of times. He could hear their shoes echo and reverberate inside, where it was dark as a womb.

Minutes passed. They watched the tunnel.

"Man," Jimmy said, "bet they ain't just holdin' hands in there."

"What do you mean?"

"Mean Lee's gettin' somethin' for hisself. Somethin' *awfully* sweet."

They watched the dark mouth of the tunnel, which to Johnny now seemed mysterious and awesome in some nameless way.

"Ooo-eee!" Jimmy laughed, squirming with glee. "Betcha Lee's gettin' hisself some nooky!"

"Well, if he is, he sure can't see it. Must be black as sin in there."

"Man, you don't have to see it, just *do* it!"

A chill ran up Johnny's neck. "Say, you think Lee's all right?"

"What ya mean?"

"I don't know," he said, unaccountably frightened. "You don't think something's happened to him, do you?"

Jimmy rolled his eyes. "Ya blown your cork?" He pointed at the tunnel. "That's *Paradise,* son. Give everythin' in my pants to be there right now 'stead of him."

As if to demonstrate his desire, he started to unload his jeans pockets. First he took out a handful of baseball cards and opening a couple of packs, handed Johnny a flat pink square of bubble gum. Sometimes just to kill time, they skipped the stuff off lakes and ponds. Jimmy had a great knack for it. His record was seven skips.

Johnny watched him open a couple of more packs and jam the gum in his mouth till his cheeks bulged like balloons and he held a mound of Ted Williams, Mickey Mantle, and Bobby Avila. Al Rosen, last year's MVP and the 1954 Cleveland Indians' best hope to help them win the American League pennant appeared and was immediately buried beneath a Dusty Rhodes.

"Hey, where'd you get all that?"

"Son, you ain't seen nothin' yet!"

He watched as Jimmy's pockets poured forth like cornucopias. Inch long Tootsie Rolls, a White Owl cigar, jelly beans, a jackknife with a dozen blades . . . Jimmy dug deeper, his face straining, and when his right pocket gave birth to a mangled but complete 52 page *Captain Marvel* comic book, Johnny exploded into laughter.

"Man! How'd you—how'd you get—all that junk in there? And where'd you get it, anyway?"

"Standard Drug."

"Standard Drug? What did you do, use a wheelbarrow to get it home?" He stopped as Jimmy grinned and rolled his eyeballs. "Wait a minute. You mean you *stole* it all?"

"Yup."

"Well, jeez, Jimmy, what if you got caught?"

"Shee-it. Ya dope, ain't nobody gonna catch me. I'm too slick. Besides, whatcha worried about? We've snitched stuff from joints lots a times."

"Yeah, but just little things, not the whole store. If you don't watch it, you're going to get into real trouble someday. Hey, you mean there's more?"

Jimmy now seemed to be in the final struggles of an excavation so deep it made the exploits of archaeologists Johnny had read about seem like chicken scratches in comparison. Without being told, he knew Jimmy had saved the best for last. This would be his grand finale, his pièce de résistance. With a grunt, Jimmy's fist emerged from the nether regions and opened like a steam shovel.

"What ya think of this?"

He gasped. Jimmy's hand held the biggest, most beautiful yo-yo he had ever seen, so glorious in its gold luster he forgot completely about Lee and the hours he seemed to have been in the tunnel with Rosemary.

"Wow!"

"Sure is somethin', ain't it?" Jimmy beamed. "And looky here, it's got little red and green jewels all over it."

Johnny didn't point out the jewels were glass. Instead, he licked his lips at the words *The Supreme* which glistened on its surface. "Looks like the sun," he said.

"Know what this baby would cost if ya paid for it? A buck fifty! And I got it for nothin.'" Jimmy slipped the string's knot over his knuckle and began doing tricks.

First he made *The Supreme* sleep. Then he "rocked the baby" by parting the string with the fingers of his other hand and rocking the yo-yo between them. The yo-yo zipped and darted, climbed and spun. At last, with the ease he did just about everything, he sent it "round the world" again and again in humming orbits, snapping it back into his hand when a movement caught his eye.

"Well, it's about time!"

Johnny turned. At long last, Lee and Rosemary were emerging from the darkness.

As Jimmy hurriedly stuffed it all back into his pockets, Johnny watched them return. Rosemary, he could see, looked different, no longer driven and compelled but assured. Her face was flushed with pride, success, conquest, and—something else. He noticed she held Lee's hand possessively, as if she owned him, and when she looked at Lee, Johnny knew that whatever price she had paid, to her it was worth it.

Then she was gone, going back the way she had come.

"Well, come on man," Jimmy prodded. "What happened?"

Slowly, Lee touched his lips.

"Hey, wake up!"

"I am awake."

"Shee-it, you look like you been dreamin.'"

"Or sleepwalking," Johnny said.

"Yeah? Well, I'm awake *now*."

"What happened?" Johnny asked.

Lee gazed after Rosemary. He touched his lips again.

"Well, answer him," Jimmy said. "Did you cop a feel? Did she let—?"

"She asked me to the dance Friday night," Lee said. "Then . . ."

"What?"

"She told me how much she liked me."

"And?"

"Then she kissed me."

"*Now* you're talkin'! Then what?"

"She kissed me again."

"Yeah, yeah, you already said that. What I want to know—"

"She kept on kissing me," Lee said. "Over and over again. She just wouldn't stop."

"'Bout time. Now we're finally gettin' to the good stuff. Then what?"

"That's all."

"That's all? Didn't ya—"

"Didn't I what?"

"C'mon, didn't you do anything more?"

Lee gazed raptly after Rosemary.

"She just kissed me."

"And ya didn't even feel her up?"

"No."

"Shee-it!"

Jimmy looked profoundly disappointed, but Lee's face glowed, transformed by something Johnny also felt. Lee abruptly shouted with delight, making the woods ring.

"Boy, ain't life grand?" Laughing, he lay down and put his hands behind his head. "Hot dawg!"

"It's grand for *you*," Jimmy said. "Say, Lee!"

"Yeah?"

"Know what I'd *really* like to do? I mean, if I had the chance?"

"Sure," said Lee, winking at Johnny. "Screw Rosemary!"

"Naw."

"Yeah? Well, you sure acted interested."

"Naw, what I'd really like to do is just take off. You know, like that Huckaberry guy Miz Simmons makes us read about. Man, wouldn't it be something? You know, just to be free as the breeze, floatin' on down the river." Putting his hands behind his head, he gazed up at the sky. "Man, ya know, I just *hate* the sixth grade. The fifth was bad enough, but the sixth is gonna murder me. Seems I can't do *nothin'* right no more." He kicked his feet in despair. "Shee-it, I'm gonna fail for sure."

"Aw, you'll do all right."

"That's easy for *you* to say. You just bat them pretty eyes at them women and they melt all over you. Shee-it, pretty white boy, talk about being a teacher's pet! And ole four eyes here, ole super Jew brain, it ain't nothin' to it for him. He's so smart they just *gotta* give him A's, see, on account he's got all the answers. Ain't that right, Roth?"

Feeling on the defensive, Johnny met Jimmy's stare, wanting only to be left alone so he could think of this new thing that had happened to him.

"Well, after all, Jim, there's no substitute for intelligence."

"Sub-sti-tute! In-tel-li-gence!" Jimmy's lips drew back with such contempt, Johnny and Lee burst out laughing. "There ya go again. Spoutin' them fancy words just to suck up to the teachers. You fat four-eyed kike, why don't you talk like everyone else for a change?"

Usually it hurt when Jimmy called him fat or four eyes or a kike, but with his black face scrunched up so comically, Johnny had to laugh. Lee joined in, and in a moment they were all howling uncontrollably. Jimmy got so bad he started to kick the dirt, and Johnny found himself struggling to catch his breath. Then he thought of something so funny he poked Jimmy.

"Say, Jim, I got—I got the answer!"

"Wha—What?"

"Stop laughing. I said, 'I got the answer.'"

"To what?" Still laughing, Jimmy barely managed to get the words out.

"To the question of how to bring your grades up. Look, you say the teachers like me. Well, I'll just tell them you're my cousin, and they'll be extra nice to you."

"You crazy, man. I'm black!"

"No sweat. I'll just tell them you're the *black sheep* of the family."

Jimmy didn't catch on at first, but Lee did. He laughed even harder, and in a moment they were all howling again. Johnny felt

good. It *was* funny, and he had gotten back at Jimmy for what he had
called him.

Then things started to go downhill.

"Hey, man, I don't think it's funny."

"What isn't?" he said, still laughing.

"The crack about me being black. The 'black sheep' jazz."

"Well, you sure were laughing at it."

"Yeah, man, but I don't think it's funny. Ain't no fun being a
negro at a white school."

Johnny looked at him. Was he serious? Sometimes with Jimmy it
was hard to tell. He could be free and easy one moment; then before
you knew it, the slightest thing would set him off. He felt a stir of
anger. After all, it wasn't as if he was the only black kid at the school,
and Jimmy had called him those things. What right did *he* have to
get mad? He was about to say something about it when he realized
things had abruptly changed. Jimmy was kneeling; Lee was silent.
He felt his throat tighten. Jimmy was fun and he liked him, but he
was also a powder keg that could erupt at any moment. Above all,
he *was* one hell of a scrapper. In school he was the toughest kid
next to Sammy Duckett, and everyone knew how Jimmy's old man
had been a top contender for the Heavyweight Championship of
the World. All at once Jimmy rose with his fists balled, and he felt
sick. Fighting scared the hell out of him.

"Come on, let's go."

"What?"

"Let's go. You think you're so funny—"

"Jim, he was just joking. Don't take it so serious," Lee said.

"Ain't none a you a negro," said Jimmy. "You don't know what
it's like. Come on, John, get up."

"Aw, Jim, I was just kidding."

"Up!"

Feeling miserable, he obeyed. He wanted to run, but there was
no escaping Jimmy, who could outrun anyone. Numb and sick, he
backed away. The first blow came as a slap, and instinctively he
brought his hands up. Jimmy danced around him, taunting him
with openhanded slaps which stung his cheeks. Then in the fierce
way that was his trademark, he moved in and put all his strength
behind a straight punch which landed right on his chin. Jolted,

Johnny shifted his feet and lashed out.

He landed high, too high to do anything. Still, he was surprised to see Jimmy wobble. Moving forward, he swung again, connecting this time on the side of his friend's jaw. An instant later he was amazed to see Jimmy stretched out on his back.

Both of them were stunned, especially when Jimmy didn't move. At last Lee went over to him.

"Hey Jimmy, you all right?"

He remained still, his eyes closed.

Lee dropped to his knees.

"Hey, Jimmy, you O.K.? Wake up!"

A bird sang somewhere in the woods. Lee looked up at him in panic.

"Holy cow, Johnny, I think you killed him!"

He felt himself tremble in horror. Couldn't believe—

Lee slapped Jimmy's face. "C'mon, Jimmy, wake up."

A groan. Then another. One of Jimmy's feet jerked.

"Whew! Looks like he's—"

Helped by Lee, Jimmy slowly sat up. Johnny found himself kneeling in relief at his side.

Jimmy felt his jaw.

"Hey, Jimmy," Johnny said, "you all right?"

Jimmy turned his head and looked at him as if he were seeing him for the first time. "Man," he said, "where'd you learn to hit like that? I ain't never been clobbered so hard by nobody!"

"I don't know. I just . . ." He gave up trying to answer as joy and astonishment swept through him. Could you beat that? He had just knocked Jimmy Wiggins on his ass! *He* had done it! He raised his fist and looked at it like he'd never seen it before. For a moment the vision returned and he watched his hand open and blossom at the end of his wrist like a flower. So it could do *two* things! Not only could it touch and shape and create, but it could also destroy. He gazed at it in amazement. Then he saw they were looking at him in amazement too. Amazement and something else. Respect. Jimmy, he could tell, was quickly revising his view of himself in relation to him. And Lee, as if to echo Jimmy's thoughts, burst out, "I don't believe it. Holy Toledo, pudgy Roth's a killer!"

"You all right, Jim?" Johnny asked again. Already pride in what he'd done was softening into concern. Jimmy, though, seemed not only to be all right but to be rapidly returning to his feisty, irrepressible self. "Yeah, I'm fine," he said, brushing himself off. "Takes more than a lucky punch to put me down. C'mon, I don't want a miss the street car."

They continued on. As before, Jimmy led while he brought up the rear. But while things looked the same, somehow they were different because of the feelings he'd had about the cardinal and Rosemary and the shocking wonder of having knocked out his friend. In a way things were the same and yet different. It was still him. He looked the same and had the same body, but now he felt heady, a bit drunk like when his father gave him a little Mogen David to drink at Passover. Now even the trees looked different, suffused with sun and intensely alive.

# Chapter
## Three

### Congratulations

"**J**immy! Jimmy! Time to get up!"

Silence. Though only six thirty, already it was so warm he'd thrown his covers off. Completely naked, he lay untroubled by his mother's summons.

"Jimmy Wiggins Jr., if you ain't up in five seconds, I'm gonna take my switch and lay it alongside your head!"

That did it. For four seconds he remained still, then in the super-energetic way he did just about everything except his school work, he leaped out of bed. Coming awake required just two seconds and followed a daily ritual. First, he yawned and knuckled the sleep from his eyes. Then like an animal he shook his lean black body and scratched one of his tiny high buttocks before opening his eyes. This morning, when he opened them, he found things pretty much the way they usually were. Bare floors. A broken chair. The rattling of mice behind the walls.

In the bathroom the toilet roared like a hot rod taking off.

Jimmy turned his head toward the sound. *He's up*, he thought. Slipping into his underpants, he left his room and looked through the doorway a few feet down the hall. There, as he had expected, his father lay already snoring again after his brief odyssey to the bathroom, a pint of cheap whiskey resting against his unshaven cheek. The bottle was empty. The bed, as usual, was rumpled and dirty, a relic of better days when his mother had taken pride in keeping everything clean and tidy.

Gazing at his father, he saw him as he'd been six years earlier, a clean-shaven man who never drank because he was always in training and prided himself on his condition. Once his father had taken him to the circus and carried him all day on his shoulder. He remembered his big booming laugh and how his father sometimes took him to the gym where he worked out.

How quick and strong he'd been in the ring! Lightning jabs. Combinations and footwork that had made him number five in the world. There had even been talk of his fighting for the championship. In those days there had been a different house which had always been clean and no rats or toilet that tried to climb off its moorings every time you flushed it. That house had been filled with his mother's laughter, and friends were always dropping in. Then as a tune-up for a possible title shot, his father had gone to Benton where he'd been destroyed in the fourth round by some nobody who had never done anything since.

Leaving the doorway he entered the kitchen, where his mother banged down a bowl of oatmeal before him.

"Aw, Ma, oatmeal *again?* Do I gotta eat this stuff?"

"Now you hush up. It's plenty good enough for the likes of you."

"Sho have had *plenty* of it," he said. "Seems like forever since I had myself an egg."

"Eggs cost money," his mother said, busying herself at the stove.

He picked up his spoon and stirred the lumpy mess, wanting to throw it against the wall, but a glance at his mother dissolved his disgust. Gray wisps of hair hung down before her eyes, and in the last couple years she had thickened at the waist. Once she had been young, vibrant, and full of laughter. Now she looked like an old woman and always complained and nagged about something. Resigned, he lifted the spoon and began eating, the smell of rust in his nose. Rust. That's all this place was. Sometimes he even smelled it when he was sitting in antiseptic classrooms seven miles away.

All at once he thought of what he had to tell Johnny Roth this morning. Boy, would he be surprised! He could just see the look on Johnny's mug when he told him *he* had been first. Wiggins the Winnah! Never one to be down for long, he dug into the oatmeal like it was spaghetti, his favorite food. Gone was the rust, his drunken father, even the sure and certain knowledge he'd be locked up all day with those snooty rich white kids who treated him like dirt just because he was poor and couldn't spell and add right. Finishing his breakfast, he bounced up and kissed his mother on the cheek.

"Boy, what's gotten into you?"

"What you mean, what's gotten into me? Can't a boy kiss his best girl when he wants to?" Moving close, he started tickling her.

"Now Jim—Jim—Jimmy, you—you—you stop it!" Laughing, she dropped her pot and struggled to free herself. Jimmy giggled and reached around her for the spot where he knew she was especially vulnerable. His mother's laughter rose higher. Desperately she tried to get away, but he continued mercilessly to tickle her. His hands darted everywhere like a swarm of bees, impossible to avoid. Finally, when it seemed she could take no more, he stopped and danced away, laughing and clapping his hands.

Angry and yet pleased and astonished by this irrepressible dynamo of a son, she watched him thump about on the cracked linoleum. Lawd, where did he get all this devilment? For a moment she felt proud and then remembered to be stern.

"Think you're so smart, huh? Make fun a your own mother who washes your dirty clothes an' slaves at other folks' laundry all day just so her fine hero of a son will have food in his belly and can go to a white boy's school. Well, I s'pose there's *some* folks who'd think they was mighty big and clever for actin' like that, but as far as *I'm* concerned, you ain't nothin' but a no 'count little nigger!"

"Aw, ma, I didn't mean nothin'. . ."

"It's all right, you just go an' get dressed. The *idea* of gallivantin' around practically naked with just your underpants on. Lawd, what will people think of me? As if I don't have enough to try me with your daddy out drinkin' and doing Lawd knows *what* every night, not bringin' a cent into this house." She flapped her hand in disgust. "Go on, git goin', or on top a everything else, you'll be late to school."

He felt a rip of anger. Why did she always have to say something mean about his father? Why, it seemed just yesterday he was lightning in the ring and would scoop him up with one hand and perch him on his shoulder. Then he saw his mother's haggard face and felt guilty. Impulsively he went over and kissed her on the cheek.

After going to the bathroom, he returned to his room and dressed in twenty seconds flat, hopping into his pants and pulling a shirt over his slender shoulders in one fluid motion. When he had everything on except his second shoe, a wisp of movement caught his eye. At the opening of a small hole, a miniature snout and whiskers poked out at him.

*Bang!* The shoe missed by inches, and he jumped up to retrieve it. "Spunky ole Samson, I'll nail yo' hide yet."

On his way out he checked his father again and found he still lay snoring up at the ceiling, the empty pint of cheap whiskey resting against his cheek. On the label the word "Old" stared back at him. Old something or other. He couldn't read the rest because the name was turned away, and he didn't want to risk waking his father by picking it up. Lately his father had begun to cuss and beat him for no reason at all.

Turning away, he returned to the kitchen where his mother unscrewed an old peanut butter jar and counted out two dimes and a quarter into his hand. The dimes were for transit fare, the quarter for lunch. Jamming them into his pocket, he kissed her cheek and bounded outside, letting the grimy screen door bang shut behind him.

It was hot outside. Though the sun was an orange wafer barely above the horizon, already he could feel the warm dirt through his thin soles. He broke into a run, cutting through a dozen yards where only an occasional patch of grass or flower grew, and sprang up the tall flight of wooden steps leading to the transit stop. He took the steps two at a time, feeling he could climb forever.

At the top he stopped and looked out over his neighborhood. The platform provided an excellent view, and from where he stood he could see block after block of houses which were little more than shacks. Many were raised on concrete blocks to protect them from rain and rats and had tin roofs which had rusted brown. Yards were hard dirt patches, sowers of blisters. Here and there chickens strutted and pecked about for god-knows-what.

By turning his head to the right, he could see even farther. Smokestacks rose in the distance, and in the yards rows and rows of tracks paralleled and crossed each other. Above everything else climbed the Terminal Tower, Cleveland's magnificent beanstalk. Ever since he had first seen it as a child, he had been awed. Even now, standing in the warm morning two months past his twelfth birthday, he could not keep from gaping at it as he thought of the excitement of riding the transit downtown with the Tower as his destination.

When the transit came, he pounced on a seat directly behind the driver. Behind him the tower shrank and eventually disappeared around a bend. Stop followed stop. The driver pushed a lever, the door hissed open, and people got on. By the time they reached Shaker Square, the car was nearly packed.

Three short stops later, right next to a Standard Drug where he and Johnny snitched Hershey and Three Musketeer bars, he jumped off and started running. He ran for a mile almost at top speed, feeling the power and energy surge through his legs and body. He did not think of the six and a half hours awaiting him in school. That he had learned to blot out; it did not exist. Now there was only the running, something he could beat anybody at, and the blazing spring morning. Finally, barely breathing hard, he stopped and waited as usual for Johnny.

Next to him a field of yellow and white honeysuckle drenched the air with sweetness. He watched bumblebees dart among them and two violet butterflies dance and chase each other without getting more than a few inches apart. Then he heard a shout and turned to see Johnny waving his hand. As always Roth looked a little comical because of his plumpness, and Jimmy shook his head in disbelief as he remembered the lucky punch of a week before. The memory vanished at once, though, and long before Johnny got close he was grinning with expectation.

"What's the big grin for?" asked Johnny. Together, they headed toward school.

"'Cause I won our bet."

"What bet?"

"Come on, man, you know. About who'd be *first*."

"You mean . . . ?"

"That's right, I beat ya. Yesterday Captain Wiggins done lost his cherry."

Johnny halted in amazement. Jimmy laughed in pride and punched his shoulder. He could see the envy on Johnny's face.

"Aw, you're full of it."

"The heck I am, buddy. Me and this girl where I live done it las' night right under her daddy's nose."

"You *serious*?"

"Yup. Did it on her daddy's bed while they was off somewhere."

He laughed again at Johnny's look. "Shoot, I missed gettin' caught by just a pig's whisker 'cause they came back early. He'd a killed me for sure if he'd caught us."

By now all doubt had left Johnny's face and they continued walking.

"Well, don't stop there! What was it like?"

"Super!"

"No kidding."

"Man, it was just great." Looking straight ahead, he rolled his eyes in ecstasy while taunting Johnny with a smirk. Roth aimed a punch at his shoulder. He quickly dodged it and burst out laughing.

"Now, don't kid me. What was it *really* like? Did she—did you—what I mean is . . ."

"Like I said, it was really great. We waited till her folks left an' used their bed."

"Yeah, I know *that*. But what I mean is, what was it like? Did you get her clothes off? Did you use something? What about—"

"Don't ask so many questions." Although Johnny was burning with excitement and curiosity, he found it difficult to add anything. What *had* it been like? A rushed thing, really, with a lot of fumbling around and little time to notice what was happening. He'd had his fly open and gotten her to pull her panties down. All things considered, it hadn't been the kind of stuff dreams are made of, but he couldn't tell Johnny *that*. Suddenly disappointed in himself and the world, he thought of the long hours ahead in school and distracted himself by poking the large pad under Johnny's arm.

"Whatcha got?"

"This?" Johnny plopped down his school books and flipped open the pad. "Remember the day we had the fight? Well, something about the woods got to me. Something about—I don't know. Anyway, since then I've been drawing things." He flipped the pages, showing Jimmy trees on a hill, blackberries and buttercups, and a bird in flight. Jimmy glanced at them with disinterest, seeing objects of light and shadow.

"C'mon, let's run the rest of the way."

He took off, running slowly so Johnny could keep up. Even so, Johnny fell behind, and he had to wait a couple of minutes for him to reach him. When they got to the school, Lee was standing astride the rounded top of the merry-go-round, his long legs parted for balance.

"Hey, I'm the King of the Castle! Got the world by the ass up here."

"If you ain't careful, you'll fall on it," Jimmy said.

"Not a chance. I'm the world's champeen. I'm the merry-go-round man!"

"Hey, Lee," said Johnny, "guess what lover boy here did last night?"

"What?"

"Got laid."

"Holy Toledo!" Lee bounded down and pounded Jimmy's shoulder. Then he did an odd thing. Solemnly, as if it were a great occasion, he shook Jimmy's hand. Johnny followed suit, and the three of them stood embarrassed for a few seconds, not knowing what to say.

"Well," said Lee finally, "I guess you're the first."

Formal recognition and congratulations made Jimmy feel better. Suddenly *he* was the one at the top of the merry-go-round in the brilliant spring morning with his whole life like a rising star before him. Surely, he had only success to look forward to! Surely, nothing could ever go wrong!

Then the bell rang.

"C'mon," said Lee, "let's get in there before old lady Simmons chews our butts off."

# Chapter
# Four

## The Broom Closet

They slid into their seats just as Mrs. Simmons was taking attendance, and Jimmy noticed that for once she didn't give him a mean look. As a matter of fact, things went well all morning and she didn't even call on him. And by gym class he found that news of his exploit had gotten around. Boys gathered about him in open-mouthed awe. Apparently he'd beaten not only Johnny and Lee, but everyone else as well. Warmed by their respect, he discovered the hasty act of the night before had actually been incomparably splendid and he himself had been a masterful seducer, wise beyond his years when it came to the fine art of loving. Not only did he excel in the bedroom, he was also supreme as a runner, beating all the other kids in the races his gym teacher organized. Only Sammy Duckett gave him any trouble, and Duckett, as everyone knew, was a *fifteen* year old who had already failed a couple grades because he was so dumb.

Best of all was the fact that Evelyn Van Deusen saw everything. "Evy," as he secretly called her, was the school's reigning queen and the angel who haunted his dreams. Though he only dimly suspected it, she was the reason his adventure of the night before had left him dissatisfied, for between him and the other girl had passed her blue-eyed, blonde-haired image—tantalizing, irresistible, not to be touched. He adored her, but did so as a miniature Tristan who avoids the object of his worship. Inside he knew she was for some reason forbidden fruit, a fact which made her more rather than less desirable.

So when he lined up with the others to race, he was sure to keep her secretly in the corner of his eye, and when he ran it was as her private knight carrying her colors into battle. Three times he vanquished all challengers, defending her honor from some dark if undefined menace. And after trotting victoriously back for the third time, he felt his heart almost burst when Evy shouted "Jimmy!" and snatched his hand. Her court, maidens lovely but not quite so fair, giggled and whispered mysteriously among themselves and stole glances at him with inscrutable eyes.

Soaring, he dashed to the showers, where he flicked his towel at Lee's butt.

"Yow!"

"He he he. Got ya, lard ass!"

"Oh, yeah? Cover your nuts, pygmy!"

Lee armed himself quickly, and they dueled back and forth the full length of the showers, snapping away at each other's vitals. The other kids scrambled for safety. Shouts boomed off the wet tiles. Rolling his towel up tightly, he soaked it in water fast and cracked its tip perfectly off Lee's thigh. Lee howled and snapped back, his towel stinging the air just an inch away.

When they returned to the locker room, Sammy was picking on Johnny again. Duckett was a bully, and what he lacked in smarts he more than made up for in meanness. Jimmy knew even he couldn't beat him, though he'd bet he'd murder him if he were Duckett's age.

As usual, it hadn't taken much to set Duckett off. Johnny had bumped him accidentally, and because he was plump, meek, *and* the smartest kid in school, Sammy had shoved him hard.

"Hey, buttergut, what'd I tell ya before about getting in my way?"

"Sorry, Sammy."

"Sorry ain't good enough. Remember what I tole ya I'd do next time?" He advanced on Johnny.

Johnny's frightened face made Jimmy want to step in, but he held back. Fair or not, you fought your own battles. He saw Johnny look around for sympathy, but many of the other boys had already had their run-ins with Duckett and didn't want to renew hostilities. Then he remembered how scared Johnny had been of *him* that day in the woods and something told him he'd better advise *Sammy* not to press the matter. Before he could, though, Lee butted in.

"Come on, Sammy, he didn't mean to bump you."

"Stay out of this, pretty boy."

"Lee's right," said Jimmy. "Don't make no big deal out of it."

Two against one changed things slightly. Sammy, the tallest boy in the room except for Lee, paused and rubbed his chin, which sported black stubble.

"Stay out of this, you guys. Ain't none of your business."

"Just let it go, and we will."

"Butt out, nigger. Get back to your shack in jig town 'fore I stomp you."

"Stay out of this, Jim," Johnny said. "I can handle it myself."

"Shit you can," he said, furious at being called a poor nigger. "Look who's such hot stuff," he said. "Mr. Dummy. Two years in the sixth grade and no end in sight yet."

"Don't call me that."

"Yaaah, dummy! You sure must like it here, ya been around long enough. By the time ya graduate, dummy, you'll be so old you'll need a cane just to go to the can." He started hobbling across the floor so comically, a couple of faces split into grins.

Like a bull pricked by a picador, Sammy turned, trying to cope with Jimmy's wit. His face darkened. Slowly, he realized some of the boys were laughing at him and bunched his fists.

"Come here, Wiggins!"

"Yah, dummy!" Darting here and there about Duckett, he felt the old craziness seize him. It was a mood he was usually only dimly aware of, a perverse tendency to take great risks. Now, in the hurricane's eye, he flirted openly with danger. Inspired by the kids' grins and rapt attention, he toyed with disaster on his slippery stage, eluding the older, bigger boy again and again while his heart pounded with a reckless joy.

Then he was hit by a stroke of genius.

"Hey," he said, "I got it! Know why Sammy ain't passed the sixth grade yet? 'Cause he's in love with ole Miz Simmons. He loves her so much he can't *stand* to go!"

"Sure!" laughed Lee. "Sammy goes for the grandmotherly type."

"Yup!" Jimmy said, hopping about just out of reach. "And ole Simmons, she sure do go for hot lips Duckett. That's why she keeps him after school all the time. Say, wonder what they do when they're all alone?"

Johnny's eyes lit up. "Elementary, my dear Wiggins. They smooch it up!"

"Right! I can see them now." Puckering his lips, he produced the sound of a long drawn-out kiss which acquired a prodigious suction as its participants strained to extricate themselves. Eventually it climaxed in an explosive smack just like a cork being pulled from a bottle.

This broke the boys up completely. Before, they had tried to hide their grins; now they burst into laughter and catcalls. Duckett spun to threaten them and finding them beyond his control, charged Wiggins.

Jimmy slipped aside and struck out. Bop. Bop! Bop! Bop! Again and again he darted away, slippery as a weasel. Once Sammy almost cornered him against the lockers, but he squirmed away, continuing to pop him with jabs. Wiggins the Winnah! See Him Move! Pow! There goes the left! Zap! A right to the chin! See him come in. Bigger. Stronger. Then at the last second, when he's almost got you, slip away, move like lightning, out-dance, out-think, out-everything the slow-moving moron, shoot out the left again just like daddy. Pow! Do it again. Zap! Zap! Now to the chin. Bop! Wiggins— Champion of the World!

As he fought, the boys' screams urged him on. He was in the ring, taking up where his dad had left off. He was the man who couldn't be stopped, who was about to win the title. It was his glorious destiny, and so sure was he of victory, his grin didn't falter even when Duckett finally cornered him and dug a fist like a sledgehammer into his ribs. Knees buckling, he managed to get away and even land another punch. It whipped through Duckett's non-existent defense like all the others: a mosquito bite he barely felt. Craftier now, sensing Jimmy's hurt, Duckett pursued and crashed a right against his jaw. Jimmy felt everything shatter in the back of his head, and the crowd's roar dissolved into a blooming buzz.

Duckett hit him again. About to go down, half-conscious yet still confident of victory, he sagged against the bigger boy, who shoved him back so he could hit him again . . .

Darkness. A sudden silence. Then light struggled back, and he found himself staring at something blue on a white background. For a while he tried to puzzle out what it was, all the time knowing he *knew* what it was, and it was as familiar as his own name. Then something clicked, and he realized he was gazing at a whistle hanging on a string against a white T-shirt.

"All right, who started this? Duckett, was it you again?"

The words had sound but no meaning. He reached for the whistle and fingered it. Then the words had meaning too and he straightened up, recovering instantly and lunging at Duckett, who Mr. O'Reilly, the gym teacher, held in his other hand. To the boys, his helplessness had gone unnoticed. They'd only seen he was in a little trouble, not that he was about to go down.

"Whoa! What do you think *you're* doing? You little scrapper, you don't know when you've had enough, do you?"

Struggling against Mr. O'Reilly's bulging muscles, he managed a swing which missed Duckett by two feet.

"See?" Sammy sneered. "It was this coon who started it."

"Yeah, and it's me who's gonna finish it too, ya big dumb jerk!"

"Enough!" Effortlessly, with immense good humor, Mr. O'Reilly kept them apart. "Now, come on, me laddies, bury the hatchet before I paddle your behinds so hard you'll have to stand sideways just to pee."

The Paddle! The room filled with awe. Made of smooth, hard, varnished oak, the "Corrector" or "Leprechaun Tamer" as Mr. O'Reilly affectionately called it, was a school legend. All the boys knew Mr. O'Reilly had made it to pledge a fraternity in college, and they spoke of it with respect. The barest possibility its polished surface might be applied to one of their own was enough to quell the most daring of rebels.

But it wasn't just its healthy SMACK! or the authority Mr. O'Reilly's powerful right arm imbued it with that inspired respect. Even more terrifying was the *thing* itself, which was carved in the shape of a dragon's head, painted red and green, and had fire flaring from its nostrils. The nostrils themselves were holes drilled to reduce air resistance so when properly swung, The Paddle was capable of a fearsome whistle prior to impact. As if even *that* wasn't enough, along the handle stretched the monster's coiled tail, whence came Mr. O'Reilly's fond, if ominous phrase, "Time to take the Dragon by the tail."

But the Dragon's fiery breath wasn't needed. Deciding that

discretion was the better part of valor, they both grumbled and touched hands. Ten minutes later Jimmy was back in class, half-listening as Mrs. Simmons read about the contest between Hector and Achilles.

Around him, a current ran from desk to desk. He could hear it, a low amperage of praise:

—Hey, Jimmy been fightin' Duckett.

–No kidding? Who won?

–Aw, O'Reilly busted it up, said he'd use The Paddle 'less they shook hands.

–Yeah? Bet Jimmy was glad about that. Duckett's tough!

—Well, Jimmy was sure boppin' him. 'Course, he looked like he was getting his butt cut at the end.

His butt cut—shee-it! A couple more seconds and he'd have wiped up the floor with the dummy! Exalting in his latest triumph, in the admiring glances of Johnny, Lee, and other kids, he easily accomplished what he always did on those few occasions when physical victory was denied him. From defeat or the prospect of it, he snatched again the mantle of invincibility. Why, hadn't he out-feinted, out-slipped, out-jived that lead-footed lug? Completely forgotten was the fact, to use a phrase he'd heard at his father's training camp, that Duckett had put him "on queer street," and if it hadn't been for Mr. O'Reilly's timely assistance, he'd have gone down for the count.

As if he'd actually scored a first round KO, a few girls turned to look at him. And could it be? Yes! Even now as he sat numb in ecstasy, Eveline Van Deusen, maiden fair, was turning to smile openly at him. At him! His Evy! For a moment her blonde hair and blue eyes were there just for him. Then she turned back to the front, leaving behind a room which for some reason he noticed was filled only with white faces.

After school, he told Johnny and Lee he'd meet them at the merry-go-round and headed for his locker. On the way a girl skipped away from a group of other girls right into his path.

"Jimmy, is it true? Did you actually fight Sammy Duckett?"

Evy! He tried to answer while one of her friends suppressed a giggle.

"The reason I ask is you must be terribly brave. The boys all say

Sammy can be positively *ferocious* when he wants to be."

One of the girls giggled again and he frowned at her, turning back just in time to see Eveline move closer and flutter her eyes. "Jimmy," she said, playing with one of his shirt buttons, "I think it's simply wonderful what you did."

"You do?" he managed to say, not certain what it was he had done.

"Yes! Simply wonderful. Why, you wouldn't *believe* the atrocious things he said to Sarah Waters. Serves him right you should beat him up."

Though no longer stunned, he did not correct her. For one thing, her praise made him glow, and for another, he could only stare at her in rapture and drink in the incomparable sweetness of her breath. Never before had he seen a white girl up so close, and this was—Evy! Still, it *must* be a dream, for she did seem to be acting peculiar. Her eyes darted excitedly between him and her friends like bright butterflies.

"Aren't you going to do it, Evy?"

"Yes, go ahead!"

"Shush!" She snatched his hand. "Jimmy, come here."

"Where?"

"In here, the broom closet."

"Broom closet? I don't know. It's—"

"Oh, *please.* Just for a moment. I've got something I *must* tell you."

Numbly he let himself be led, dimly aware the girls were following and openly giggling now. Eveline's eyes seemed to be everywhere, to dance constantly about in bright, restless excitement. He could see little else of her except her eyes. They were all over, lingering nowhere. Now they were on his face, now on her friends, now on the closet door as she reached to open it. At the last moment something made him pull back, but the door was already opening.

Inside it was dim, though the door was still open a little. The closeness magnified their breathing, which seemed a bond between them.

"Jimmy."

"What?"

"You like me, don't you?"

"Sure."

"I know you do. All my girlfriends say so. They all say you like me *very* much."

"Uh, guess I do."

"I *know* you do. And you know something?"

"What?"

She moved closer and played with his shirt button again, her eyes fluttering. "They say you'd like to kiss me."

"I—"

"Oh, there's no use you denying it, Jimmy Wiggins. To tell the truth, I like you too. You're cute. And just to prove it, you can once if you want to."

"Can what?"

"Why, kiss me, silly. You know you want to. Isn't that why you're always looking at me?"

He tried to answer but couldn't. She had exposed his adoration, yet he felt joy. She liked him too!

"Well, what are you waiting for?"

Between them there passed another girl, the one who had groaned beneath him. She passed like a shadow, sullying the white purity of Eveline's features. He felt himself yearn toward her, yet froze.

"Well," she huffed, "if you won't kiss me, I'll just have to kiss you. But first, you *must* close your eyes."

He swallowed and obeyed, waiting for the miracle. Then, when it seemed he had waited forever, he opened his eyes, blinked, and saw her. She was at the door, her eyes now different. Her mouth twisted horribly, slashing her lovely face.

"You ugly nigger, did you think I'd let you even *touch* me?"

A moment later the door slammed behind her and he heard the lock click.

"Evy?"

Groping for the knob, he found he couldn't turn it.

"Evy?"

In total darkness he heard faint laughter and shook the knob violently. "Evy, let me out! Please!"

Looking down he saw a sliver of light, and a new understanding began to form in his rising panic. She would not, could not, do this! There must be some mistake! Striking the door, he screamed her name over and over, pounding the hard wood to deny the horror of what she had done. Finally, when he could do it no longer, his knees buckled and he slipped to the floor. Curled up on his side, he lay with the cold tile against his cheek, staring blindly into nothing as he started to cry in the blackness.

# Chapter Five

## Collection Day

**S**mack!
  *Smack!*
*Smack!*

A flash of light. Another white rocket in the sun. This time, though, the angle was awry, the missile out of control. Rising from the sidewalk, it climbed on a line that would take it out of this galaxy altogether. Dropping his bag he streaked across the lawn, darting perilously close to Mrs. Williams' petunia bed where he leaped up and at the last instant stuck out his hand.

*Smack!*

Descending to Earth, he stood lean and graceful in the sun, the rolled up copy of *The Cleveland Press* with its crew of Dick Tracy and Mandrake the Magician safe in his hand. That had been close!

He reclaimed his bag and after hoisting its burden of newspapers to his shoulder, went to the front door by taking the more orthodox flagstone route designed for the purpose. When Mrs. Williams, a close friend of his mother's, answered the bell, he handed her paper over.

"How much do I owe you, Lee?"

"A dollar and seventy-five cents, ma'am."

Though she paid him promptly every week, she always asked how much it was. Accepting the coins she doled out from a tiny purse, he punched her card and smiled politely. In the background he could hear her radio gabbing away about communism and Joseph McCarthy, who was some big shot that had gotten in trouble.

"I'll see you next week, Lee. Be sure to say hello to your mother now for me, won't you?"

"I will. Thank you, Mrs. Williams."

Mrs. Williams was the last of his house customers. Ahead there remained only a stretch of apartment buildings along Van Aken Boulevard. Since each of the buildings accommodated five or six customers, he could finish his route quickly even though they represented the bulk of his trade. The only problem was, between him and freedom there rose an obstacle. Mrs. Futch.

He froze in the act of launching *The Cleveland Press* toward Venus. Every day it seemed harder to sneak past her. At first she had just smiled when he collected. Then she had gotten friendly and started to joke about how "pretty" he was. Lately, however, she seemed to be actually waiting for him, so even though he tried to sneak past, she still caught him half the time. And today he could not possibly avoid her. It was collection day.

Putting her out of his mind, he breezed through each building in a matter of minutes. One customer, Mr. Daniel, answered the door drunk as usual, and the news he was three weeks overdue didn't exactly please him. *Whadya mean overdue? Goddamn it, paid ya just last week!* Politely, as his mother had taught him, he absorbed the man's abuse, and when Mr. Daniel stopped for air, he showed him just as politely where he had stopped punching his card three weeks ago.

Usually that was enough for his few difficult customers, but this time Mr. Daniel was not pacified or chastened by Lee's faint air of moral superiority. Aware his best tactic had failed, he half-listened while Mr. Daniel accused him of outright swindle and moved slightly so he could see around him. Three years ago when he had started his route, he'd found you could learn a lot if you just kept your eyes and ears open. A newspaper route was like a stage drama. Behind each door was a story. Sometimes when they opened their doors, they shamelessly fed you slices of their lives. Today he spotted a nylon stocking on the floor. From past observation he knew Mr. Daniel lived with a girlfriend who threatened to leave him if he didn't stop drinking and get a job. Maybe she had just done that and left a stocking behind. If so he'd better wait till next time when Mr. Daniel was feeling friendlier.

Mr. Daniel was one thing, Mrs. Futch quite another. The closer he got to her apartment, the more he thought of her. Why did she tease him in such a manner? And why did he feel so shy and

embarrassed when she did? It wasn't exactly a *bad* feeling. In a way
her attentions pleased him. Still, he was used to feeling confident
and in charge, and it bothered him when things were different.

By the time he reached her building his mouth was dry, and
the carpeted hallways were so soundless he could hear his heart
pound. First, he collected from Mrs. Bishop. Then Mr. Fisher. They
both smiled and paid without protest. Mr. Fisher even gave him a
couple dollars and flapped a magnanimous hand.

"Keep the change, sport."

Next was *Mrs. Futch*. He thought of skipping her but rejected the
idea. Heck, he'd only have to collect tomorrow. He swallowed and
pressed her bell.

He heard the chimes ring in her living room. That was something
else which distinguished her from his other customers. They
accepted the bells which came with their apartments. She wanted
*chimes.*

When there was no answer, he sighed with relief. Looks like—

The door opened and she stood there, plump and attractive.
He noticed she was wearing sandals, tight toreador pants, and a
lilac blouse with the upper buttons left open. She wore the blouse
casually on the outside of her pants, and the cuffs bunched in a flare
of lacework at her wrists. Altogether, he had to admit she was some
looker!

"Well, howdy, lover! What brings you my way?"

Blushing, he handed her paper over and fumbled at the ring of
cards on his belt. It didn't come.

"Collection day, Mrs. Futch. You owe . . ."

Struggling, he managed to free the cards, but the card puncher
in his jeans was caught. Finally he rescued it. "A dollar and seventy-
five cents," he said, finishing his sentence.

"What for?"

"Uh, the paper."

"Is that *all* you want?"

"Ma'am?"

"I said, 'Is that *all* you want?'"

He frowned. What was she getting at? "Oh, yes, a dollar and
seventy-five cents. You owe for just one week, Mrs. Futch."

"Please, don't be so formal."

"Ma'am?"

"You don't have to call me Mrs. Futch, you know. Besides, it sounds so much like something else, something not so nice." She winked. "If you get what I mean."

He felt his face warm. She laughed and poked him.

"Call me Lilah, O.K.?"

"Lilah?"

"Uh huh."

"Sure, O.K. I mean, if you want."

"Oh, I do. Anyway, let me get my purse."

She left and he waited, wanting to run away and finish his route.

"Lee," she called.

"Yes, Mrs. Futch?"

"Could you come here, please?'"

"Ma'am?"

"I said, 'Could you come here, please?'"

He paused. Only on rare occasions had he been asked to enter an apartment, and it was always just inside the door. She was calling him from where the *chimes* were. Nervously he ventured inside.

He found her in the living room, which was voluptuous in every way and reflected a woman who liked to indulge herself. To his left he saw a small alcove in the wall with golden chimes of different lengths in it. Stunned, he moved out across the plush carpet like it was thin ice, blinking at velvet drapes and porcelain figures on a wine table.

"Mrs. Futch?"

"Lilah."

"Oh, yeah." He lifted his arms, the cards in one hand, the puncher in the other. "Lilah."

"That's better," she beamed. "Now, why don't you give me those silly things? I get the jitters just watching them."

Before he could protest, she took them and dropped them on a table. He felt her look him over.

"How old are you, Lee?"

"I just turned thirteen a week ago," he said proudly.

"Thirteen?" She came over. "But you're so tall. Wanna know something, Birthday Boy? You're as tall as *I* am. And so cute, too. Bet all the girls go for you."

He blushed and looked away, remembering his mother's warnings never to enter a customer's apartment. God, why didn't he get out of here? He wanted to but couldn't seem to move his feet. He gazed at her, just inches away.

"Actually, I don't go much for girls."

"Oh, my!" she said, breaking up. He felt instantly foolish, like a kid before a grownup. "Well, 'actually,' I don't think that's going to be a problem for long. Believe me, honey, I've seen lots of 'em in my time, and you were born for it. Won't be long before it'll be second nature and you'll have us all eating out of your hand." She reached out and patted his cheek, her voice going softer than anything he had ever heard. "And your skin's so smooth too, just like a babe's. Yessir, just like a babe in the woods, like I used to be."

He frowned and stepped back. "I'm not a baby!"

"Of course not," she smiled, somehow close to him again even though he had moved away. "You're a man, aren't you? I was just remembering, that's all. Just remembering things the way they used to be a thousand years ago before I lost them. Things I miss and can't get back."

"I don't . . ."

"No, of course you don't," she said hastily. "I'm sorry. Ole Lilah is just feelin' sorry for herself. Don't let it bother ya, huh?" She smiled and patted his cheek again. "Anyway, you sure are a good-looking kid."

Though embarrassed by this latest compliment, he tingled with pleasure. He felt split in two. Half of him wanted to run from her warm breath and confusing words. The other half felt proud and flattered. Automatically a smile sprang onto his face, showing his even white teeth. She shook her head in wonder and then snapped her fingers.

"Hey, how about some ice cream?"

"Uh, no thanks. Don't want to put you to any trouble."

"It's no trouble. What would you like? Vanilla, chocolate—"

"No, really, Mrs. Futch. I—"

"Lilah."

"Yeah, uh, Lilah. I—anyway, I got my other customers you see, and—"

"*Relax*, honey. You act like I'm gonna bite you. Don't you want to be friends?"

"Well, sure, but—"

"Good. Then just plop yourself down on the sofa. Won't take but a sec. Then you can—Say, I know! How about pistachio?"

"Sure, it'll be—"

She was gone. Feeling unreal he went to the sofa, which proved to be as soft as his mother's. The cushion sank beneath him so his knees rose to eye level. He felt trapped. Why was he still here? He couldn't believe he'd let her talk him into staying and yet, here he was! Trying to sit up, he blinked about at his surroundings, feeling half asleep. A sheer black negligee hung from a bedroom doorknob, its hem just touching the deep pile of the carpet. Everything about the room exuded a feminine excess and indolence that answered to something inside him. Stretching his hand out, he unconsciously stroked the velvet cushion beside him.

Suddenly she was back, bearing a silver bowl which she ceremoniously placed on the coffee table before him. Struggling up, he found it contained two scoops of speckled green ice cream circled by a fringe of delicate cookies.

"Well, dig in!"

"Oh, sure."

He took a small taste and found it to be the most delicious ice cream he'd ever had.

"Good, huh?"

"You bet!"

"Well, it better be. It's from a snooty specialty shop and you wouldn't believe the price. Go on, hop to!"

He forgot her and devoured it. His spoon rang continually inside the bowl, giving off sharp 'pings!' The cookies were also delicious, fragrant and wafer thin. Before he knew it, the bowl was empty.

"Want some more?"

The look on his face was enough. Taking the bowl, she refilled it and returned. This time he didn't have to be asked.

When her fingers grazed the back of his neck, he started a little and felt his spine tingle. But he was more comfortable now and the ice cream was so delicious, he didn't want to stop. Besides, her touch was gentle and soothing and seemed a part of what he was doing. *Pistachio*. He had never eaten anything this good, and the word itself seemed magical and exotic. When he finished the second bowl, he was almost as disappointed as after the first, but this time she didn't offer to refill it. Instead she picked up the napkin and patted his lips.

"What is it?"

"Drop of cream."

"Oh, thank you, ma'am."

She smiled.

"What's so funny?"

"It's just you're so polite. You know, you must have called me 'ma'am' a hundred times since you came in."

"Well, my mother's always taught me it's important to have good manners. You know, like calling adults 'sir' and 'ma'am.'"

She touched his knee. "I thought we agreed you were going to call me Lilah."

Somehow the idea no longer seemed so strange.

"How about your brothers?" she said. "Are they little gentlemen too?"

"Don't have any brothers. Or sisters either. Just mom."

"No father?"

He dropped his gaze and looked away. "He . . . left mom when I was five. We don't know where he is."

"So there's just you and your mother," she said, patting his knee. She moved closer and he could see her sympathy. It seemed incredible now that he could ever have been spooked by her. She was so nice. Tired of trying to sit up on the soft cushion, he lay back.

"It's not so bad," he said. "Mom's real nice, just like you. We do everything together."

"Still, you ought to have someone. A boy needs a father."

This time the pain was worse when she mentioned his father, who he wasn't even sure he remembered. "Well, how about you? Is there a—Mr. Futch?"

"No. Or in a way there is. A hundred Mr. Futches."

*"A hundred?"*

"Hmm hmm. Give or take a dozen. All of 'em eager little beavers dropping in to help me keep up this place." She looked around at the luxurious furnishings. "A hundred sweet Mr. Futches with money in their fists and nothing to do except help old Lilah here live it up in the grand style. Plumb out of the kindness of their hearts."

The bitterness and loneliness in her voice reminded him of his mother whenever she mentioned his father, and instinctively he took her hand just as he did his mother's at such moments.

"I'm sorry."

"Why?"

"Because you've been hurt."

"My Galahad," she said. "Christ, a kid. Who'd have believed it? A wet-nosed, thirteen-year-old kid." Then her voice went soft again, and she was so close he could smell her. Her breath was a sea. He closed his eyes, then opened them, gazing at her in trust, loving the touch of her, the sound of her. "Baby," she crooned, collecting him to her, "my pure sweet beautiful baby. Listen, do you know what I'm going to give you for your birthday?"

"What?" Had he said it? It hardly mattered. He closed his eyes again.

"I'm going to give you for free what all of them have to *pay* for, baby. And you can have it anytime you want." Gently, she kissed his eyes, his cheeks. "Remember that, honey, all the ice cream you want and all sweet ole Lilah can give you. For *Free.*" Cupping his chin, she pressed her lips down on his, and he felt her begin stroking his thigh. A moan escaped him and his eyes opened in yearning, then closed again. He felt her hands move over him, undressing him like a child, and a little later he lay perfectly still while she did other things. "Now, listen," he heard her say, "don't do anything. You don't have to do anything at all."

# Chapter
## Six
### The Merry-Go-Round Man

Hours later, running home, he stopped on a hill overlooking the playground and gazed down at some kids who had gathered near the merry-go-round. Even from a distance he recognized Jimmy Wiggins because he was black, and it occurred to him that lately Jimmy had been acting funny, like he was sad or something bad had happened to him.

This was not true of *him*, however. Without being aware of it, he sensed he had found what he had been not so much looking as waiting for. Call it a purpose, or what he was born for. Call it what he could do well. Whatever it was, he paused, his body graceful with assurance, lean and loose in the late afternoon.

Then he whooped and ran down the hill, his empty newspaper bag flapping like a banner behind him. When he got close he saw that Johnny Roth and Sammy Duckett were at the center of the group and Duckett (horror of horrors!) stood boldly tapping Mr. O'Reilly's formidable paddle against one of his hands. Probably he'd snatched it from his office, and if Mr. O'Reilly ever found out who took it, he'd kick Duckett's ass from here to China.

"O.K., you chickenshit bastard, hand it over."

Uh oh. Duckett was picking on Johnny again. He looked across at Jimmy, signaling him with his eyes, but received only a dull gaze in return. Well, darn if he was going to get in this one. He'd better stay clear.

"You've got no right to take my lunch money," Johnny said.

"Aw, listen to the little lawyer. Well, I've got something here says different." Duckett tapped the paddle against his hand. "Come on, fat ass. Cough up."

"It's not yours. You have no right."

"Tell ya what I'm gonna do, punk. I'm gonna give you three."

"Leave me alone!" Johnny edged backwards, his lower lip trembling, and looked at Jimmy for help, but Jimmy was looking elsewhere. Then Lee saw him turn his way and glanced away uneasily, wondering why Duckett picked on Johnny so much. Maybe it was because Johnny was plump, wore glasses, and did queer things like draw pictures all the time. Why, even now he could see a couple of those art books Johnny had started lugging around with him lying in the grass. *The World* of *Cézanne. Fauvism.* No wonder kids thought Johnny was an oddball and picked on him. God knows, there was always some bully who'd pick on others just because they were weak or different.

Duckett laughed. "Look at him! Another second and he'll be blubbering! O.K., here goes. One . . ."

"That paddle's not yours!" shouted Johnny. "You stole it from Mr. O'Reilly's office, and when he finds out—"

"Yeah, who's gonna tell him, crybaby? *You?*"

"Maybe."

"Yeah? You and whose army? Shit, you're such a chickenass you ain't gonna do *nothing.*" He turned to a supporter. "Hey, Ward, what does O'Reilly call this thing, anyway?"

"Calls it lots of things. A pandybat, dragon, Leprechaun Tamer—"

"No, the other one. Somethin' about makin' things right."

"His 'Corrector.'"

"Oh, yeah, 'Corrector.'" He slapped it against his thigh a couple of times and advanced on Johnny with a menacing grin. "Well, maybe I'll just do a little correctin' of my own here. Come on punk, bend over and spread 'em. One . . ."

Lee saw the red and green dragon on the paddle flash in the late afternoon sun. *Poor Johnny. Looks like he's going to feel the Corrector's sting and burn from the breath of the dragon.* He could hear air whizz through the holes in the paddle as Duckett swung it for effect, and felt guilty for not trying to stop it. Then, as the dragon flashed again and Duckett opened his mouth to say "two," an image of Johnny in the woods darted through his mind. For a split second he wondered if he was worried about the wrong fellow and if someone should tell Duckett about the time Johnny had laid Wiggins flat with just one punch. But it was too late to interfere. Johnny was backed up all the way to the tree, and Duckett was poised over him.

"Two!"

"Leave me alone!"

"Three!"

The dragon flashed for a last time. Duckett brought it down . . .

Then Johnny did a curious thing. Reaching up, he caught Duckett's wrist and wrenched the paddle away. Turning, he hurled it so it spun end over end for a long way in the sun.

Duckett stood and blinked at his hand in puzzlement. A moment before it had held a weapon. Now it was empty. He glanced at Johnny and frowned. Then he sneered and pushed him. Johnny stumbled back. Duckett followed and lashed out. Johnny slipped it and off balance, still retreating, threw his first punch. It landed on Duckett's forehead and stopped him. Lee saw him drop his fists and a look of surprise enter his face. Never before had Lee seen such surprise. It was as if Sammy had seen something incredible, something absolutely beyond his ken which no one else would believe because he could not even believe it himself. Then Johnny, for the first time, was moving forward. Lee saw him set his feet and his fist shoot out and the punch, not an off-balanced slap this time but a straight shot, take Duckett on the side of the jaw. Even as it landed an immense change seemed to register in the order of things. Lee felt something sting his arm and looking down, saw three teeth scattered in the dirt. When he looked up Johnny was standing before a bleeding Duckett, his soft body no longer so ridiculous. Johnny swung from his knees and Duckett actually seemed to *rise* from the ground as he exploded against the tree and came off it, his mouth a gaping wound.

Johnny hit him again.

Duckett went down like a spike being driven into the ground, and as quickly as it had begun, it was over. The boys stood stunned. Even more amazing than the fact that Johnny was an unexpected winner was the ease and rapidity with which he had gone through Duckett. Not only had he won, it had been a colossal mismatch!

It was Lee who snapped out of it first. Whooping, he grabbed Johnny. Then Jimmy hugged him and pounded his back. Johnny himself seemed unable to believe what he'd done.

In seconds they were all shouting and slapping his back. A couple of his more casual friends started to congratulate him and then hesitated, conscious of his new status and their failure to come to his aid. Emboldened by others, though, they soon swarmed about him too like he was a conquering hero, unaware that from his sudden transformation he had changed back to his usual self.

"Way to go, Johnny!"

"Wow!"

"H-Bomb Johnny!"

"Kid Dynamite!"

"Did you see Sammy hit that tree?"

Along the street some boys were passing. One shouted over at them.

"Hey, what's going on?"

Lee megaphoned his hands.

"ROTH JUST CREAMED DUCKETT'S ASS!"

"What?"

They all laughed at the look on his face.

"I SAID, 'ROTH JUST CREAMED DUCKETT'S ASS!'"

"Man, you crazy?" They all ran to join them.

A couple of the boys finally thought to check on Duckett and after some effort, managed to rouse him and lead him away, clutching his ruined mouth. His departure broke the mood. Shaking Johnny's hand and slapping his back for one last time, the others drifted off, leaving a string of "nice fight, Johnnies" and "See you tomorrows" behind them.

When they were alone, Lee jabbed Johnny's shoulder.

"Man, talk about being a fighter! Johnny, you don't ever have to worry about being picked on again! Ain't *nobody* you can't lick!"

Johnny shook his head. "I can't believe it."

"Well, it's true," said Jimmy. "You went through him like crap through a goose!"

"Yeah," laughed Lee, dancing around like Jimmy usually did when he was excited. "And did you see him bounce off the tree when Johnny smacked him? Wham! Jesus, who'd think you'd be such a killer? You don't even *look* like a fighter!" Moving closer, he began pumping fake punches at Johnny, giving his nose healthy swipes between them like he'd heard pros did. "Come on, hot shot, let's see your stuff!" (Swipe.) "Bam! There goes a left!" (Swipe.) "Boom! A right! Esner's got him now! He moves in, throws another right . . . Roth's on the ropes, looks like he's finished . . ."

"You really want to fight?" laughed Johnny. Glowering, he raised his fists and moved forward, trying to look as mean as possible.

"Oh, no!" Lee skipped away in mock horror. "Save me, somebody, save me! Hey Roth," he taunted. "Heard your old lady just *gives* it away!"

That did it. Johnny took off after Lee, who found refuge behind the merry-go-round. Johnny ran around and around it, trying to catch him, but Lee was too fast. Nor could he go over it. If he did, Lee would be in the next county by the time he reached the other side. So all he could do was laugh and run around and around, stopping now and then to rest and swap insults.

"Come on, you yellow? Stand and fight!"

"I'm right here, slowpoke, come and get me!"

Finally Johnny urged Jimmy to use his speed to catch Lee for him, but Jimmy seemed not to care. Which was odd. Usually it was Jimmy who sparked their horseplay and did wild things. Thinking about it made him dizzy, as if he was only now feeling the circular chase of the last few minutes. Stumbling to the merry-go-round, he sat down on it.

"Hey, you all right, Johnny?" asked Lee.

All of a sudden the events of the last half hour crashed down upon him. The fear. The fight. The unexpected victory. The praise afterward. Elation and nausea flooded him. He leaned forward on the seat, his stomach racked by dry heaves.

"Hey, you all right?" they asked simultaneously, both of them touching his shoulders.

"Yeah."

"You sure? You aren't going to throw up, are you?"

"Man, get off his case," said Jimmy. "Can't you see he's sick?" He patted his back. "Just take it easy. Take some deep breaths."

Trembling, he gasped at the air. Surprisingly, he *did* feel better. What had one kid called him? H-Bomb Johnny? Huh, he liked that. Then he remembered the feel of Duckett's teeth against his fist.

"There's just one thing," he said, raising his head.

"What?" said Lee.

"Duckett. I hope he's all right. Jesus, I knocked out half his teeth."

"Hey, man," said Jimmy, "you worried about *him*? Don't you know the punk tried to make you eat dirt?"

"Yeah, but—"

"Well, stick it. That kind of talk's for losers. Be nice and folks'll just walk all over you."

Lee looked at him. "What are you so cheerful about, anyway? You've been acting funny all week."

Jimmy dropped his gaze.

"Nothin.'"

"Well, stick it yourself, then. No one wants a sourpuss around him all the time." He touched Johnny's shoulder. "Sure you're O.K.?"

"Yeah, I'm fine."

"Good." All at once he thought of Lilah again. Imagine forgetting her and all that had happened! Having remembered, though, he felt better than ever and impatient with anyone's problems. Why be glum? Why worry or be down about anything? Exuberant, he yanked Johnny to his feet. "C'mon, you deadbeats, cheer up! Tell ya what. Bet I can beat ya both to the top of the merry-go-round."

"Aw, that's no fun," said Jimmy.

"'Fraid you'll lose?"

"It's not that. Ain't got time for no kid games."

"I'll buy the next pack of smokes if I lose."

"Big deal."

"Oh, come on," said Johnny, feeling well again. "Stop moping around and give it a try. Shoot, all you black kids are regular monkeys, anyway. You'll probably reach the top before Lee and me even get our hands off our dinks."

They all laughed. Jimmy looked a little like his old self.

Lee backed up. "And my bet's only half of it," he said. "Whoever gets there first is the *real* King of the Mountain. This is no kid's game."

Jimmy brightened. "Yeah?"

"Sure. Whoever wins is Champ for life! I mean, this ain't just another game. This is the real McCoy, the one for all the marbles." Surging with confidence, he pointed at the merry-go-round. "Whoever gets to the top is the real Champeen! For the rest of his life he's on Easy Street! Everything's rosy and he's a winner!" Inspired, he shook his fist at the summit. "Believe me, whoever gets there first has got the world by the balls!"

Jimmy jumped up, his face glistening as he looked at the merry-go-round. Shit, wasn't he the fastest? Didn't none of them stand a chance!

"That's the spirit, monkey!" yelled Johnny.

They laughed. Shoving and jostling each other, they lined up thirty feet away. "O.K., ready you guys?" said Lee. "On your marks . . ."

They tensed.

"Get set . . ."

The wind snapped up. Jimmy's lips tightened.

"Go!"

They exploded forward. Jimmy reached it first and started up. Lee pulled him back. Johnny butted Lee aside and forged ahead. Then they were in a mad scramble and clambering over each other with murderous intent, each trying to climb over or dislodge the others. Their breathing rang in each other's ears, and because of their efforts, the merry-go-round started to spin clockwise in the sun. Suddenly Jimmy broke free. Kicking Johnny back, he grabbed the top, his shoes frantically thudding against the green wood as he strained upward. Lee countered by yanking at his belt and Jimmy's shoes slid back just as Johnny wedged himself between them and drove forward like a ram. For a moment they were all equal, piled on each other in a mass of flailing arms and legs, neither able to advance or lose an inch without the others. Then amazingly, with ease and alacrity, Lee climbed over them and scaled the summit. A moment more and he stood looking triumphantly down.

They got off and gazed up. Johnny shielded his eyes against the sun, which was behind Lee and almost at the horizon. Jimmy swore, his lips moving silently as the merry-go-round spun. Now Lee's back was turned to them, and they watched him pump his arms and shoot them his rump in insult. When he had almost reached them again, he spread his arms and whooped. "Hey, you guys, I win! Ya-hoo! Got the world by the balls up here!"

At last the merry-go-round stopped. Astride its summit, he stood directly facing them. Mutely they watched him pound his chest in a crowning outburst.

"Hey, you bums, I'm the King of the Mountain up here. *I'm* the merry-go-round man!"

# Part
# Two
## 1958

# Chapter
## Seven

### The Fire Escape

Through the window he could see the fire escape. Made of iron and rust, it formed a diagonal slash against the brick rows that constituted the wall of the building. At the moment he was trying to decide how he should paint it. Metallic gray against orange red. A bold slant against the precise symmetrical tiers. "Tension" and "antithesis" the book he had been reading called it, yet there was a unity of form and idea which went beyond their opposition. And the rain, the gray rain, the dark watery spatterings which had begun a few minutes after he had entered the room? How could he capture the streaking and dripping of the rain? Closing his eyes, he drew the image inside his head, using line and color and texture to catch the impressions he pursued and sought to coalesce.

Someone put out a cigarette in an ashtray, jarring his inner canvas. They had been talking about him, part of his mind realized. *The boy dreams in his classes. The boy walked out of school again and did not come back.* And worse: *The boy does not draw pretty pictures. The boy does not do what we tell him.* As his father would say, raising his gaze to heaven, "Ribono Shel Olom, what do You want from me?"

He did not want them to break his contemplation of the picture he was drawing inside his head. He did not want them to take him away from it with their criticisms and complaints. Resolutely, the part of his mind that was aware of them tried to ward off the intrusions which would disturb the part that was not. But it was hopeless. The ashtray rattled again. Opening his eyes, he discovered not the wall and fire escape he had been trying to draw, but Mr. Farragut watching him.

"Well, John, aren't you going to answer my question?"

Hopelessly he gazed back at the principal who sat behind a desk which looked like a forest of pen and pencil sets. "Fat-gut Farragut" the kids called him. But close up you soon learned there was nothing funny about the neat bow tie that rode snugly on his Adam's apple or the stiff, close-cropped red hair resembling a Fuller brush. Mr. Farragut, as any of his former guests could attest, was a tough customer with all the humor of a hawk in chicken country.

"What?"

His father sighed to his right. Daydreaming again. When would he learn to stop making it so hard for himself?

Luckily, Mr. Farragut was patient. "John, I just asked you why you left school at lunch and didn't come back."

Knowing the question didn't make it any easier. What could he say? Removing his eyes from Mr. Farragut's candy-cane striped bow tie, he glanced to his left at Mr. Murdstone, his cadaverous-looking art teacher, who sat holding what appeared to be some of his drawings. Sitting between him and his father was like being caught in a vise.

"I don't know," he said.

"Don't know? This is the third time you've left. Surely you knew you'd be caught. Why did you do it?"

Being asked the same question again didn't help. What could he say that they would understand or accept? Even though he was sixteen years old now and in the tenth grade, he still couldn't get along with them. If anything, it was getting worse.

"I guess I just wanted to get out," he said. "Sometimes school gets . . . well, it feels kind of like jail. And I get bored."

"Like jail, hmm, I see. And bored too. Well well. *Splendid.* Your attitude explains as well, no doubt, why you don't pay attention in class. Obviously we have failed you."

Damn it, why couldn't they see it had nothing to do with them and they shouldn't take it so personally? Mr. Farragut's plump lower lip quivered. Any moment now his bow tie would snap off like a grenade.

"I didn't mean it that way."

"John," his father said, "where do you go when you leave school?"

"Oh, I just go."

"Yes, but where?"

"Here and there."

"John," his father said, "I want an answer. Now tell me: *where do you go?*"

"Uh, sometimes I ride the rapid transit."

"The rapid transit? Where do you go?"

"For a ride."

"Where to?"

"Well, sometimes I go to Cleveland."

"*Downtown* Cleveland?"

"Yes."

"And what do you do there?"

"Walk around."

"Walk around?"

"Yes."

His father paused, rapidly losing his patience. "John, you will answer me at once! Why do you go to Cleveland? What do you do there?"

He swallowed. So he'd finally been cornered, just as he should have known. He closed his eyes and opened them. Outside, the rain had stopped. The fire escape glistened in the sun. He swallowed again, anticipating his father's anger.

"The art museum," he said. "I go to the art museum."

His father's cheeks hardened. Mr. Farragut frowned.

"And what do you do there?" asked Mr. Murdstone, speaking for the first time.

"I look around."

"Look around? What do you see?"

Marble corridors echoed beneath his feet. Moving past a Cubist exhibit, he entered the room where the nudes were. Forms leaped out to meet him, forms caught between sensualism and spiritualism, earth and heaven. His footsteps faded. Something was happening to his eyes. Something had been happening to his eyes for a long time. He felt them reach out to touch, to feel. He was falling into the forms, drawing them in his mind—

"John!" his father said.

"I draw," he answered. "I make sketches of pictures I see in the galleries. And later . . . later I draw them at home from memory, sometimes in oils, sometimes . . ."

He stopped. He had said too much. There had been no need for it.

As if to worsen matters, Mr. Murdstone passed the drawings to his father. "These are some I found in his locker," he said. "Mr. Farragut has already seen them."

Expressionlessly, his father went through them. "I can't say I've seen these before, but I've seen some just like them."

"Then you knew he was drawing?" asked Mr. Farragut.

"Oh, yes," he said, shrugging and making a gesture of resignation Johnny recognized as part of a heritage thousands of years old. "My son, the artist. You should have seen his room before I ordered him not to do it anymore. Paint on the walls and floor, paint everywhere. Sometimes his mother and I couldn't even enter his room, it was so filled with drawings."

"If you ordered him to stop, how could he continue? Art class here lasts only fifty minutes. Mr. Murdstone found dozens."

Again his father shrugged. "My son is . . . resourceful. This foolishness of his, he knows how to deceive his mother and me so he can pursue it. Gentlemen, I own a building with thirty apartments. Once I found he had actually set up a gallery in a vacant one and was painting there. Another time I found his etchings in one of the cellars." He shook his head. "Believe me, gentlemen, it injures me deeply to tell you these things about my son. His mother is at her wits' end, and my only comfort is that his grandfather, may he rest in peace, is not alive to see it. Sometimes, and this it grieves me most to confess about my son, he has even stolen money from his mother's purse to buy these things he says he must have. Paint, brushes, and other such *narrishkeit*."

"If you'll excuse my saying so, Mr. Roth," Mr. Murdstone said, "I don't think John's interest in art is quite the waste of time you think it is. As a matter of fact, some of his drawings . . ."

His father waved him off. "Pardon me, Mr. Murdstone, but I come from an Orthodox tradition and received a strict yeshiva education. I may have let things slide, especially when it came to acceding to his mother's wish that my son be given a goyische name like John and attend a public school, but to me drawing is foolish, unmanly, and a waste of time. At its best, as a diversion, it is nice, but only if it produces attractive pictures you can at least recognize. At its worst it is childish foolishness, a pollution of one's spirit, a dangerous endeavor inspired by the sitra achra, the other side, which can take John away from his studies and religion. And when the things he draws are ugly and you can't even recognize them, when you find an eye here, a hand poking out there, then—"

"Chagall and Picasso did the same—"

"No, Mr. Murdstone, give me no Chagalls and Picassos. Better my son should be a ditch digger than an artist."

Mr. Murdstone started to reply but shrank into silence at a glance from Mr. Farragut. Johnny sat quietly, glancing from the cadaverous-looking Mr. Murdstone to his father, who resembled Moses carved in stone. Funny, it was like he wasn't even here. For all it mattered, he might as well be playing hooky again. Yet *he* was the subject of it all. Why didn't someone ask him what *he* wanted? And what right did they have to open his locker and take his sketches? He looked at his father again. To him, the only art with value was the kind you found in the Torah and on packages of matzoh, and he was about as humorous as the dour-faced rabbi he had engaged to teach him. A thousand years of Talmudic tractates and commentaries and then smicha was what his father had planned for him. Rebbe John Roth, complete with beard, earlocks, and phylacteries. Well, what could you expect from a frustrated real estate broker who'd had to forfeit his own dream of becoming a rabbi in order to support a family and parents from the old country?

"If you'll indulge me a bit further," said Mr. Murdstone cautiously, "John did some other drawings I'd like you to see. He was working on them in my wife's English class and she took them away. I've asked her to bring them here." He checked his watch. "Can't imagine what could be keeping her."

Mr. Farragut shot him a warning glance. "Mr. Murdstone, I hardly think they would serve any purpose. Mr. Roth has already made his position clear. Besides, the real question is, how do we get the boy's cooperation?" He flipped open a folder. "Seems to me it shouldn't pose any real problem. According to tests, his I.Q. is quite high. As a matter of fact, it's exceptional. One fifty-eight." He snapped his fingers. "Motivation! That's it! All we've got to do is give him a positive goal. Make him see the necessity for better grades if he expects to graduate and pursue an advanced education."

Mr. Murdstone swallowed. "Mr. Farragut, I don't really think it's that simple."

This time the principal shot him a glance like a guillotine, but Johnny didn't notice Mr. Murdstone was cowed by Mr. Farragut the same way he was by his father. Actually he hadn't heard a word in minutes. Oh no, the drawings Mrs. Murdstone had taken from him! What if his father saw them? How private they were! The idea of *them* pawing through those drawings with shock and disapproval, not to mention his father's disgust . . . He started to protest, then realized how futile it was. How personal those pictures were. They represented something new he'd been trying and were not meant for anyone to see! He had hid them in books on Delacroix and baroque expression and meant to look at them only for a moment. But he had gotten so absorbed, he hadn't heard Mrs. Murdstone come to his desk. If it had been anyone else, he wouldn't have given them up. But she had simply held out her hand and like a fool, half his heart had fallen into it.

At that moment there was a knock, and Mrs. Diana Murdstone came in.

# Chapter
## Eight

### Diana in the Rain

Instantly the three men rose, all smiles as she favored them with a smile. Without knowing it, he had risen too and was openly staring as Mr. Farragut introduced her to his father and gallantly found her a seat right next to his desk. Only when she was seated and still smiling up at them, did they sit down.

Briefly the mood lightened, and even his father made small talk. Johnny, though, stiffened with excitement, for he couldn't imagine anyone more beautiful. And she knew it, too. The way she moved and brushed sometimes against the older boys . . . Lee Esner claimed she was hot to trot and bragged that sooner or later he'd add her to his list. Around school her alliance with Mr. Murdstone was a constant source of wonder and speculation. What could such a piece of cheesecake see in a pile of withered old bones? Why, the match defied all rules of nature and common sense. Murdstone even rattled when he moved like a dried up shuck from an ear of corn. Sometimes, when the stags at Shaker High were especially spicy in their reflections, they'd speculate about Mr. Murdstone's hidden talents as a lover. On such occasions their laughter turned bawdy and was laced with envy and hatred.

At the moment, though, it was neither of these two sentiments that glowed in Mr. Farragut's eyes but something appreciably warmer. By inspired strategy he had maneuvered himself so he was within striking range of Mrs. Murdstone, whose crossed legs revealed half of one of her thighs. Laughing brightly, she joked and patted Mr. Farragut's plump hand, swinging her head so her hair swirled freely behind it.

To Johnny, the gesture captured so much about her. Virgin and whore. That was how he saw her. In one movement she had caught them all, yet done it with such a natural forwardness no one could object. Even his father, he was surprised to see, seemed charmed and was smiling through his beard. Yet according to Jewish tradition, women were supposed to stay in the background and not interfere in men's affairs.

She rose quickly, her high heels forming oval impressions in the carpet as she swept across it. "Here are those drawings you asked for, Harvey."

Instantly her spell was broken. Mr. Murdstone received the drawings and flipped through them while Johnny cringed. His sketches! He had forgotten them! Then he remembered there was one drawing, one in particular which he must not, *must not* show them. If he did—why, he couldn't even begin to imagine his father's reaction. Just the knowledge that *she* had seen it, that she must *know* what he had been trying to do, had kept him awake nights. In the dark he had buried his burning face in his pillow and pounded the mattress with his fists.

Scarcely breathing, he watched Mr. Murdstone deliver his drawings to the principal, whose nostrils flared as he started through them. In the meantime Mr. Murdstone was using phrases like "a precocious feeling for the human form," "a sense of anatomy," "a talent for shading and chiaroscuro." Mr. Farragut wet his lips, his candy cane striped bow tie seeming to harden beneath his chin. The office was silent. After a minute Mr. Murdstone's voice began to falter and seem less certain. "Interesting quality . . . course I'm no expert . . ." Finishing, Mr. Farragut passed the drawings to his father, whose head snapped back in shock when he saw the top sketch. Johnny saw him look at him in anger and then force himself to continue. It was brutal to watch. Watching him, Johnny felt foul and unclean.

When he was through, his father stood and placed them on the principal's desk.

"Tell me, Mr. Farragut," he said, "do you encourage this kind of art work in your school?"

"Of course not, Mr. Roth. I'm as shocked as—"

"Tell me, Mr. Farragut," he said, "do you encourage your art teachers to teach this kind of thing? Perhaps you use naked women in class? Hire them off the streets and expose sixteen-year-old children to them for the sake of . . . for the sake of . . . what do you call it? Aesthetic appreciation, maybe? Artistic—"

"No, of course not," Mr. Farragut said. "Let me assure you, I'm as dismayed as you are."

"Then how can this be? How—"

"Perhaps from his imagination," said Mr. Murdstone. "Or from paintings he has seen. At any rate, it's hardly as serious as you make it sound, Mr. Roth. After all, this is 1958, and the drawing of nudes is a tradition that goes back thousands of years."

"Not among *my* people, it doesn't," his father said. "Not among *my* people. This is for the *goyim*." He pointed a rigid finger at the stack on the desk, struggling for control. "Nudes you call it. *Nudes*. Well, I call it something different. I call it naked women. I call it obscene filth."

"Mr. Roth," Mr. Murdstone began.

"Mr. *Murd*stone!" said the principal.

Mr. Murdstone caught the ultimatum in Mr. Farragut's voice and collapsed like a pricked balloon. At the same time, Johnny's father made a one hundred and eighty degree turn and glared down at him.

"And I tell you here and now you will not turn my son into a *shaygetz!* Maybe I had to give up my rabbinical studies to support my family and parents, but not John. Ribono Shel Olom, what do You want from me? Naked women, why it's—"

Suddenly he remembered he was in the presence of a woman and turned to apologize. Johnny saw his anger change instantly to mortification and contrition. To Orthodox believers like his father, sordid subjects like nudity were especially taboo around women, whose purity must never be compromised.

"Pardon me, Mrs. Murdstone," he said, "for exposing you to such an indelicate matter. And . . . let me personally apologize for the behavior of my son. It must have been most unpleasant for you to have seen such . . . such . . . indecent material. I can only suggest in his defense, not to excuse him, you understand, that he must have been influenced by these boys he has fallen in with. This Esner boy, for example. And the black boy, Wiggins I think his name is. Believe me, my son used to be a good boy and an excellent student of the

Torah. Such a mind he has! He could be a brilliant Talmudist, perhaps a phenomenon. He could do much to preserve our heritage and to teach those less gifted than he. But because of such playmates, he has been corrupted. Why, would you believe I don't even recognize my own son anymore? He studies most reluctantly and because of them, he even gets into fights and comes home dirty and bloody."

Johnny straightened in his chair. This was going too far. Now his father was attacking his friends! What was worse, he was being denied even the integrity of his battles, for his father was saying his friends forced him to fight. It was like he wasn't man enough to do *anything* on his own! Why, if he were to draw this scene he'd have to erase himself from it completely because he was so insignificant. He was merely the reason everyone else was here.

Because his father had both attacked his friends and treated him as a child whose scraps were engineered by others, he forced himself to do now what he had never done before: challenge his father.

He rose to his feet. "It's not true," he said. "Lee and Jimmy have nothing to do with my fighting!"

"John, sit down!"

"And the same goes for my drawings. No one made me do them!"

"John, you will not—"

"Yes, I will. You can't stop me!"

"John, you will not talk about this! Mrs. Murdstone—"

"Excuse me," Mrs. Murdstone said. "I have one more drawing to show you."

His father turned. "One more?"

"Yes. Perhaps I shouldn't have waited, but I felt it should be considered separately." She reached down beside her chair and produced a large piece of sketching paper that had been folded twice. Rising, she handed it to her husband.

"Thanks, Diana."

Mr. Murdstone unfolded the drawing while Johnny, still standing, thought of the weeks he had spent making dozens of sketches culminating in this one. Yet even it left him unsatisfied. Still, it was by far the best, and for some reason he knew the five foot canvas he had stretched on a plywood frame and hidden in one of the cellars of his father's building would receive and magically transform it.

Mr. Murdstone had half opened it now and moved his hands to open the second fold. Johnny turned his head to look at Mrs. Murdstone. Diana: Goddess of Love. Virgin and whore. He had drawn her that way, naked and pure, naked and wanton, half-reclining on top of the green merry-go-round at the old school. Her magnificent hair streaming in the wind, she smiled mischievously out through the rain at the observer who would be yearning up at her. However elusive that smile had been to him, however fleeting the impressions he had striven to capture, there had never been any doubt about what he should call the picture. It had come to him at once.

He would call it, *Diana in the Rain*.

Mr. Murdstone had it open now and gazed at it for a long moment without expression. Then, slowly, he turned his head and looked up at him. Johnny gazed back in amazement. The man's face looked ravaged, betrayed, stripped naked. Whatever he had seen in the picture had torn aside some veil in his life and revealed to him truths he had hidden from himself. A moment more and the face changed again. Johnny saw hatred enter Mr. Murdstone's face, hatred for him who had exposed him. Johnny looked, seeing an enemy now where before there had been a friend. *You bastard,* the face seemed to say, *I defend you and plead your case, and look what you do to me*. Then the hate was gone and the face merely looked hurt and empty, the face of an old man. Mr. Murdstone turned and rose to hand the drawing to the principal.

He was down!—bracing himself on one knee while the picture skidded across Mr. Farragut's desk. Mr. Farragut grabbed for it and then rose to help him. By this time, though, Mr. Murdstone had recovered and regained his chair.

Assured that Mr. Murdstone was all right, the principal examined the picture. Immediately his eyes went to Mrs. Murdstone, whose smile caused him to blush. Guiltily, he glanced at her portrait, not knowing what to do until Johnny's father rose impatiently and confiscated it.

Johnny watched him. Despite his fears, he thought excitedly of their various reactions when they had seen his picture and of the pleasure he would have later when he tried to capture their expressions. And how would his father react? Would his face be destroyed like Mr. Murdstone's? Would his father look at him as an enemy? Or would he perhaps blush like the principal and turn red like a cherub in heat? No: rather, his father would recoil at once and show even greater disgust than before.

But his father did neither of these things. Instead he did what struck him as funny: began apologizing to Mrs. Murdstone, who hardly seemed to need it. "I'm so sorry, Mrs. Murdstone. Believe me, I can't begin . . ."

To Johnny the whole scene flashed upon him like a group portrait. There was Mr. Murdstone, his dead hands in his lap, and Mr. Farragut, lust and embarrassment struggling for supremacy in his face. His father was all contrition. From the way he looked, you'd think he had drawn the picture. And what about Mrs. Murdstone, Diana? How did she look? What was in her face? Shifting his gaze, he encountered an elusive Mona Lisa smile. Yet he felt that at any moment he could break its code, probe its secrets.

"All I can do, Mrs. Murdstone, is to tell you how deeply I deplore my son's conduct."

"Please, Mr. Roth, it's perfectly all right. Don't give it any more thought."

Any moment now and he would have the answer. Mrs. Murdstone's smile roved the room, repeatedly touching on the three men. Then her eyes met his and like a lightning bolt it struck him. *Why you bitch,* he thought, *you're enjoying this!* An instant more and he knew it all, knew she had arrived late and saved this drawing for last because of the attention it would bring her. Yes, she loved the principal's lechery and subtly taunting her husband with the fact of her unfaithfulness.

Then her eyes met his again and she did something incredible. She winked.

His father began to chastise him anew for his misconduct. It seemed he had been even more remiss as a father than he had thought. His son's behavior was truly unthinkable. Well, there was only one thing to be done: he must apologize at once to Mrs. Murdstone and forswear forever this foolish drawing, which had led him astray and caused others so much heartache.

He had received his father's commandments before of course, but this one seemed to be carved in stone and to leave him no way out. Besides, it was absurd. Far from being hurt, Mrs. Murdstone was delighted and flattered by his drawing. And as for Mr. Murdstone, he was sorry but he had to draw what he felt, didn't he?

Then his father ordered him to do something he had never done before: *promise* he would not draw anymore.

He could promise him anything, of course, and then continue to draw just as before. But for some reason this time he did not want to submit. Maybe it was because of his father's ultimatum or the presence of the principal, Mr. Murdstone, or his deliberately seductive, secretly cruel wife. Whatever the reason or reasons, he felt threatened by the idea of making a false promise. Maybe it would compromise and betray something important to him. And what did they know about his drawing? What did they know about what he'd been trying to accomplish? Why, even Mr. Murdstone didn't understand his drawing. Far from insulting Mrs. Murdstone, he had meant to praise her.

He took a deep breath and forced himself to meet his father's eyes.

"I can't do it, abba."

His father didn't appear to have heard him correctly. "Can't? Of course you can."

"I *won't* do it. I won't give up drawing."

"John, this is unthinkable. I won't tolerate your disobedience!"

He felt his will buckle and almost go under. Imagine standing up to his father this way. It was unthinkable! He took another breath.

"I didn't mean to hurt Mrs. Murd—"

"You will apologize."

"No."

"You will apologize to Mrs. Murdstone, and then you will promise not to draw anymore."

"I can't."

"Apologize."

Just beyond his father, he could see Mrs. Murdstone's glittering eyes and slight smile.

"No."

"John!" his father pleaded, "why must you do this? Why can't you be like other boys?"

He hung his head, seeing something else now besides anger in his father's face, a frustration and pain that were almost unbearable. In his own way, his father was trying to make sense out of his behavior in order to reach him. Johnny bit his lip, hating the unhappiness he was bringing him.

"John, I've tried to understand but I can't. Why must you be different all the time? Why can't you behave?"

His father was right. He *was* different. He did not think as other boys, was not interested in the same things they were. If only he could be the same. He hated being a freak all the time. But if he was like they were, he would have to give up his painting! Still, look at the suffering and hurt in his father's face. He knew he was bringing him much pain. Maybe he should do what he wanted. Grief-stricken, he felt himself begin to collapse again and turned to Mr. Murdstone for help.

"Mr. Murdstone, please! You know my drawings are good. Please tell him."

Mr. Murdstone stared back without recognition, his face blank and lifeless. Then it was ugly with hatred. He looked away.

"John, I will *not* wait any longer."

He was all alone. What could he do? They were all watching him, waiting. Outside it had started to rain again, and he could see the rain spatter on the fire escape. He considered running and smashing through the window. How far of a jump was it to the fire escape? Ten feet? Twelve? Maybe he could make it. Escape them.

His father took a step toward him.

And in that moment he knew something. His father was right. His friends did make him fight. It was always they who got him into trouble, for he was too scared to do it himself. There was something soft in him, something that let him get pushed around even though when driven to it, he could beat them all up easily. That was the irony and pain of it: his right hand held *two* gifts. Not only could it create, but when closed into a fist, it could also destroy. For years now, no one had been able to stand up to it.

They were still watching him. Against his will, he started to cry.

"There's not one of you who sees me, who sees me at all. To you

I'm just a . . . You don't even know me!"

"John, stop this. You're making a fool of . . ."

Tears. More tears. One puddled at the bottom of his right lens, and he thought crazily of removing his glasses to clean it. But he had no handkerchief. He felt his chest clench and wanted to hide. He knew he was crying and worst of all, making a fool of himself before *her*, Diana in the Rain. He just couldn't stop. It was as if the rain were a flood, and he were swept along by it. "Don't any of you know me," he shouted. "Don't any of you understand!"

His father slapped him. He felt the sting. Blindly, he raised his fist. His father saw it and stepped back, eyes widening. Ribono Shel Olom, what do You want from me? It was his father who always gave him orders and never understood, who he hated most. Yet he loved him, loved him deeply. Now, half of him wanted to kill him. But he couldn't do that. It would be unthinkable to hit his father! What . . . what could he do?

He found himself at the door and tore it open. Looked back at them.

"Go to hell, you bastards!"

In the hall the tile floor rang. He stumbled into someone and shoved him aside, not even hearing the shout of protest. Then, through tears, he saw the words. *In Case Of Fire Break Glass.* Ripping the hammer off the wall, he glared at the red box with its glass front. Yes. By God, they'd see him now. He'd make them, even if they kicked him out of school! Swinging the hammer, he saw the glass shatter and swung again. Somewhere a horn started to blare, deafening, awesome, insistent. Striking the box one more time, he threw the hammer away and ran. As he stumbled down the stairs, he heard shouts fill the building and a teacher call ineffectually for silence.

# Chapter
## Nine

### Indian Attack!

Three days later he had occasion to be concerned again with a fire escape, only this one was attached to the side of the Colony Theater and he was standing on it. It was eight o'clock at night, and he was in the process of sneaking in without paying.

Derring-do and chutzpah require a thick hide, however, especially when you're standing where you have no business being, and every minute there are people walking by who gawk up at you. To Johnny, it was like they all knew what he was up to. He might as well be blowing a trumpet.

Damn Jimmy! What was keeping him? Self-conscious, he lit a Chesterfield and tried to act nonchalant when a little girl asked her parents what the "man" was doing up there. He couldn't quite pull it off, though. To make matters worse, the couple paused to observe him on his iron perch.

Finally they left, and not a moment too soon. Low down on the other side of the metal exit door, he heard the *tap tap tap* which was Jimmy's signal. Immediately he rapped in return. The door opened slightly, and with relief he flicked the butt away and slipped inside.

He crouched on the carpeted floor of the balcony, looking at Jimmy who he couldn't see yet.

"What the hell kept you? I felt like a clown out there."

"Aw, one of them ushers looked 'spicious, so I had to wait."

"Yeah, well it's no picnic—"

"Shhh!"

Eighty feet away, on the other side of the balcony, a flashlight appeared and probed the darkness.

"Shit!"

"Shhh."

Kneeling, he felt his heart pound. Why had he done this? If he were caught, his father would kill him. Besides, he had all that other trouble right now and was getting too old to let Jimmy talk him into joining his kid games. The flashlight swung slowly like an evil eye. Now it was pointed right in their direction! He was about to run for it when the usher who held it turned it off.

"Man, that was close!"

"Thought he had us," Johnny whispered. "Where's Lee?"

Jimmy's white teeth gleamed. He could see him clearly now in the darkness.

"Aw, he's downstairs, workin' hisself up to a little nooky."

"No kidding. Who's the skirt?"

"No one we know. Some Catholic babe."

"Catholic? Hey, that's great. Don't think he's nailed one of them yet."

They both laughed. "Yeah," said Jimmy. "Lee sure bounces 'em. Girls can't help themselves when he's around."

They moved to the brass bar stretching along the entire front of the balcony. On the screen Jimmy Stewart moved through a tense scene from a western. The music swelled dramatically and became taut with suspense.

Wiggins climbed on the ledge and put a foot up on the rail.

"Jimmy! What are you doing?"

"Gonna walk the tightrope, man."

"What, are you crazy? You'll get killed!"

Jimmy ignored him, and as the screen exploded in gunplay he created his own drama. For God's sake, stop! Was he crazy? Breathless, he watched Jimmy's other sneaker rise and mold itself to the rail as he lifted his hands over his head for balance.

Afraid even to breathe lest he cause him to fall, he watched Jimmy nimbly move along the bar. Halfway across, right beneath the dust-laden beam from the projectionist's booth, he executed an amazing little turn and started back.

When he'd almost returned, it happened. Poised above disaster, Jimmy's foot slipped and his hands tilted to one side. He was going to fall! Choking, Johnny watched him teeter over the abyss. One leg came up slowly, rising higher and higher as he fought for control.

Then, miraculously, it descended and Jimmy skittered the rest of the way and hopped off.

"Jesus!"

"Nothing to it, man."

"Are you *crazy*? You almost fell."

"Naw, just a little jig to make things interesting. Part of the act."

"Part of the act? Look, if you're going to pull stunts like that, you'd better get yourself some wings."

"Cool it. I'm like a cat on a high wire."

"Yeah, well there's no net down there. Keep it up and it's going to get you killed."

"Fat chance."

He gazed at him in disbelief. A little jig. Didn't he know it had almost been curtains? How could he be so calm? He started to say something, but Jimmy was pointing over the balcony.

"He's down there."

"Who is?"

"Lee. He's right under us, in back. You just can't see him. Here."

"What? Oh." He felt Jimmy slip him a handful of pellets. "What are they?"

"Jujubes. Snitched them from the candy counter."

"*Jesus,* Jimmy. One of these days they're going to catch you and throw away the key." He raised his hand to his mouth, but Jimmy stopped him.

"Hey, whatcha doin'?"

"Going to eat some."

"Shit, man. I didn't steal 'em to *eat*."

"What, then?"

"Wait till the music gets real loud and let 'em have it. Blast 'em out a their seats."

Johnny gazed down at the dark figures. It looked like a packed house. Why did he let himself get into these things? He was going to get caught for sure.

At the moment, things had simmered down considerably on the screen. Stewart was riding peacefully along on his horse, and the blonde in the covered wagon next to him was sizing him up with a look he was too dumb to notice.

Shots rang out, filling the theater.

Indian attack!

Jumping up, they threw their fistfuls of hard candy down into the audience. Johnny wasn't sure, but he thought he heard someone cry out.

"Hey, don't waste the stuff!"

They turned. Lee had snuck up behind them.

"Don't sweat it," said Jimmy. "I stole nine boxes."

"Nine boxes? Holy Cow, why didn't you just take the candy counter with you?"

"It wouldn't fit up the stairs. Here, be my guest."

"No thanks," said Lee, declining a box. "I prefer to get my kicks other ways."

"Yeah? How's that Catholic babe, anyway? Score yet?"

Lee winked. "Son, I've been doin' the dirty with her for *weeks*. Guess she gets starved for lovin' at that Catholic school she goes to."

"Well, don't wear it out."

"Don't worry. Anyway, I got to hustle my tail back. I told her I was just going to check on you guys." He punched Johnny's shoulder. "Get in O.K.?"

"Yeah, but we almost got caught."

"No kidding. What happened?"

"Aw, one of the ushers was sniffin' around. Thought for a minute he saw us."

"Which one?"

"Shit, I don't know," said Johnny, glad for the chance to use a little profanity. "All we could see was his flashlight."

Lee considered the matter. "Well, it was either Jackson or Parker. If it's Parker, it's O.K. He's an all right guy. Won't ever turn any of you guys in. On the other hand, Jackson'll screw you to the wall just to make points with the manager."

More shots sounded. Down below, Stewart had managed to draw the wagon train into a circle and was firing into a swarm of charging Indians. War paint filled the screen; the theater reverberated with whoops. An arrow whizzed by Stewart, embedding itself in a barrel just six inches from his ear. Dauntless, he drew a bead on the offender and squeezed off a shot. Another redskin bit the dust.

Lee shook his head. "Bullshit. All bullshit."

"What you talkin' about?" asked Jimmy.

"Man, don't you ever sit up close?"

"Yeah. So?"

"Well, try it some time. Know what you see? Vaccination marks. Nothing but vaccination marks. All the Indians got 'em. But the thing is, see, they didn't have vaccinations for smallpox then. At least, the Indians sure didn't get them."

"What's your point?" Johnny asked.

"I don't know," Lee said. Usually he was not the kind to get introspective or to worry his head about things, but he felt temporarily bothered. One day he had sat in the front row and happened to notice all the Indians had vaccination marks. Ever since then he had looked for them. Sometimes they covered them up, but usually they just left them. Unaccountably he thought of Mrs. Futch, the pro he had lost his cherry to when he was thirteen, and all the girls since then. All easy, most of them practically throwing themselves at his feet. Briefly, his handsome features sagged.

"I don't know," he answered. "Sometimes it just all seems phony and too easy, like none of it's real."

"Uh oh," Johnny whispered. He had spotted the flashlight again.

Instantly they crouched. The beam revolved in the dark like a turret light used in prisons to catch escaping convicts.

"Let's run for it!" Lee whispered.

Johnny stopped him. They were twenty feet from the carpeted slope leading downstairs, and he could see they'd be nailed before they got halfway.

The beam stopped revolving and swept to the balcony seats above them, where it exposed rows in broad swaths.

"Here goes!" said Jimmy, getting set.

Too late! Like radar, the light shot to them. They watched it grow larger. Larger and larger. Jimmy turned to Johnny and swore. They were done for!

# Chapter
## Ten

### Powwow in the Balcony

The flashlight, and the hand holding it, emerged from the darkness.

"It's O.K.," exhaled Lee, "it's Parker!"

Above the flashlight a face materialized. Johnny recognized Parker, a senior at Shaker who was celebrated for his dry wit.

"Well, well, look what's playing in the balcony: *The Three Stooges*."

They rose to meet him. Parker doused his light.

"Hey, sure am glad it's you," Lee said.

"You better be. Jackson would turn his own mother in just to score points with Pincombe. What brings you boys up here?"

"Just gabbing."

"Well, let's move back a bit, huh? I don't want this to make the Society Pages in the morning."

They followed him away from the front rail, where it was darker. Parker crouched beneath a NO SMOKING sign and passed a pack of Kools around.

"We'll light up here, gents, but please, don't set the fort on fire."

Parker's lighter flared. As he lit them up, they each caught a glimpse of his deadpan face.

"Like I said, you're lucky I'm not Jackson. If I was, they'd be fingerprinting and making mug shots of you boys about now." He glanced at the screen, where a tomahawk was slicing through the air. "How many of you Injuns sneaked in, anyway?"

"Just me," Johnny said. "Jimmy opened the door."

"Yeah," said Lee. "He had to let the old rabbi in."

"How's that?" said Parker.

"Aw, John's daddy wants him to be a big shot rabbi when he grows up," said Jimmy.

"Indeed." Parker regarded him expressionlessly. "Now what kind of a job is that for a nice Jewish boy?" he said.

Lee and Jimmy laughed. Johnny frowned. "For your information, it's a tradition that goes back thousands of years."

"Really?" said Parker, not giving away a thing. "As an old choir boy at St. Francis, I thought all you Jews became lawyers or doctors, not to mention loan sharks."

"Not really," he replied. "That's no more true than the popular belief that all Catholics make good ushers and want the Pope to be President."

"Touché," laughed Lee. "That's telling him!" But Parker just crouched there, impervious and reflective.

"So you're Roth, huh?"

"Yeah."

"Huh, you wouldn't be the one who caused the hullabaloo Tuesday, would you?"

Jimmy and Lee looked at him. "Yeah, I guess I am," he said, hoping Parker would drop the matter.

"Well, that was a droll incident. Has Farragut conveyed his distress to you?"

"I believe the gentleman did register his sentiments," Johnny said, trying to imitate his style.

"I bet he did. I bet he did. As a matter of fact, he was squealing like a stuck pig when I saw him. He has a colorful opinion of you."

"What the hell you guys talkin' about?" Jimmy asked, carefully putting his cigarette out. "Hey, man, I'm out of weed. How 'bout passin' the ole peace pipe?"

Johnny swallowed as Parker gave him a smoke. Better it should come from him than Parker.

"I was the one who tripped the fire alarm Tuesday," he said.

Jimmy's and Lee's mouths fell open. "You? What for?"

He shrugged. What could he say? "I don't know. For kicks."

"Kicks?"

"Yeah, it was pretty dead around the joint, so I thought I'd shake things up."

"Aw, c'mon!"

"No, it's true," Parker said. "He was spotted."

Johnny almost gagged with delight at their stupefaction. With great effort he kept his face straight, finding he enjoyed his bravado and their speechlessness. Casually, he took a drag and flicked a nonexistent ash from his sleeve.

"Boys," he said, "you'll be happy to know I had a cordial session with 'Fatgut' afterward. He was inclined to give me a week's vacation, but my father talked him out of it."

Now even Parker seemed impressed by his act. If they only knew the truth: how *they* had forced him to run bawling from the principal's office and break the glass in anger and frustration. He was *some* hero. What would they say if they knew the real story and how pathetic he'd been? If they knew Mr. Farragut had decided not to expel him for a week only on the condition his father take him to a psychiatrist?

Now that he had started to bullshit, he wished he hadn't. Jimmy and Lee were all over him, pressing for details. Was 'Fatgut' mad? What did he say? Was he really going to kick him out of school? Had *he* been scared? After all, Farragut was one tough mother when he wanted to be.

Lee, especially, with his typical "Holy cows" and "Crimmeys," was hard to avoid. "Crimmey, John, you know every now and then you do something which really surprises me. Why did you *really* turn in the alarm?"

"I told you, for kicks."

"Aw, c'mon. Holy cow, that just ain't your style. *Wiggins* might do something dumb like that 'cause he likes to take chances, but not you. There's something you're not telling."

*You bet your sweet ass there is*, he thought. *Like my father has taken away my paint and brushes and I'm on probation at school and they're all against me, every last single one. But I'm not going to tell you that.*

"I'll tell you later," he hedged. "Anyway, haven't you forgotten something?"

"What?"

"Your sweetheart."

"Holy Toledo, I forgot all about her!"

"Who's this?" asked Parker.

"Aw, Lee's got a broad pantin' for him downstairs," Jimmy said.

"Lee's *always* got a broad pantin' for him downstairs," Johnny said.

"That so?"

"Yep. Lee's a real Casanova. Always on top. The ladies just can't resist him."

"Do tell," said Parker. "That kind of combat must get pretty wearing after a while."

"Not one bit," Lee said. "Like the boys say, I'm on top. I'm the merry-go-round man!"

"Merry-go-round man. What's that?"

"Aw, it's a game we played once," said Jimmy.

"Yeah, on a merry-go-round," Johnny added. "And the guy who gets to the top first wins and is on top for good. For the rest of his life he's got it made."

"How do you play this quaint game? You boys do it much?"

"That's just it," said Johnny, explaining for them. "This game is different from all other games. You play it just once, and there's no doubleheaders on Sunday."

Parker shook his head, apparently feeling more questions would be a waste of time. At the moment, he was more interested in the girl.

"She's Catholic," Lee volunteered when asked. "Goes to St. Catherine's."

"Yeah? Well, remember *I'm* on the Pope's team too. What's her name? Maybe I know her."

"Theresa Walsh."

Parker allowed a long cool whistle to escape through his teeth. "Theresa Walsh? I do know her. She's a knockout. We used to take baths together as kids, and even then she made your eyes pop out."

"Yeah, well these days she makes something else pop out," Lee laughed. "The girl can't get enough of it. She's a real nympho!"

"So I've heard," said Parker, a small note of envy entering his detached air. "But be forewarned. St. Theresa has a knight who seeks to protect her virtue, what little of it she has left."

"Yeah, who's that?"

"St. George, otherwise known as her brother."

"Aw, I've handled brothers before."

"Not like this St. George, you haven't. He may not wield a sword, but he carries a reasonable facsimile: a switchblade."

"Shoot, all those Cathedral Latin guys do. It's part of their get-up."

"Yeah, but George likes to stick his into things, especially guys who get too close to his little sister. Believe me, he's *mean*. He's already cut up some guys who've messed around with her. And I mean, hurt them *bad*. He's got this real blind spot, see, this real jealous blind spot when it comes to looking out after his sister's honor. I'm a Catholic too, and I can sympathize with his sentiments. But with him it's an obsession."

"Umm. Maybe I better be careful."

"I highly recommend it."

"Or introduce her to someone else. Maybe you, Parker."

Parker permitted himself a slight grin. "Now there's a thought."

"Or maybe Jimmy here." Lee turned to him. "How about it, Wiggins. You don't have anything against Catholic girls, do you?"

"Shee-it, I don't want to mess around with no switchblade."

"Crimmey, what happened to your sense of adventure? Don't let Parker here scare you. We'll just go downstairs and see how she feels about it. She'll do anything I ask her."

"It would be rich," Parker said.

"Huh?"

"Oh, nothing. I was just wondering what her reaction would be to you slipping her Amos 'n Andy here in the dark."

Lee and Johnny howled. Then they stopped. Without knowing it, Parker had gone too far. Way too far. Wiggins' hackles were up. He had always been sensitive about his color, and though they had never talked about it, they both sensed that four years before something had happened to Jimmy that made him extra touchy on the subject. Parker had made just one joke, but even so, Wiggins was ready to hit him.

"Yes," said Parker, "I wonder how she'd—"

"Maybe we should slip her a Jew instead," Johnny joked, trying to turn things into safer waters.

"*There's* a thought," Parker said. "You know, if there's one thing Catholics love more than negroes, it's Jews."

"Sure," Johnny said, "and maybe I could set her straight about a few things."

Lee looked at him. "You wanna? She would if I asked her."

"Aw, I was just—"

"C'mon, you're such a hot shot. Let's just zip downstairs and I'll set things up. You'll be in like Errol Flynn in no time."

They were all looking at him now. Suddenly, he realized *he* had gone too far.

"Naw, like I said, I was just kid—"

"No guts," Parker said.

"Ya know, Roth," Jimmy said, "you're just a big bullshitter. All that crap about turning in a fire alarm. Shee-it, you don't have the guts to do it."

"I *did* turn it in."

"Then *prove* it."

"Yeah," said Lee. "C'mon, you can't fuck your fist all your life, can you?"

Johnny blushed, his mouth tasting like chalk. Damn it, why had they slam-bam turned on him? What was happening? He felt himself being manipulated again, forced to do something he didn't want. Damn it, why didn't he just say no and walk away? Fuck them. Why should he care what *they* thought?

"I dare you, jelly prick," Jimmy said.

Though he felt frozen by fear and embarrassment, a keen blade of excitement cut through him. Could he? *Could* he? Unlike them, who had long since lost their virginity and bragged repeatedly about it, he had never touched a girl before, never even kissed one. What would it be like? And more important, what would it be like not to be so different for a change, to have something in common with them?

Lee noticed his pause. "C'mon, you'll be in paradise before you know it."

"Watch out for Brother George," Parker said.

"Aw, John can take care of himself," Lee said, standing.

"Do tell," Parker smiled as he inventoried Johnny's plump features.

Jimmy jabbed his shoulder, a little harder than necessary. "Let me tell ya something, Parker, Johnny can take care of hisself. Maybe he don't look like no Joe Louis, but there ain't nobody he can't handle. Believe me, *I* know."

"Damn straight," Lee said.

Finding himself on the outside looking in, Parker shrugged. "If you say so."

Jimmy rose. Apparently it was all decided. They had decided for him. Johnny looked at them looking down at him, feeling as if he were in Mr. Farragut's office again, an airtight bottle where he couldn't breathe.

"Well, John?"

*To hell with them. I'll just walk away. I don't have to prove anything to anyone.*

They stood there waiting. The silence was getting long. Much too long. He coughed.

*Can I do it? Maybe I can. Prove I've got guts. Prove I'm not different.* He felt excited. *What would it be like? I've never even touched a girl before. Maybe I CAN do it.*

"Ain't got all day," Lee said. "Movie's almost over."

Numbly he rose. Finding his cigarette had burned down to the filter, he put it out against the brick wall with shaking fingers, careful not to set the fort on fire.

# Chapter
## Eleven

## The Fox and the Hounds

**W**alking downstairs, he actually had to look to locate his feet and was mildly surprised to find them attached to his legs. He still felt sick with horror. How had he gotten himself into this?

At the bottom Parker lifted the purple braided rope and they ducked beneath it into the lobby, where they marched him past a cold drink machine and a candy counter with a yellow sign advertising buttered popcorn. Esner had him by his right arm, and Wiggins, laughing that soft, throaty, mocking laugh which always infuriated him a little, had impounded his left. The message they conveyed was clear: *Don't try to escape, son. Just come quietly.*

Behind him, Parker sent a parting cheer. "Break a leg!"

*Run, you dumb jerk! Get out of here!*

What made it especially bad was—he could. Even though they had him by both arms, he knew he could shake them off with ease. In a way it was funny. Though he looked like a plump pushover and had the will of a marshmallow, there was a power in his fists and shoulders, in his whole body, that shouldn't be there. Ever since the day four years ago when he'd decked Jimmy with one punch, he had periodically been reminded of that power. True, he couldn't run fast, and halfway around the track he was already winded, but if he wanted to stop this abduction, he'd have to do little more than flex his muscles.

Like a lamb, he let them lead him to slaughter.

The girl sat alone in a back row. When they reached it, Lee released his arm so he could give her the word. Wiggins remained behind, still laughing mockingly. Like a dedicated cop trusted with a prisoner, he tightened his grip.

What kind of girl does this sort of thing with a guy she's never even met and in the dark where she can't even see him? And what kind of a jerk goes along with it? Appalled, he watched Lee return up the long dark row.

*Please let her say no! Let her have some class.*

"She's all yours, buddy," Lee whispered. "Get it while it's hot!"

At the same moment, he felt him slip something into his hand.

A rubber.

Mechanically, he jammed it into his pocket and stood paralyzed at the start of his long journey. *Who am I kidding? I can't even move!*

A poke from behind got him started, and he stumbled forward rusty-legged like the Tin Man in *The Wizard of Oz.* He was totally unprepared for anything: talking, thinking, even breathing. He only knew there was a dim figure sitting in a chair, and its face was turned to the screen. He didn't even hear the blood-curdling yells of apaches or check to see how Stewart was doing.

When he reached her (all too soon!), he collapsed in the chair beside her. What should he say? He tried to speak. He must say something! What? What? The girl hadn't even turned her head. Dazed, he wondered if she was a dummy or mannequin they had stuck here for a joke. Maybe Parker had helped set it up.

All at once she turned and kissed him, her arms going around his neck.

*What the hell is this? No introduction? I might be a chimpanzee for all she knows.* Pulling back, he gasped for air. Even in the dark he could tell she was pretty.

"Hi," he said.

"Hi," she said and embraced him again.

*Consider yourself introduced. Pretend you're old lovers.* Overwhelmed by a sense of unreality, he felt disembodied. *This can't be happening! I'm dreaming.* Maybe he was still standing on the fire escape, waiting for Jimmy to let him in. Unconsciously he pulled her to him. Her lips were soft, her breath sweet. She held him closely. He found himself beginning to like it as she caressed his hair.

She pulled away.

"You Lee's friend?"

"Yes."

"I'm Theresa."

"John Roth."

"Hi, Johnny."

He started to answer but she was kissing him again, this time *French kissing.* Her tongue slipped between his lips. She found his right hand and placed it on her breast while his heart boomeranged inside him. *I can't believe this! What do I do now?*

A voice jabbered in his ear. Jimmy.

"What?" he said.

"I said, you're in trouble. Her brother's here, and he's got his gang lookin' for ya!"

He sat up. With perfect clarity he saw the second showing of the movie had long since begun and Stewart had gotten himself in hot water again. War whoops rent the theater, and savages completely encircled his wagon train. A tomahawk sliced through the air . . .

"Run, man, he's got ya surrounded!"

It was too much. Stunned, he might have sat all night watching the Indians if *she* hadn't started to whimper. "He'll kill me! Oh, sweet Mary, he'll kill me if he catches me here!"

*Kill you? What about me? I'm the one he'll be sticking his switchblade into!* Snapping alert, he spotted two figures roaming the far aisle of the theater. Another was coming his way up the near aisle. He saw it pause to scan the seats. Jimmy was right; he *was* surrounded!

"Quick, the exit!" Jimmy said.

He rose and stumbled out the way he'd come. It seemed to take hours. Some seats were down, and he kept banging into them. It was a dream he'd had many times: the monster loomed just behind him while he kept slogging through quicksand. At any moment, he expected to feel a blade in his back. Maybe they'd scalp him!

Finally he gained the aisle where Jimmy waited, forty feet from the approaching figure. Had he seen them yet? Johnny saw the red exit sign and grabbing the crossbar, crashed through the door, knowing he'd just betrayed his position.

He found himself in the alley, right below the fire escape where he'd waited for Jimmy what seemed a thousand years ago. He looked up, half expecting to see himself still standing there, dreaming all this. *Momma, what is that man doing up there?*

The exit door crashed open, and a kid his age burst into the alley. In the second the boy stood there, Johnny's thoughts seemed to move unbelievably fast, as in a dream. He saw everything: the shiny, pointed stiletto shoes, the black, neatly pressed pants, the glossy silk Italian shirt with *The Cossacks* emblazoned on one of its sleeves, and the 'duck's ass' haircut, brushed and slicked back on the sides. All this, he knew, was the uniform of the hoods who went to Cathedral Latin. The only thing missing was his switchblade, and it was probably in his pocket right next to a set of brass knuckles.

The kid's mouth opened, swallowing half the air in the alley. He dashed back into the theater.

"George, I found 'em! They're in the alley!"

Jimmy shoved him.

"Run that way! I'll get some help!"

He ran in terror, only something was wrong. Something stuck to his hand and held him back. He shook at it.

*Ribbono Shel Olam, it's the girl!* Dodging some garbage cans, he realized she'd attached herself to him like a leech ever since he'd left his seat and was clinging to him for dear life. God, he might as well be waving a flag to let them know where he was. He stopped.

"Let go!"

"No!"

"I can't—"

"He'll kill me—please!"

He considered shoving her away so he'd have a chance. A thought hit him. *Bet it'd be ten times harder to shake her off than Jimmy and Lee. And maybe I couldn't do it!*

He heard shouts, footsteps in the night.

"C'mon!"

A sidewalk. Curb. A street to cross. Another alley. A dog barking at his heels. More garbage cans. Shouts and footsteps getting closer. Should he look back? No! Objects passed him in a blur. He realized it was night. And all the time the girl was crying, wasting her precious breath crying the same thing over and over. *Sweet Mary, he'll kill me, Sweet Mary he'll* . . . He wanted to shake her off, smash her against a wall so he could set sail, let fly, run like lightning in a wind of panic, drive his feet one after another against the ground. If he was free, he might have a chance, and if they caught him anyway at least it wouldn't be because he was dragging *her* with him.

In the middle of a street, she collapsed against him, unable to run another step but still holding on and crying hysterically. He thought of throwing her off, even slamming her against the ground to get free. After all, she'd have to see her brother sooner or later. Yet he couldn't do it. Across the street he recognized a field and half carried her toward it, just beating out a row of trucks rumbling toward them. On the other side, he stopped before the stone wall stretching along the front of the field. It was half a foot shorter than his height of 5'10", and he picked her up by the waist and swung her over it, depositing her in the deep grass on the other side. Then he swung over it himself and lay beside her.

Gasping for breath, he watched the street through a broad crack in the wall. His whole body was drenched in sweat and as his blood pounded in his ears, he saw the trucks rumble by in an unending line. It resembled a train, and he had never seen anything like it. Truck followed truck, all different and without order. Budweiser Beer . . . Pepsi Cola . . . Wonder Bread Helps Build Strong Bodies Twelve Ways . . . Armour Ham. Then came two that would have struck him as funny under different circumstances. Mogen David Wine and Stein's Matzoh Crackers. *Hey, abba, how's that for running with the goyim!* If he got out of this, it might be because these trucks had come by when they did and stopped his pursuers.

Finally the trucks passed and he could see *The Cossacks* on the other side of the street. For a few moments, the gang just milled around. Then one of them started to organize things. He posted two to stay across the street in front of the field and directed the others to split up into two units and patrol the sidewalks that ran around it. Johnny counted about a dozen of them, and in the moonlight he could see their stiletto shoes and glossy shirts clearly.

Master of the Universe, it's going to be one bitch of a night. He was so scared now he could feel fear writhe like a snake in his belly. It was enough to make him get religion. Abraham, Isaac, and Jacob. Maybe there was something in it. Maybe he should have gone for the whole *megillah*, studied Rashi, Ibn Ezra, and all the other sages more devoutly and listened to his father, who wanted so deeply for him to become a rabbi. If he had listened to his father, maybe he wouldn't be here right now, about to get his throat cut. Yes, maybe that was the difference between believers and nonbelievers. If he were a believer, he'd be home right now, sound asleep with the Torah under his pillow. It's only goyim and apikorsim who skulk about like rats at night and wallow in their own terror. Yes, that must be it. It was too late now for a foxhole conversion and besides, to be honest about it, he hated religion, did not know or care if there was a God in the sky or not; did not, as he sometimes admitted to himself, even care if in the vast scheme of the universe the cockroaches were kings. To him religion was his father's stern face and commandments carved in stone.

Still, there had been times when his faith had brought him deep happiness, such as at his bar mitzvah, the ritualistic coming of age, when he had read flawlessly from the Torah. He remembered his father's tears and how closely he had embraced him, overjoyed his son was now a man. Then there was Simchat Torah, the day which celebrated the yearly-end-and-new-beginning of the consecutive weekly readings of the Torah in the synagogue and the continuing cycle of worship. Lying on his stomach watching the moonlight spangle on the gang's shirts, he recalled the frenzy of the event. How joyously his father and other men had danced with the scrolls! He remembered his own exaltation and how he had felt knowing God was after all a living God, that He wasn't just a thousand years of Talmudic logic-chopping and endless minutiae of Jewish law pertaining to everything from food preparation to the frozen procedures of Yom Kippur and other Holy Days. God, the law-giver, had a sense of humor, too! He could understand joy and rejoicing and fervor that was blood warm. Did it not follow, then, that despite all the other things, Judaism was a living religion?

But most of it was painful and demanding, so alien to everything within him. Well, doesn't the midrash say all beginnings are hard? Maybe he should grit his teeth and try again. What does the Old Testament say about stiff-necked or hardhearted people? Maybe he should loosen up a bit and let Yahweh enter his heart, perhaps ask Him to deliver him from George. Maybe he should give Him another chance. Maybe, indeed, he should even do his father one better and become not just a fanatic but a student of the kabbalah and its mystical lore. Maybe he should counter his father's Orthodox, rational mind and insistence on scientific text criticism with a religion that at least had some warmth and feeling. Magic and Miracles, Visions and Trances, Angels and Demons, Numerology and Chiromancy. Yes, his father might like such seasoning. And who knows, maybe if he had been a mystic, he could have fashioned an amulet or chanted an incantation holy enough to save him from this Angel of Death. Well, don't fret. Maybe the messiah will come and rescue you from George in a chariot of fire if you only have faith, if you only repent. Yeah, well screw it. It's too late to change now. Here's a divine lesson you can sink your teeth into. God helps those who help themselves. In other words . . .

*You better save your own ass.*

The girl touched him.

"George," she said pointing. "My brother."

He looked at the one who had dispatched his troops so efficiently. What had Parker called him? St. George. St. George and the Dragon. Lying there he thought of another dragon, the one on Mr. O'Reilly's paddle which Sammy Duckett had tried to beat him with when he was twelve. He remembered how he had taken that dragon away from him and then surprised them all, especially himself, by virtually dismembering Duckett with his fists. Well, it wouldn't be so easy this time. As he watched, something glinted in her brother's hand, and he saw the switchblade. It looked at least a foot long. George stood hungrily tossing the knife back and forth from hand to hand. Johnny saw him stare directly at him and felt the hairs rise one by one on the back of his neck. Could he see him through the wall? Could he penetrate this darkness? He held his breath, afraid even to breathe.

It was then, lying flat on his belly in the darkness with her brother seeming to stare right into his eyes, that he realized the significance of the gang's name. The Cossacks. He recalled his father's dark stories of how their saber-flashing bloodbaths had slaughtered countless Jews throughout history, among them three hundred thousand in the Ukraine during the mid-seventeenth century. And now, in another century, in a different guise, the slaughter continued. It appeared you couldn't escape your heritage because history always repeated itself, and regardless of how he felt, he was a Jew after all. Only this time there was a difference. This time it was a pogrom of one, and he was the intended victim.

He swallowed, sweat stinging his eyes, and glanced at the girl. So this was what he got for being on the fire escape tonight and letting them talk him into seeing her. This was what he got for trying to prove he wasn't different, or a freak. Well, perhaps if he said a prayer. If he could only think of one.

Nudging a companion, George stepped off the curb and walked wolf-like toward them.

# Chapter
## Twelve

### Stars Over Eden

*Uh oh. Better get moving.* Shivering, he edged backwards and urged the girl to follow.

They moved into the interior, away from the sidewalks and streetlights. If he was lucky, they would patrol the sidewalks around the field for a while and then leave. At least he *hoped* they would. After all, they probably hadn't seen them go over the wall and couldn't be sure they were in the field. Luckily the field was dark, and even if they were surrounded again, it was over half a dozen times as large as the theater and far more complex. There were ravines, trees and thickets that leaped out of nowhere. Anyone who entered here after dark would almost certainly get lost and stumble around endlessly unless he knew the place cold. Which he did. Confidently, holding the girl's hand, he moved expertly through the darkness, glancing at the stars piercing through the branches overhead and thinking of all the times neighborhood kids met here at night. There was Andy Yesso, whose father owned a butcher shop nearby on Buckeye St. and who stole beer and cigarettes for their meetings. And Jim Parsons, the real tall lean kid who was always telling dirty jokes and pissing on the fire to douse it. What had happened to Parsons anyway? Oh, yeah, he had stolen one too many hubcaps and ended up in reform school.

Now, in the dark, after an evening which had started with his sneaking into the Colony Theater, he was walking alone through that same field with a girl whose brother wanted to kill him.

The girl's hand tightened in his, and he felt her give him all her trust. She was counting on him. This knowledge changed the way he felt. *He* was the one in command now, so he'd better show some guts. Words he had not realized he had memorized occurred to him, and he whispered them in prayer.

"Thou shalt not be afraid for the terror by night; nor for the arrow that flieth by day. Nor for the pestilence that walketh in darkness; nor for the destruction that wasteth at noonday."

Moving confidently around a deep hole, he glanced at Theresa. She was a lovely girl with dark hair and soft features, the kind you dreamed about. Had he really kissed her and felt her breast? His spine tingled.

A briar patch lurked ahead. He skirted it and turned to the right. In seconds they were in a clearing located in the center of the field. He felt safe here, as safe as he could with her brother's gang stalking him in the night. He pointed at the remains of a dead fire.

"This is where we meet."

"Are we safe?"

"As long as we sit tight and wait them out, we are. I don't think they'd be dumb enough to come in here after us, especially since they probably don't even know for sure we're here."

"You don't know George. He'll try anything."

He reached in his pocket, beneath the rubber, and dug around until he found some matches and what remained of the pack of Chesterfields. Surprisingly, he felt confident in himself, maybe because this experience was so different and she was so dependent on him.

"Smoke?"

"I guess so."

He lit her cigarette, then his. She touched his hand.

"You've got strong hands."

"Think so?"

"Sure, I felt them when you lifted me over the wall. You did it like I was a feather." Her gaze ran over his chest and shoulders. "You're strong."

He took a puff, excited.

"What's with George, anyway?"

"Huh?"

"I mean, why's he out there hunting us like . . ."

She shrugged. "He just don't like me foolin' around."

"Meaning boys?"

"I guess so. He's got a thing about it."

"A guy I know says he's real mean and has even cut up a few guys who messed with you."

"Yeah, that's George all right. He takes religion seriously. Keeps telling me it's a mortal sin to do what I do and if he catches me he's gonna hurt me bad. You ought a see this strap he's got."

*To do what I do.* He swallowed nervously. What surprised him was that she seemed so indifferent now that she was not in immediate danger. Still, she'd have to go home.

"If you know he's going to hurt you, why do you keep . . .?"

"Seeing boys?" She smiled. "I don't know. Guess I just like them." She moved closer. "Besides, he keeps spoiling my fun. You know somethin'? Sometimes I think I do it just 'cause he keeps after me all the time. It's like he thinks I should be the Virgin Mary or somethin.'"

"But then you get whipped."

She took his hand and pulled him toward a patch of grass. "Let's not talk about it, huh?"

"Sure, but it seems kind of fun—"

"Here's a nice place," she said.

He sat beside her. "What I mean is . . ."

She put her arms around his neck.

"There is one thing, though."

"What?"

"Well, one night about a year ago I was in bed when I heard him come in my room. He must a thought I was asleep."

"So?"

"I don't know, he did somethin' real creepy. He just stood there for the longest time. I didn't dare open my eyes, but I didn't have to. I *knew* he was standin' there watching me."

"So what happened?"

"Nothin'. Finally he just left."

An idea stirred, but before it could form, she pulled him down.

He responded differently this time and kissed her hungrily. Then he found his glasses got in the way and knelt to remove them. She lay beneath him, a mystery waiting to be explored, a new world. She reached out for him and he sank down upon her, nuzzling her throat. There was a slight hollow there, and he felt like a small animal burrowing in. Then she took his hand and placed it on her breast again. He felt the soft flesh beneath the fabric and caressed it. She started moaning. "Oh, Johnny, Johnny, Johnny, Johnny, Johnny, Johnny." She began moving beneath him. In shock he remembered Lee's words, "She's a real nympho," and all the dirty jokes he'd heard about "nymphomaniacs." The first time he had heard the word he couldn't even guess what it meant and had acted wise while the other kids snickered. *Nymphomaniacs. Man, they can't get enough. I tell you, they just can't stop! Get their hands on you, pal, and you'd better stitch your fuckin' pants shut.*

Was *Theresa* a nymphomaniac? He rose to get a better look, and she used the opportunity to remove her dress. There was a soft rustling, a whisper in the night, and then she was wearing only laced panties and a bra. She turned around to hang her dress on a low hanging branch.

He gazed at the long naked bow of her back. Gauguin had been wrong. His Tahitian girls were flat cardboard figures in comparison. His eyes reached out, tracing the inexhaustible shadings of her form. He could never master it, never capture the full sweep and contour and texture of her spine, its long downward curve and plunge beneath the elastic of her panties. Still, he must try, no matter what his father wanted, no matter how many times he took away his paint.

She turned back and slipped out of her underwear, her smooth limbs flowing like water. The universe caught in his throat. She sat there naked for him, leaning slightly back on molded arms. He saw the delicate surge of her breasts, her bud-like nipples, the V-shaped valley between her thighs. Her throat was a white column dappled by moonlight, a spire of form. Unconsciously he stood up, wanting to paint her with his whole body and sink into her milky iridescence. His fingers found his shirt buttons and then his belt buckle, hastening to remove the last obstacle to his yearning. Her eyes followed their progress.

"Gee, Johnny!"

He looked down, seeing it as a bold tower, a passionate ache rising from his core. Proudly he stepped forward.

"Hey, you're gonna use somethin', aren't you?"

Her words checked him. He had to think twice before he

remembered the rubber in his cast-off pants and retrieved them. The first pocket he tried turned out to be the wrong one, and though the second one was right, he had trouble getting it out. He managed to get the foil of the wrapper in his hand, but everything was bunched up. Something was wrong. Her question had marred the magic. He seemed to have regained all his old clumsiness. When he got the thing out, he promptly dropped it, and when he groped for it, he couldn't find it. *Oh, no, No, this couldn't happen! Where is it? Please don't—*

Just when his horror and humiliation threatened to choke him, his fingers brushed the wrapper. His whole being flooded with relief. But he had to hurry. He had lost precious time. Would she wait for him? Luckily, he got the wrapper open with no trouble at all, but when he tried to get the thing on, it wouldn't go. He looked down at *her* petulantly looking up at *him*. Any moment now she'd tell him to stick it in his ear. At the same time, he started to wilt. Panicking, he fumbled at the thin sheath, frantically trying to slide it down his shaft before it fell completely along with his expectations. Then— miracle of miracles!—he thought desperately of *reversing* the damn thing and it slipped down like butter. A moment more and he was rampant again.

It was easy then for him to lie down and take her in his arms, to stroke her smooth breasts and thighs. He had often wondered how it would be his first time. Often, in more honest moments, he had admitted to himself he would probably be nervous and clumsy. He did not find it so. Deftly, his fingers moved up her soft flesh and parted her thighs, seeking entry to the last, secret place, the mecca of all his fantasies. He found her moistly waiting there for him, an oasis among dunes, and groaned when her hand took him in return. She commenced to stroke him with experienced fingers that made him throb in delicious pain just short of exploding. His own fingers probed deeper, found the hard little nub of her center. He kissed her everywhere, her lips, her breasts, her navel, wanting to paint her with his whole body. *Theresa I want you I want you please let me—*

Her voice cracked hoarsely in his ear. "Now?" she pleaded. *"Now?"*

Half delirious, he knelt between her thighs and with her help, their loins joined. Instantly she began to grind herself against him and dig her nails into his back. She wrapped her legs around his waist; he cupped her buttocks and drove harder, deeper, thrilling at her salty taste and utter abandon. Then she was licking his ear and panting words he could not believe, words he had never thought any girl could use, pleading with him to do things, things he had only heard hinted at in jokes and snickers. His breath rose against the dam and blasted through it. Crying, he felt his body grow tight as a bowstring and then release, grow tight and then release as she joined him . . .

Later he lay gazing up at the glittering lights of the Big Dipper.

"Johnny?"

"Huh?"

"I'm gonna see you again, aren't I?"

"Sure."

"You mean it?"

"Sure, why wouldn't I?"

"I don't know. It's—"

"What?"

She didn't answer. He turned his head.

"Come on, why wouldn't I mean it?"

"I don't know. It's just—"

"Tell me."

"Well, it's just that once boys get, you know, what they want, they don't . . ."

She sat up, hesitating while she took his fingers and toyed with them. He felt the night wind wash him with an infinite number of fragrances. Somewhere nearby there must be a magic garden. He smelled apples and oranges, limes and pomegranates, quince and citron and grapes. Somewhere close by grew jasmine and rose blooms and purple bougainvillea and lotus blossoms that intoxicated the senses, causing forgetfulness, and listening closely, he could hear sparkling water in a marble fountain cascade on opulent blossoms which opened to drink the rain of paradise. A nightingale burst liquidly into song, enchanting the very air with loveliness. His mind reeled, spun momentarily like a child's dreidel he had once seen. Beside him, Theresa's dark eyes watched him, demure now instead of wild.

"It's just once they get what they want, they treat me cheap and tell other guys. Even if they stay they're different."

He turned and pulled her down to him. "Don't worry, I'm not like them."

"It's just I'm so *tired* of their laughing at me and telling jokes. I can't help what I—"

"Hey," he said, "it's all right." He held her and kissed her forehead, but he didn't really know what he could do. Besides, his thoughts were elsewhere now and he felt almost disembodied as he gazed up at the stars, wondering how he could paint them when they were so far away. *Billions and billions of miles. How can mere paint capture the rings of Saturn or stretch across light-years? Surely it's too far to reach in any canvas. And what if—what if—there's something up there wondering the same thing? Maybe an artist who doesn't look like me at all and whose art is completely different?*

He felt himself drift up toward the stars, which shaped all men's destinies. Hadn't he read that man was no more than a blind helpless product of cosmic forces? And long before he took his first step or uttered his first word, the stars had already decreed his whole future? He closed his eyes, surrendering himself to immense voids where he was mere stardust, a dream of endless peace.

Then Orion, that vast warrior, burst upon him. How splendid he was in his glittering pursuit of the gigantic bull who was his eternal foe! Imagine, the universe itself was divided between the hunter and the hunted and was forever about to ring with the clash of Titans. And what were he and all the Georges, who stalked him now in the night, but infinitely pale, small, and fleeting reflections of this glorious spectacle in the skies?

"Johnny, aren't you listening to me? Wake up."

She had been complaining bitterly about how her brother "kept after" her. Coming back from the stars, he realized they shared something. She had a brother who sought to impose his will; he had a father. Both wanted to dominate them, assumed automatically they had the right, and couldn't care less what they wanted. And the consequence was, both of them would probably catch holy hell tonight for staying out so late. His father, indeed, had been quite clear on the subject: *Stay away from those boys, John, and be home every night by ten or I'll lock the door!*

Frightened, he started to get up. It must be *way* past ten! She clung to him, though, and he kissed her in a surge of tenderness. She returned it desperately, and before he knew it, they were doing it again.

Afterward, he led her out of the field. When they got near Buckeye St., he crept forward by himself to check things out. Across the street he saw a familiar sign, *Groucho's Delicatessen*. In both directions the street was well lit by the streetlights and clearly empty. It seemed a safe bet they had left long ago.

He turned back reluctantly to get her. In a way the field had been a refuge and dark sanctuary for him, a magical self-enclosed world where he'd had the most wonderful experience of his life. He would be sorry to leave it. Taking her hand, he felt close to her. She had shared their experience with him, and from now on it would be Theresa's field in his memory.

They left the field and crossed the street, his heart exulting. Wait till he told Jimmy and Lee! As Lee would say, "Holy Cow!" He felt like dancing. In front of the delicatessen he stopped and kissed her. She clung to him.

"Well, good night."

"Walk me to A&P, O.K.?"

"I've really got to go."

"Please! It's just a block."

He scanned the street. What the hell, another ten minutes wouldn't make any difference. Might as well be hung as a wolf as a sheep, anyway.

He took her hand and they headed up Buckeye. A couple of times she squeezed his hand and flashed him a smile. He felt warm and soft inside. Once he thought he heard a sound but when he looked back, he didn't see anything except the stores and bright streetlights. All too soon they stood in front of a short wall separating them from A&P's parking lot. He kissed her for the last time.

"Well, now I've *really* got to go."

"You'll call me?"

"Sure, don't—"

A sound. He turned around and saw the flash of the switchblade. There were two of them. Her brother, the taller one, moved forward with the knife, a hard smile on his face.

"O.K., you motherfucker, I've finally got you. And now that I do, I'm gonna cut your balls off!"

# Chapter
# Thirteen

## Surrounded!

He leaped the wall and hit the concrete already running, not even knowing yet he had reacted. By the time his mind caught up, he had made ten yards. He drove his legs as fast as he could, running on his toes to squeeze the last particle of speed out of his body, running in the nightmare of a dream.

Only this was no dream! George was going to cut his balls off! He saw the switchblade. Its glitter. Its sharpness. George would slice him up like butter. He saw George's face. Mean, sadistic, beyond restraint. He had heard talk about what hoods like that could do. What had Parker said? George had hurt some kids *bad*!

The parking lot rocked crazily before him. He had covered nearly half of it now and dimly sensed it served not only A&P but also a Rexall and a Dairy Queen. Should he look back? No! Only what difference did it make? He couldn't run fast. Any second now he'd feel the knife enter his back.

Instinctively he headed toward the lane to the right of A&P because it offered an escape. Down that lane and across the street beyond it there was an apartment building he knew where he could hide. He was getting closer and closer, the first agony of fatigue tugging at his lungs, and miraculously, George still had not caught him! Was it possible? *Did* he have a chance?

A car screeched out of the lane with blinding lights. Horrified, he veered to his left. Ahead was the drugstore, a driveway—

Another car exploded out of the driveway, tires screaming, lights blazing. Hearing their hoots, he swung insanely about as new headlights bounced onto the parking lot off Buckeye. Car after car after car. The Cossacks were circling him, just as the redskins had circled Jimmy Stewart's wagon train. He heard their whoops, their shrill, happy, mocking cries. Too late he realized he had underestimated George and had been seen and followed ever since he'd left the field.

Something happened to his eyes, a new mode of seeing. Around him flashed the bright net of their headlights. He knew they were drawing closer and were toying with him, *knew* their whoops were meant to terrify. Still, what struck him most were the signs as he dodged and weaved and retreated ever further. His eyes lingered on their trivia. *Life Savers—3 f o r 13¢ . . . Band-Aids 39¢ . . . Lovable Bras from $1   . . . Old Spice Giant Tube 49¢ . . . Dairy Queen 19¢ Sale All Malts And Shakes . . . Campbell's Tomato Soup 7¢.*

Finally, exhausted and driven to bay, he found himself like a pilgrim at a demonic Wailing Wall, backed against a cosmic promise that *3 Magnificent Corona de Luxe Cigars* could be purchased for just 50¢.

The Cossacks had him now. The net was tight. Less than twenty yards away, cars screeched to a halt, and boys with shiny shirts and greased-back hair piled out. And walking toward him down through the center of the ring came George, grim faced and dragging Theresa with him. Her face was livid with fright, and he wondered if the same look was on his own. The only way to tell, though, would be to feel his face, and he felt too drained to do even that.

It was a surreal circus—horrible, unreal. Or maybe it was real in a way he hadn't grasped yet. The ring of faces clapped shut behind George and his sister. They reached him and stopped.

"What's your name?" George said.

"John."

"John what?"

"John Roth."

"Roth?" Sneersnarlsmile. "That's a kike name. You a Jew?"

*Oh, God, on top of everything else, he hates Jews. Better play dumb.*

"What's a kike?"

Sneersnarlsmile. "Don't act dumb. You know what a kike is. It's a Christ Killer."

He knew it would be suicide not to lie, but as he gazed at George, he smiled perversely.

"Ribona Shel Olam, George. Why do you ask?"

"Bitch!" Like lightning, he slapped his sister. "As if you haven't done enough, now you've done it with a dirty Jew!"

Slapping her was too much. He stepped forward. George's hand shot up and the switchblade gleamed. His other hand beckoned him.

"Come on, come on! Want it, you stinkin' Jew? Then come and get it! Let's see how brave you are."

He almost fainted. *What's wrong with me? I almost ran onto his knife!*

"Why are you making such a federal case out of it?" he heard himself say.

"What ya mean?"

"I mean all this," he said, waving at the faces. "What the hell, George, so she spreads her legs for one more guy. If you don't mind my saying, it's just another slice off the old loaf. Dig?"

A rumble ran through the gang. *What the hell am I doing?* he thought, *trying to get myself killed?*

A kid moved forward. With a glance Johnny saw he had two distinctions. The first was that he had a crew cut and was dressed differently, wearing jeans, engineer boots, and a black leather jacket with zippers glittering like jewels. The second was that he was one of the biggest sonofabitches he'd ever seen, weighing over three hundred pounds.

"George, remember what you said you was gonna do?"

"What's that, Kelly?"

Johnny saw Kelly look at him. He didn't like his smile. For all he knew, he was one of those who thought Jews killed goyische babies and used their blood in matzos for Pesach. He glanced about at the gang, thoughts bombarding him as his mind seemed to race insanely the wrong way down a one-way street. Why did they hate him so much? What had he ever done to them? Weren't Christians supposed to stand for love? After all, Jesus had commanded them to "love one another." Even more, how could people hate others just for being different, just for having a different religion or skin color? Was it prejudice, superstition, ignorance, intolerance, or were they just plain mean?

He didn't have time to explore the matter further, for Kelly was jabbing his finger at him. "George, you said the next guy got cute with her you'd doctor like a cat. Said you'd cut it off personally an' serve it to him on a platter."

"He's right, George," someone said.

"You sure did."

"Yep," George agreed. "I did, didn't I?"

*Castration!* He choked and thought of falling to his knees. *Do anything! Beg, wrap your arms around his legs.* Yet he didn't do it. Despite his horror, he felt a grin coagulate on his face and slipped George a wink.

"St. George to the rescue, huh?" he said. "With a switchblade for a sword and his sister the maiden in distress. Sorry, George, it just won't wash."

"What the f—"

"Poor George," he said. "Didn't you know? *You* are the dragon."

Something flickered in George's eyes. "Man—"

"It just won't work, you know," he heard himself insanely repeat. "You can't have her, George. But if you really do want to protect her from the dragon, maybe it's your own dick you should cut off."

He saw his words strike home like a rapier. For an instant George was naked, naked to himself, to the truth he wouldn't admit. Terror filled his eyes. Then something else happened, and George's face was like Van Gogh's last self-portrait: demented, decadent, sick of soul as he confronted his own personal *dybbuk,* the demon within that desired his sister. Johnny shook his head, trying to clear it of the image.

The movement saved him. Growling, George slashed at him, only to have the knife deflected by Johnny's wrist.

"Hey!"

"Gonna kill you!"

"Wait! Give me—"

"Hold him, Kelly. We'll see how tough he is without his balls!"

Kelly lumbered forward with hands like ham hocks. If he got them on him . . .

"You're a coward!" he shouted desperately. "You're yellow!"

"Grab him, Kelly."

"You're a coward!" he shouted. "Yellow! Afraid to fight me!"

"Aw, bullshit."

"Bullshit, nothing," he screamed, aware of George's hesitation. "Where would you be without—without—your knife and this ape to back you up? You're afraid to fight one Jew!" he taunted. "C'mon, you Pope's ass. Think you're so tough? Then prove you don't need a dozen guys to make you a man. Or is that what it takes: twelve Catholics to carve up one Jew!"

George moved back. "I don't need any help with *you*." He nodded at one of the gang. "Bobby, toss me your knife."

A knife sailed through the air. George caught it and flicked it open so the six inch blade caught the moon's glitter. Theresa stifled a scream, her eyes bright with fear.

"Here," George said.

"What's that for?"

George sneered. "You said you wanted it to be man to man. Well, here's your chance."

"I wasn't talking about knives."

Snickers ran through the gang, and a tall pimply kid with a cigarette dangling from his lips made clucking sounds like a chicken.

"C'mon, Kelly," said George, "let's get this over."

"Wait, that's not fair! You're used to knives. I'm not!"

"Chicka . . . chicka . . . chicka—"

"Stop it! You want to show how tough you are? Then let's use fists."

"Aw, fists are for sissies," George said. He pinched Johnny's cheek and made obscene smooching sounds. "C'mon, sweetie, let's drop them panties and in a few seconds you won't be taking advantage of no more little girls."

Johnny slapped his hand away. The gang hooted.

"Ooo-eee!"

"Tough! Tough!"

"Watch it, George, ya got a regular Marciano there."

"How about it, George?" he pleaded. "Let's use fists."

More hoots. For some reason the idea of him fighting their leader with fists was now even funnier than if he tried a knife. George looked around at them, laughing and sharing their amusement. Grinning, he seemed so different from the haunted, stricken figure of a few minutes before.

"Let's get this straight," he said, "you really want to fight *me*?"

"Oooh, baby, you don't want to fight *Georgey*," the pimply kid said. "Only cat can whup *'im* is Kelly."

"Sure," another said. "That's 'cause Kelly's the Frank-en-stein mon-ster! Only thing can zap him is some lightning bolts from the sky."

"You *sure*?" George grinned. "You want to fight me?"

"Yes." He raised his fists, noticing Theresa was gone. Had they taken her away? He wanted to look but didn't dare. It seemed so strange that the girl who had caused all this might not even be here.

"O.K., sucker," George said. "Then I'll cut your nuts off afterward. Here goes!"

Johnny braced himself for the first blow, determined to block it and counter with his own. It was always like this, he realized feverishly. Sooner or later he always ended up with his back to the wall, pushed there by others. It was the pattern of his life. There was some softness in him which let him get manipulated and shoved around, forced into a corner. Damn it, why had he let Jimmy and Lee get him involved with the girl? He hadn't wanted to. *Lee* was the one who should really be here! He felt a spark of anger and tightened his fists, feeling the pressure of his thumbs on his index fingers. Always the same. Sooner or later he found himself sick with fear and with just his fists between himself and destruction. What was George except another Duckett, meaner perhaps and twisted, but essentially the same? Well, he'd had it. Wanted a fight, did he? Then by God . . .

The parking lot acquired a sponge-like quality and he found himself in Mr. Farragut's carpeted office again, his back against another wall. The face too had changed. Now it was his father's. Dimly, with that dual awareness his mind sometimes split into, he realized he was riding a high wave of hysteria. *No, it couldn't be!* He shook his head, trying to dislodge his father's face, but it remained. *Quick, I've got to—*

His father's fist shot out and he tasted blood. Strike back! But he couldn't. He couldn't hit his own father! *Loved his father hated his father loved his father . . . fight!* He saw his father's hard, inflexible face, always so certain, always so right, and angrily started to swing. But he couldn't. He was his *father!* His father hit him again and he felt his head strike something hard behind him and again and again he hit him and something hard at the back of his head and *I can't hit my own father!* And this time his father hit him in the belly and he doubled over and now his father was in close his knee shooting up into his groin and he was down and he was dead.

He lay on his side, wondering if he had been knocked out. He didn't think so, because he had been studying the ghostly sheen of moonlight on the concrete. It had been close, though. George's punches had knocked his head against the wall, and the impacts had done it. Without the wall, he wouldn't be lying here.

Knowing it was George who had hit him made him realize he was coming out of it. But his progress was too slow. Too slow for what? He sorted through his mind, intrigued by the question, and reached the conclusion he needed to do something fast. If he could only figure out what it was and why he had to do it. Above, the marble face of the Madonna appeared just as he had seen it on statues before Catholic churches. The features were meek, mild, filled with mercy, sweetness, and serenity. But there were no eyes. Abba, why don't statues ever have any eyes? Then there were eyes and the features flowed and lost their whiteness, became George's, who he found was kneeling over him with a knife and the strangest look. The hand with the knife dropped from sight, and he felt it search below his waist.

Then he knew what he had to do and why he had to do it. Horror was a quick-working injection, but would it work quickly enough? George was busy now, having found his target. The hand holding the knife dropped. Suddenly he felt his hands and feet again. The back of his head hurt. Quick! He twisted his body, trying to get away. George straddled him, and he felt cool air on his genitals. The use of his legs returned. Thrashing like a fish about to be gutted and beheaded, he managed to roll George partly off. George dropped his blade. Jackknifing his body, Johnny shot his legs out and caught him in the chest, knocking him backwards. Frantically he got a knee beneath him and scrambled up.

He tingled like an electric circuit, all connections restored. George jumped up.

"Eat 'im up," a gang member snarled.

"Kill the Jewfuck!"

George unleashed a barrage of punches which he slipped and caught on his elbows and forearms. Everything seemed fine; everything worked. To test things, though, he dispatched a light jab. George took it on his temple and seemed to reflect. Yes, he felt just fine. He dropped his hands and raised them again, closing them into fists before his chest with the left one extended seven or eight inches ahead of the right. He savored the tautness of his clenched knuckles, the power he knew was in them. Dancing, he drew a canvas around George's face and then forgot the canvas. Now there was only the face before him, and he concentrated on making it fall. That it would fall he had no doubt. Always, always, the face would fall. In the past three or four years he had been driven back by many such faces. Some had been black, some white, some fat, some lean, but whatever the case, whenever they had smugly, arrogantly driven him back *too* far, they had fallen with alacrity. And although he had always been sick with fear and reluctance, the ease with which he had made them fall had always astonished and awed him.

This time, though, it was different. His body sang with anticipation, and for the first time he understood what hate really was. Hate was hunger, and violence or destruction had a rich meaty taste. One could bury one's snout in it and if lucky, gorge himself to his heart's content. Still, against one like George, whose tepid undisciplined blows were rapidly losing their steam, it would not do to be a glutton. The feast would be over too soon. Blocking a blow, he thought of Mrs. Murdstone, his English teacher, and how she had quoted Brutus:

> ". . . And, gentle friends,
> Let's kill him boldly, but not wrathfully.
> Let's carve him as a dish fit for the gods,
> Not hew him as a carcass fit for hounds."

Very well, then, he would sport with George, cut him down bit by bit. He remembered how helpless he had been just a minute before and how mercilessly George had straddled him. If he had recovered just a few seconds slower . . . His lips tightened. *All right, you would-be sisterfucker, this time I'm going to push back!*

He shot out a couple of jabs, taking care to keep them light.

George's head snapped back. He screamed and rushed. Johnny pinned his elbows to his sides and grinned, making smooching sounds as George had earlier. Then he contemptuously pushed him away.

He began to pick up the pace, delighting in the way his punches shaped and molded George's body, turned it this way and that to suit his whim. It was as if George were a block of marble and his fists delicate chisels giving it form. *Rat-a-tat-tat. Rat-a-tat-tat.* Was *this* what he had been born for? Just to use the power in his fists? He circled George outrageously, gave him a playful cuff on the ear from behind. Maybe *this* was his destiny, not the painting, which everyone despised. His fists at least had a place in this world. However much he had tried to avoid using them, people did respect and fear them. And what better proof could there be of the value of his skills than his being so often called upon to display them? Besides, there could be no doubt of their lethal excellence. His artistic skills were debatable, to say the least, and so far his work had been dismissed by his superiors as obscene, ugly, and ridiculous. In fact, his father didn't believe in painting at all and had confiscated his tools like a Nazi. Maybe his father was right. Maybe he *was* a disobedient ingrate.

Whatever the case, thinking of his father had an odd effect. Moving in, he drove a right into George's face, accidentally breaking his nose.

It erupted like a fountain. Blinded, with blood raining down his face, George reached out. For what? Sympathy? A helping hand? In the past it had been at this point, when he had his opponent at his mercy, that he had softened and felt sorry. It did not happen now. Drilling yet another punch into George's ruined nose, he watched him collapse.

Looking at the gang, he placed his foot on their fallen general. It felt good. Damn good. Drunk with conquest, he wanted to rub their faces in it. They in turn just stared back, fumbling with their switchblades and trying to believe this illusion. Could it really be *George* lying there? One of them held a tire chain but had forgotten about using it. Like the others he stood mesmerized.

*I'm tired of being a schnook, a patsy, a plump, four-eyed jerk everyone thinks he can pick on and push around. This time I'm going to be the bully. This time I'm going to push back!*

He scanned their faces. George had been tasty, but only an appetizer. Now he was ravenous for a succulent entree of massive proportions. Years of being humiliated and forced into corners raged within him, requiring catharsis, the purging effect of bare knuckles on jaws and teeth. Who *would* it be? One by one he rejected them. All were unworthy, all that is, except for Kelly, the sluggish behemoth, the *bulvon,* to use his father's word, who had been so eager to have him neutered. Yes, Kelly was made to order, a chateaubriand for kings. The fact he was a giant made him irresistible.

"What are you looking at?"

"Huh?"

"I said, what are you looking at, you stupid tub of shit?"

Stupid or not, Kelly got the point and lumbered toward him, arms open in a mammoth embrace. Johnny rushed.

"Sweet Mary," somebody said, "he's goin' for Kelly!"

Close up, Kelly was even bigger than he had thought, so big he had to leap to hit him. But he succeeded, and the impact carried them both back against the drugstore's window, which quivered and almost broke. Kelly's arms swooped down, squeezing him in a terrible vise.

Behind him, the gang returned to something like its old self. If their leader's fate had come as an inexplicable wrinkle in the smooth fabric of their existence, then at least things were returning to a predictable pattern. For Kelly had him now. More fearsome even than Kelly's blows was his legendary embrace, which had never failed to crush those who had strayed into it.

Reassured, they swapped smirks and waited. When the time for Johnny's collapse had come and gone half a dozen times in as many seconds, they began to fidget and look at each other. Then they noticed that Johnny had freed his arms and was working on Kelly's ponderous belly at close quarters. Soon Kelly began to comment on the punches' effect. Great shuddering sounds assaulted their ears. Kelly sagged. As they watched, his arms drooped and their intended victim stepped clear.

Johnny came out feeling fuller and more complete than ever before. Ducking under a sluggish right that cut a huge swath, he dug a left into Kelly's side and felt it cave like an avalanche. He darted around him, blasting whole chunks away from the mountain. His fists were equally potent bombs, and with delight he ripped away, no longer clumsy and convinced he was doing something alien to his nature. Now it was as natural as breathing, a gift, a blessing that his fists did his bidding so faithfully. Still, he made the old mistake of underestimating their effectiveness. A right to Kelly's heart brought to pass an unprecedented wonder. One vast sigh escaped him as if through an enormous puncture and as Johnny watched, Kelly settled to his knees like a god in ruins.

Nearby a couple of the gang were retching. Another kept saying "Oh, my God," in awed tones as if he were praying. Resisting the urge to hit him again, Johnny placed a finger on Kelly's forehead and pushed, causing their idol to tip over and lie still.

Even yet he was not finished but turned and charged them. The first who got in his way suffered a broken jaw. The next dropped instantly. Johnny waded on, lashing at faces and bellies.

So great was the gang's surprise, they were almost routed. Then some of them realized he was just one man and surrounded him. Two jumped him from behind. One caught an elbow in the ribs. The other found himself airborne.

Still, he was going under. Swarmed over, exhausted, he flailed away at a cataract of forms. One jolted him with an uppercut. Another tripped him. Staggering up, he tried to dislodge a forearm wedged across his windpipe.

One of the gang drew his knife. Unlike the others, it was a homemade shiv, a product of love and hours of honing that had earned for its owner a reputation which left even his friends uneasy.

Sensing a kill, he circled closer and closer, advancing from the fringes to a point where he had only to wait. The blade rode on his thigh like it was a part of him. A crack opened in the flesh around his target. He slid through and raised his hand.

His wrist exploded in pain. He turned, finding a big black man.

"Now, that wouldn't be kosher at all, would it, sonny?" The man smiled, snapping his wrist like a pretzel.

Although dazed, Johnny sensed the waters subsiding. With the last of his strength, he deterred a foe with a leaden punch and found, miraculously, he had time to breathe. Also, he discovered a muscular black man was shooting punches with a precision he admired even in his weakness. *I've seen him before,* he thought . . . *but where?* Barely able to lift his hands, he watched a tire chain approach. Panther-quick, the black man caught it and raked it across its owner's mouth.

Moments later the lot rang with departing footsteps. Tires screeched off into the night. The man grinned at him, showing bare gums and scar tissue that brought him almost, but not quite, to the point of recognition.

# Chapter
# Fourteen

## The Ancient Mariner

**N**ow there were just three left in the whole parking lot: himself, the black man, and. . . Jimmy Wiggins!

"Hey, Johnny, you all right? Looks like we got here just in time. Man, you was really bangin' them cats! Who was that *monster* ya flattened? Jeez, he was the biggest—"

"Boy, give him a chance to catch his breath," the man said.

Johnny sat, or rather *plopped* down like a blob of gelatin beneath the *3 Magnificent Corona de Luxe Cigars* sign. Bluebottle flies buzzed about him. Along Buckeye, the bright streetlights had acquired ghostly halos as if the night were feeding back to them their own radiance. The night itself smelled late to him. *Late.*

*God, so much has happened tonight. Is this really me sitting here?*

He leaned his head back against the wall, his body a ripe harvest of dangling ganglia and shattered synapses. One of his knees started trembling spastically. Jimmy sat beside him and touched his shoulder.

"Hey, man, you all right?"

"He will be, soon as he takes a swig of *this,*" the man said, putting a pint of whiskey in his hand.

"No thanks, I—"

"Go ahead, boy," the man said, firmly pushing the bottle back. "You need it."

Johnny looked at the old man on the label. *Old Granddad.* Trembling, he managed a small sip.

"Not like that." The man tipped the bottle so its contents sloshed down his throat in an insistent stream. Against his will, he took three large swallows.

"Feel better, son?"

J.C. on a Bicycle! His belly blazed with fire. He gagged and coughed. Then the coughing stopped, and he felt instantly better, warm and lined with fur inside. Without asking, he lifted the bottle and took two more swallows while the man, kneeling in front of him, chuckled softly and ran a hand through his neat, marcelled hair. Johnny grinned back and handed him the bottle, his body beginning to flow like a silken and velvet river. He felt his sweat cool in the breeze and accepted the cigarette proffered by Jimmy as if it were a victor's wreath. He took a drag. Delicious!

He threw back his head and laughed.

"What's so funny?" Jimmy asked.

He tried to answer but couldn't. Imagine! Hours and hours before the night had begun with a typical Shabbat meal. Challah, kreplach, gefilte fish, pot-roasted chicken and Manischewitz wine so cloying his taste buds were sated after three or four sips. (Why was Jewish wine always so sweet?) As always, they had worn yarmulkes and his father had recited the Kiddush, and tonight, he had stumbled over the Hebrew in the prayer book, causing tension and a solemn disapproval to register on his father's face beyond the brightly flickering Shabbes candle. Ida, his mother, a dutiful wraith who existed in her husband's shadow and who he associated with a line from Wordsworth ("Her voice was always gentle and low"), had betrayed only one emotion during the meal. That had been a meek look of gratitude when her husband had said:

"The kreplach are good tonight, Ida."

Other things had been good tonight too, or at least had turned out better than expected. Sneaking into the theater. Jimmy Stewart and the Indians. The chase. Theresa, who had reaped his virginity in the woods (Good Riddance too, and what would his father say about his wooing a *shiksa?*) Then there had been the nightmarish renewal of the chase in which time and reality had been a surreal kaleidoscope of new forms and patterns of perception. The gang. The horror of almost being castrated. The fight, which for the first time, he had actually sought and welcomed, and his rescue by this black man who seemed so familiar. And last of all, there was this bottle of balm in the middle of the night where he sat incandescent with life. What a night! How could he even begin to make them understand what it all meant to him? Hiccupping, he realized he was half-drunk and reached for the bottle, only to find the man's hand quicker than his own.

"Whoa! Save some for the old man!"

Johnny watched the leathery lips wrap around the bottle's neck and the Adam's apple bob. The man drank like it was water. Johnny turned to Jimmy and saw him watching the man anxiously. Of course! It was Jimmy's father, who had once been a contender for the Heavyweight Championship of the World. Years ago, at school, Jimmy had been a celebrity because of his father, but that was all gone now.

"Boy, I'm sure glad you turned up when you did," he said. "How did you find me?"

Jimmy reluctantly removed his eyes from his father. "I called my dad and we searched for *hours*, man. I knew you was in real trouble."

"How'd you know that? How'd you know I hadn't gotten away?"

Jimmy spat. "You crazy? Man, them cats was swarmin' all over the place. Up and down Buckeye. Shee-it, their leader, uh—"

"George."

"Yeah, George, he even had his gang goin' round and round the big field we meet in like they was soldiers. Don't know why the hell he'd want to do that."

Johnny grinned. "'Cause that's where we were."

"You kiddin'? Shoot, if I'd a known, I'd a gone in after you." He paused. "Wait a minute, did you say, 'We'?"

Johnny felt himself blush.

"Yup."

"You mean, jus' the two of you went in? *Together?*"

Johnny blushed again, only this time he turned crimson with the joy of guilt.

"Why you . . . sonofabitch!" Jimmy laughed, bug-eyed. "Here I'm worried about you gettin' *killed* an' lookin' all over for you, and you're losing your cherry and couldn't care less." He turned to his father, who was also laughing in soft throaty delight. "How about *that*, dad? If I'd a known, I'd a led them into the field personally an' helped them whip his ass."

"And they'd have needed your help too," Jimmy's father said.

"Haven't you told me for years how your friend here can handle himself?"

Jimmy spat, apoplectic with enthusiasm.

"*Handle* himself? Shee-it, that ain't the half of it! You saw him yourself. He was mowin' em down like a buzz saw!"

"He was for a fact." Jimmy's father smiled and looked at Johnny in appraisal. Despite the wonderful languor spreading through his body, Johnny noticed how different the father was from the son. Mr. Wiggins' English, for example, seemed carefully polished and consciously correct, as if he had taken diction lessons to impress people. Each word was pronounced clearly with every syllable clipped to a fine precision. Jimmy's speech, in contrast, consisted of slurred words and murdered grammar. Not only that, his ripped T-shirt and dirty jeans contrasted jarringly with his father's neatly pressed trousers, white shirt, vest and tie. With his ruffled sleeves, trimmed mustache, and styled, pomaded hair, Jimmy's father was what Johnny had heard kids call a "dandy." Yet when they laughed in their soft, throaty way, they seemed stamped in the same mold and more similar than different.

All at once Mr. Wiggins reached out and took Johnny's arm. Johnny felt him test his forearm and work and massage his way up to his biceps.

"How much do you weigh, boy?"

"About 190."

"And you're how tall? Five ten?"

"Yes."

"Five ten, hmm. That means at least six feet and two ten when you're full grown. Trimmed down, make it one ninety-five. And that's a conservative guess. You could be bigger." Mr. Wiggins dropped Johnny's left hand and picked up his right, which he also examined. "Good hands. Broad flat knuckles, nothing to break. Fighter's hands. Perfect for breaking things."

What was he getting at? Johnny looked at his right hand, the one he painted with. It *was* crude. The palm was a club, a slab of flesh, the fingers thick stubs. Funny he had never noticed it before. There was no delicacy in the hand, no finesse, no beauty. Surely it was not a hand designed to paint. Yet it had felt love in the brush, a caress in its bristles, had felt transformed merely scraping a knife on a palette or when it used turpentine to thin the paint. . . . No, he was wrong. This hunk of muscle, which was so different from his soft belly and hips, was obviously not meant to paint. For that matter, as his father had pointed out, who had ever heard of a Jewish painter? ("But abba," he had asked, only to be ignored, "what about Chagall? What about Modigliani, Soutine, Pascin?") Well, maybe his father was right. Such a thing *was* unthinkable! But if he was not to paint, then what? And why was Jimmy's father looking at him so closely?

"Johnny," Mr. Wiggins said, using his name for the first time, "have you ever thought about fighting?"

"Fighting? I just did."

"I don't mean that way." He smiled. "I mean professionally."

"Professionally? You mean for a living?"

"Yes."

He shook his head, this last development in the long jumble of crazy events comprising this night finding no niche in his brain whatever. The man was daft! What was he talking about?

"Don't look so confused. There's money to be made in it, and I think you could go a long way."

He still felt like Alice in Wonderland. "A long way. Where to?"

"Maybe to the top, who knows? It depends on you, on how much talent you've got, how much guts."

Jimmy was looking at his father anxiously again. Johnny took another drag of the cigarette Jimmy had given him, recalling how it had been Jimmy who had given him his first smoke. *Then* he had gotten dizzy, even sick. Now he held the smoke deep in his lungs and savored it lustily. Yes, he had come a long way. Especially tonight. And why *not* a Jewish boxer? It at least made sense. There had been Jewish boxers before. You could name them. There were the Max Baers, the Maxie Rosenblooms, the Barney Rosses. They had come over from the old country, from their Russias and their Polands and like other ethnic groups before them, had survived by hammering out their destinies in roped-in rings, in square traps that could, for a precious few, be catapults to the stars. The canvas there at least had a purpose. But a painter's canvas? What could it do for a Jew, with his hereditary fear and taboo of graven images except collapse beneath him? A Jewish artist? *Feh!* Except for him and a few others, who could name even *one*?

Still, the idea of boxing was ridiculous. "Me, a fighter? You've got to be kidding."

"Boy," Mr. Wiggins said, his eyes intense, "don't you even know what you did?"

"What?"

Mr. Wiggins shook his head in surprise and tossed off a quick drink. "When I got here there were nine boys against you. *Nine.* Some of them had knives and chains. And you damn near took them, son. You damn near took them all."

"But that's not *boxing;* it's just alley fight—"

Before he could finish, Mr. Wiggins was shaking his head impatiently. Jimmy, Johnny noticed, was watching his father with increasing alarm.

"No, it's not *just* alley fightin'. I mean, sure you ain't no boxer yet, and you sure as hell ain't in no kind a shape. You wore out mighty fast, looked like. But we can take care of that. A couple months trainin' and conditionin', and I'll have you ready for the Golden Gloves. Not a fighter? Boy, if you ain't the most natural, god damned, *borned* fighter I ever saw, then my ole brain's *soaked* in this juice I keep pourin' down and I don't know my ass from my elbow. Didn't you *see* what you done to that big one? Talk about David goin' up against Goliath! And you took him apart like he was a stuffed doll!"

Amazingly, Mr. Wiggins' correct speech had vanished, and in its place was a patois distinctly his own. Johnny waved his hand disparagingly.

"Oh, he's big and strong, all right, but basically he's just an ox. He's what my dad likes to call a *bulvon, a golem.*"

"Gol . . .?"

"*Golem.* It's somebody who's only half-formed, and a *bulvon's*—"

"Naw naw naw naw naw. Don't put yourself down. The cat was *dan-ger-ous!*" Mr. Wiggins snapped the bottle up and grabbed some feisty gulps. Air bubbles boiled in the caramel liquid. "Lemme tell ya, boy, ya really got it. I mean it. Just like I did the night I went up against 'Sailor' Levy."

"Dad!"

Mr. Wiggins shook off his son's hand and gazed over Johnny's shoulder into some lost moment in the past. "It was in March of 1948, and the word was out I was due for a title shot. I mean, *everybody* knew it! *Ring Magazine* had me ranked number five. And that was no slouch year, neither. There was Louis and Walcott and Charles. Anyway, I was ranked number five, and my manager, Chauncy, comes up to me one day and says—"

"Please, dad," Jimmy said, "don't tell it no more. It don't—"

"—says Joe, we gotta get ya ready for Louis. Ya need a tune-up bout." His gaze became unfastened from the wall and found Johnny, who was reminded of the Ancient Mariner. How many times had he been driven to tell this tale, and how many listeners had been mesmerized by it? "That's what he called it," Mr. Wiggins said. "It was supposed to be just a 'tune-up bout,' marking time and gettin' ready, you might say, for the real thing. A light workout in a ratty ole civic center in a jerkwater town, with some sweet coin for my troubles and nothin' but jivin' and good feelings comin' back. Oh, it was supposed to be a piece of cake, it was."

Johnny opened his mouth to say something, but like the Wedding Guest in Coleridge's poem, he found himself hypnotized. Jimmy's face, he saw, was filled with despair.

"A piece of cake," Mr. Wiggins repeated, savoring the phrase, "and it *was*. I mean, from the moment I entered that locker room, I knew it was my night. There was a leaky shower goin' drip drip drip all the time an' as I changed, I started to dance and move around to it. Ya know, give it the ole shuffle. An' man, I was so *smooooooth*, like I was an oiled machine made for just one thing or a pot a honey just oozin' out sweet and ripe, an' as I worked it round an' peppered the air with comba'nations, I just knew I'd never been so good. I mean man, there comes one time in your life when ya just *know* you're at your peak, your ab'slute peak, an' nobody has to tell ya. It's like ya been stuck for a long time on a kind a plateau, and all of a sudden the clouds clear way an' ya break through to a high place ya never been before. An' I mean you're on top, an' nobody can touch ya, an' the only thing bad about it is that it ain't *Louis* out there waitin' for ya, it's only some palooka in a jerkwater little town where the locker room smells like piss an' has a shower that goes drip drip drip all the time . . ."

Mr. Wiggins paused for breath and rose, his eyes still holding Johnny's to his own.

"And then after I changed, an' Billy Joe taped ma hands an' tied the gloves on an' rubbed me down an' I done some shadow boxin', we finally got the word. I can remember it like it was yesterday. Chauncy and Billy Joe went ahead, see, to clear the way 'cause the place was packed an' everybody was there cheerin' for their home town white boy. An' I felt *good*, man, I felt so *good* 'cause I knew I was roarin' an' was gonna show them crackers what a *real* fighter was an' it'd be the sweetest thing ever happened to me an' the only thing wrong, the only thing wrong at all, was that it wasn't *Joe Louis* himself out there 'cause then it would be for all the marbles 'stead of a tune-up in some nowhere little dump 'gainst a punchin' bag who wasn't even ranked. And when we got near the ring I saw he was there first just like we agreed, 'cause I'm the champ an' the other guy waits for *me*, see, an' Chauncy holds the ropes an' I slip through an' they're booin' all the way up to the fuckin' rafters 'cause I'm the king nigguh that's gonna chop down their white hope an' I give 'em a real show, test the ropes an' flex my muscles an' dance round an' flick jabs out one two three like lightnin', man. Then I stop an' look over at him an' smile. An' ya know what I see? There's this skinny white guy twenty pounds lighter than me. Pasty white he was, an' so scared I could see 'im *shiv*-uh!"

Abruptly he stopped, his black face shining with sweat. With a sweep of his arm, he seemed to conjure the whole scene from the past. The ring. The crowd. The smoke hovering like a cloud in the rafters above. Even the smell of liniment. When he spoke again, it was in a whispered incantation that summoned vanished wonders forever lost.

"And then, the announcer was proclaimin' our names, an' it was Jimmy Wiggins out of Cleveland, weighin' two twelve an' a half, wearing white trunks an' ranked number five in the world! An' of course they booed. Lawd, how they booed! An' I danced round an' waved and pumped the air with punches to give 'em a show, an' as I moved round I heard 'im say Dave 'Sailor' Levy, an' of course the crowd blows the roof off cheerin' cause he's their boy an' I'm a nigguh an' they got big hopes for 'im even though he's even *lighter* than I thought, only one eighty-eight. Then we're meetin' in mid ring an' I'm givin' 'im the ole grin as they give us the instructions, an' let me tell ya, I've got the 'Sailor' really shakin'! Lawd, how he do shake! I see 'im swallow an' I'm wonderin' why they call such a white mouse 'Sailor' when I notice he's got a dragon tattooed on his right shoulder like some of them sailors do, an' I pat it once to let 'im know I'm real nice an' gonna put that ole dragon to sleep quick an' painless, an' he swallows again like he's about to gag. An' as I stand there I look up at the crowd an' the ceilin', an' it's like never in my whole life have I seen things so sharp and clear. Up on the wall high above the seats they've got this sign for chewin' tobacco that ain't been sold in twenty years. BRIGHT LEAF it says, WHEN YOU WANT THE FINEST, an' I just have time to read it when it's time to go back to my cornuh an' remove my robe an' have Chauncy slip the mouthpiece in. Then the bell rings."

*Clang!* Had a bell actually rung? Holding their breath, they watched him move forward.

"Well, I come out smokin', full of the ole nick, but I know if I let myself go, I'll have 'im on Queer Street in just thirty seconds. So I lay back, see, dance round 'im like *this.*"

They watched as Mr. Wiggins did a head fake and shifted his feet so he was miraculously pointed in a new direction. His left fist shot out.

"Bam! An' lemme tell ya, was that cat surprised when I hit 'im practically from behind! I mean, I was *fast!* Nevuh nevuh nevuh had I been that fast before! It was like my legs was springs. The way I bobbed my head, the speed in my fists . . . I tell ya, I could a taken 'im out any time I wanted or carried 'im all night, an' for three rounds I was a tiguh on a leash, man, givin' them rednecks a show like they ain't never seen before. An' at the end of each round Chauncy an' Billy Joe flash me this big grin in the cornuh 'cause they feel it too an' know I'm ridin' high an' when the bell rings for round four I rush out an' pin 'im into a cornuh 'cause I'm a tiguh see, an' a tiguh's gotta eat, an' I jab 'im real good and get 'im set up for the kill when he accidently throws a left hook which ain't got enough punch behind it to squash a grape."

Abruptly, Mr. Wiggins' hands dropped, and it was as if he actually wore gloves. Johnny heard Jimmy sob beside him but couldn't look away. Instead he watched Mr. Wiggins' eyes open wide like those of a bewildered child who asks once again the same unanswerable question.

"Well, it wasn't as if he *hurt* me or nothin'. It was just that it made me blink an' kind a pause, only for a second, ya understand, though I don't know why 'cause like I said, it didn't have enough behind it to hurt a *fly*. Maybe it was jus' the surprise. Anyway, I'd about got it all back an' started a punch when I see he's not there an' I'm about to look round when *bam!* somethin' hits me on the side of the jaw an' I see we're in the center of the ring now an' I move toward 'im an' it's like quicksan' or somethin', I can't get nowhere or feel nothin' and all round I can see 'em screamin' only I can't *hear* 'em, an' he hits me again an' the only thing I know is I'm lurchin' round the damn ring like I'm a clown in a dream an' all them stupid rednecks is standin' on their feet screamin' 'cause I can see their moufs are open an' the Sailor's glove fills my face again big as a pumpkin an' I don't know a thing more till I look up an' see the referee count ten over me an' Chauncy and Billy Joe stumble through the ropes with their faces filled with horror an'—Oh Lawd, I've lost! Oh Lawd, I've lost! He's done beat me!"

He was on his knees, his muscular thighs straining at the costly fabric, and Jimmy threw himself at his father and held on.

"Naw naw naw. Don't tell it no more, daddy. It don't—"

"Oh Lawd, I've lost! Lawd—"

What was *happening*? There were tears on Jimmy's face and a horrible emptiness on his father's. Johnny's gaze struggled from one to the other, trying to make sense out of this last, last craziness of a long night. He felt like he was in the ring himself, as baffled and overwhelmed as Jimmy's father. Before him, Jimmy in his dirty jeans and T-shirt clutched his stylishly dressed father, trying to save him, but save him from what? His father knelt as if in prayer. *What did it mean? What was it about?*

"What happened after that?" he heard himself say.

Mr. Wiggins' eyes found his, still searching and groping for an answer to his mystery.

"We figured—decided—it was just a fluke, an accident. One of those one in a million things that just happens. So we went back into training and laughed it off, and two months later I fought again in New Orleans."

He was calmer now, his language correct and grammatical again. Yet he still seemed drained, weighed down by an immense weariness.

"And what happened?"

Mr. Wiggins smiled weakly and shrugged. "I was doing fine for the first five rounds and led on all the judges' cards. Then in the sixth he hit me with no more than an ordinary right hand lead, and I couldn't get it back. This time I went down three times instead of just one. It went into the books as a TKO."

He paused, about to give his own requiem.

"I don't know. I don't know *what* happened. I've never been able to figure it out. I never won again, and a year later I quit the ring."

"I see." Cold sober, Johnny started to rise and was surprised when Mr. Wiggins, with a surge of his former intensity, stopped him.

"That's why, when I saw you handle yourself tonight, I was impressed. Boy, I think you can go places, and maybe if you have the heart for it, you can go all the way! Reach what I—what I never quite . . . Look, give me a month. There's no one who knows more than I do about fighting. I'll have you ready for the Golden Gloves before you know it."

"Is that what you do—train fighters?"

"You bet. Just ask around. They all know Jimmy Wiggins."

Johnny looked at Jimmy for confirmation because he had heard one of the football players at school laugh at Jimmy and say his father was a drunk who operated an elevator or did other odd jobs when he wasn't out of work. But Jimmy was still watching his father with that pleading, desperate look which made him look away.

Still, what did he have to lose? No one cared about his art or wanted to see it. And certainly no one had come forward to show him how to paint or what techniques to use. Whether Jimmy's father was a blowhard or the real thing, he at least showed a willingness to teach him something worthwhile. Covering a canvas with paint *must* be foolishness. Hadn't his father told him so often enough? Hadn't it already made him and his parents unhappy and gotten him into enough trouble? Fighting, on the other hand, always seemed to be in demand and to have value.

"How about it?" Mr. Wiggins said, holding his hand out.

*The Merry-Go-Round Man.* Why was he thinking of that now? He looked at Mr. Wiggins' blasted face and thought of how high he had climbed, almost to the top. Then when he had seemed on the verge of reaching the summit, he had fallen back. And if the rumor was true, he had fallen ever since. Before him, Mr. Wiggins' hand waited, rock steady in the moonlight. An expensive ring gleamed on one of his fingers, and as he contemplated its evil eye, it seemed like all the other times he had been manipulated and controlled against his will, forced to conform to someone else's conception of him. Again he was in Mr. Farragut's office, helpless against their collective interrogation. Again it was like he wasn't even here, or at best was a bit player, the mere excuse for their gathering. Would he ever be able to run his own life, make his own decisions, stand up to them?

He raised his eyes to Mr. Wiggins' pencil-line mustache, which broke upward as he smiled.

"What do you say, son?" Mr. Wiggins said. "The sky's the limit."

"Sure. Why not?" Wiping his hand against his pants, he accepted the other's grip, feeling the strong fingers tighten around his own and wondering what he had gotten himself into *this* time.

# Chapter
# Fifteen

## No Sale

**E**ven from the woods Jimmy could smell the tantalizing aroma of corned beef and pastrami that reached him from Groucho's Delicatessen across the street. *Kosher,* Johnny Roth called it, winking at him whenever they passed the shop. Jimmy did not know what the word meant except it was something funny Jews did to food to make it smell good.

Only today it smelled like sour iron, and he could not have eaten a spoonful of manna to save his life. The thought of what he and Curly were about to do lay like an anvil in his stomach. He had stolen before, of course, but only kid stuff. This was the real McCoy, a robbery at midday using a gun.

His *gun.* Did he have it with him? For perhaps the twentieth time he felt his jeans pocket for the bulge of the .45 revolver. Yes, it was there, as wicked as ever though it contained no bullets. *That* he had insisted upon after Curly talked him into using a gun. At least this way there was no chance of anyone getting hurt, though the idea of going into the store waving a heater to scare the old Jew still made him squirm. Somehow it didn't seem right. His mind slipped again into Curly's lingo. Either they should pack a rod and be willing to use it or forget it. To his relief, Curly had readily agreed and called him smart. They'd *both* use empty guns. It was a bright move. All they'd have to do, Curly said, would be to poke them at the old kike and he'd fork over everything in the register.

Speaking of Curly, where was he? Cautiously, he raised his head and scanned the street, looking for Curly's casual gait. No dice. There were black kids coming his way along Buckeye, but even from a distance he could tell they lacked Curly's distinctive swagger. Then he realized Curly was too smart to be seen on the street just before they pulled a heist. Of course. He'd come another way. Curly was smart! Hadn't he cased the joint to begin with and had the idea of robbing it at two o'clock, just after the lunch rush was over and all the money was fresh in the till? Talk about smart! They'd hit the old geezer in the early afternoon lull and escape with a bundle just like they did in those crime comic books Curly was always reading.

He fixed his eyes on the shop. *Groucho's Delicatessen. Bagels. Kosher Meats. Orders To Go.* A woman left the place holding a paper bag with doughnut shaped rolls cresting at the top. What was it Roth called them—bagels? Wonder what they'd taste like.

A train whistled in the distance, and he thought of a rousing spiritual they sang in the Baptist church near home. How he loved those negro voices, tired yet transfigured by faith and joy.

*Dis train boun' fo' Glory*
*Dis train . . .*
*Dis train boun' fo' Glory*
*Dis train . . .*

The whistle faded, mournful and sad.

*Dis train don't carry no gambler*
*No fo' day creeper or midnight rambler*
*Dis train, Oh Hallelujah*
*Dis train . . .*

He frowned and shifted his body to get a crick out of his leg. Maybe he should go home, call it off. Guiltily he remembered he was supposed to be in Johnny's corner that afternoon. Johnny had reached the semi-finals in the local Golden Gloves tournament, and his father expected him to handle the sponge and relax him. What was he doing here? He was letting them both down. He fidgeted and glanced uneasily about. Lawd, what if someone spotted him here? What if they—

There was a wisp of sound, and Curly slipped beside him like a weasel.

"Take it easy, man. Be cool."

"Jus' jumpy, I guess."

"Huh, any more jumpy you'd be pissin' your pants."

"Hey, I'm cool, man."

"Well, ya better be. Don't want no punk walkin' in there with me."

Curly's doubt hurt his feelings. "Cut it out, will ya? I'm all set to go."

"Uh huh. Anyway, looks like we gotta wait some yet."

Across the street two men entered the shop. Curly watched the men. Jimmy watched Curly. Curly's scalp, almost bald in the autumn sun, accounted for his name and made Jimmy think again of a weasel. It was as if Curly were a sleek slippery animal that sneaked through woods and bushes and whose weasel-shaped head was ideally suited to burrowing into the ground and through crevices in rocks. Maybe that was why he was almost bald. Still, while there was something about him you couldn't trust and had to watch, there was also something that inspired respect and made you follow him. Jimmy gazed at his smooth, almost featureless face, determined not to appear yellow and marveling again at how much of a hold the other boy had gotten over him since they had met three weeks ago at the gym where his father was teaching Johnny how to box. He was just two months older, and yet it was like Curly was a grownup he had to obey.

"Fuckin' Jew, we gonna grab a pot a your gol'.'"

A soft breeze ruffled the leaves. Jimmy stared at Curly's patient profile, astounded by his words. He could remember when *he* was the one who was so sure about things, but lately he seemed to have lost his confidence. Just when had he lost it? He couldn't say exactly. A month ago? A year? Or was it earlier, when he had first found out what it meant to be black? He didn't know. Maybe it was a gradual thing. And why had he lost his confidence? He didn't know that either. All he knew was he had to get it back, and this was the only way he knew how.

The sun burned down through the trees. A few leaves fell, the first victims of autumn. Gold leaves. Orange. Red. A furry green caterpillar nibbled away at a leaf before his eyes. Curly nudged him.

"Git ready."

With shaking fingers he felt the .45 in his pocket. The butt was hard. Bullets or not, you could crack a man's skull with it. He looked at Curly, waiting for his move and determined not to look frightened.

"Let's go."

Numbly he crawled through the bushes after Curly and got to his feet. The shop seemed deserted. Now was the time.

Curly entered first. He followed, blinking in the dim light and managing to make out a slanted glass case in which various meats and cheeses were displayed. Behind it on the wall hung a sign written in Yiddish.

*Mit mazel ken men alles.*
With luck, everything is possible.

Where was the owner? There wasn't a soul in sight. Curly, though, didn't hesitate but slipped silently to the counter where a tiny old man sat reading.

Curly cleared his throat.

The old man kept reading. Was he deaf? Now that Jimmy was close, the owner didn't look tiny so much as shrunken and shriveled up, as if every drop of blood had been drained from his body. There wasn't an ounce of flesh to spare anywhere. Everything seemed stripped away, leaving skin over a human skeleton.

"Hey, mister," Curly said.

The old man looked up. "Yes?"

"Like to buy somethin.'"

"*Something* I got. A bad back, a double mortgage, a wife who gives me no peace. You would like to be more exact, maybe?"

"To eat."

"Ah, a little something to nosh! Why didn't you say so?" He went behind the display case and grinned at them, his bony features crinkling. "What will it be, boys? Gefilte fish, corned beef, potato pancakes? Please, I have all the dainties. Everything from knishes and knaidlach to farfel and flanken and sturgeon you would not believe. Just ask. Everybody tell you Groucho has the best food at lowest prices in town. And strictly kosher!"

The old man's queer talk and vitality stunned him. It was as if a cadaver had come to life. And what life! Even Curly seemed put back. Jimmy found himself pointing lamely at the case.

"Give us some of them."

"Ah!"

The owner snatched up a paper bag and snapped it open. Jimmy saw he held a handful of the doughnut shaped rolls he had noticed earlier.

"How many?"

"What?"

"How many? A dozen? All? Please, I need a number!"

"Uh, six."

"Six! A big spender I got yet. You make my wife happy, and all my creditors will bless you. This winter I retire to Miami Beach, thanks to you."

Queer old man! Why didn't he shut up? The old man handed him the bag.

"Something else? Creamed cheese, a little lox, maybe?"

"No thanks."

"You sure? Better you should buy some lox and cream cheese to go with them. Or maybe a little herring—"

"No thanks," Jimmy said, trying to cut in. "These'll be just—"

"Say, boys!" the old man said, snapping his fingers. "Do you know what a bagel is?"

"Look, mister," said Curly. "Just—"

"Well, I'll tell you. It's a doughnut with rigor mortis!"

The old man cackled and doubled up with glee. Curly drew his gun.

Jimmy watched, forgetting *his* gun. Instantly, all merriment left the man's face. He seemed to understand at once.

Curly waved his gun at the register. "Open it."

The register rang and the drawer slid open. *No Sale.* The owner stared at them with eyes of flint. Curly grabbed the bag from him and emptied it on the floor.

"Fill it."

The owner didn't move. Curly stepped forward and shoved him back. Plates crashed to the floor. Curly reached over the counter and began emptying the register into the bag, his eyes fixed on the old man. The owner lunged forward and grabbed Curly's hand.

"Let go!"

The old man hung on. Curly tried to pull free. The owner sank his teeth into Curly's wrist.

"Jimmy, get this fucker off me!"

The old man held fast like a terrier. Could this really be happening? It was supposed to be a simple job, a pushover. Could it really be Curly calling *him* for help? Curly held helpless by a little old man?

Curly screamed.

Belatedly, like a zombie, he stumbled forward and tried to pry the old man's jaws from Curly's wrist. Something skidded across the counter—Curly's gun.

"Gimme your gun!"

He reached in his pocket and dug it out. Curly grabbed it with his left hand and brought the butt down on the owner's skull. Once. Twice. Three times. The man held tight. Curly hit him twice more, raising the gun as high as he could and bringing it down with all his might.

What happened next was a nightmare. The owner let go. Curly was free. Then the old man had *his* hand! Jimmy pulled back, but it was like a claw. A moment later he found himself on the floor, trying to escape from the horror jabbering above him.

"You pisher, I'll teach you to steal from me!"

"Let me go!"

"Little Nazi, I'll kill you!"

"Get off me! Help!"

Saliva spattered his face. He pushed backward but now the other talon had him, binding him to the floor with superhuman strength. Where did he get it? He was just a frail old man!

"Help! Curly!"

Curly was at the door with the bag of money. He saw him hesitate and then dart forward. Curly chopped down with the gun again and again, smashing the owner's skull with heavy thuds that rang in the shop. Finally the thing above collapsed on top of him, but Jimmy still couldn't get away. He struggled to escape the claws and spittle, stabbing his feet in panic at the floor to drive himself out from under what seemed now to be a corpse. Finally he got a leg free, then another, and scrambled up.

"Curly, where'd you go? Don't leave me!"

It seemed forever before he could get himself to move. He was alone, alone in a shop with a dead man, and his feet were plants rooted deep in the earth. *Run!* He stumbled to the door, hearing a bell jingle above his head as he fumbled to open it. Finally, after several tries he succeeded and fled, only to run full tilt into the barber's pole next door, a red and white peppermint stick six feet tall. Stars exploded in his head, and he fell.

"Curly, don't leave me!" Curly was gone, had abandoned him. He staggered up, heard a whistle. Down the street a policeman was pointing at him, yelling at him to stop. Stop, hell! He turned and ran, at last finding his legs as the whistle shrieked again behind him.

His feet blazed. He was flying. Yet when he snatched a look behind, the policeman seemed closer. He turned into an alley and streaked down it. Oh, no! There was a high wooden wall at the end studded with fight posters. He timed his steps as he ran and leaped up, trying to grab one of the painted boards at the top, but his fingernails clawed wood and ripped down through a boxing glove tied with gold laces. JIMMY WIGGINS VS. JOE LOUIS FOR THE HEAVYWEIGHT CHAMPIONSHIP OF THE WORLD. He blinked his eyes, but he still saw his father's face, a younger face with gloves confidently raised before it. It couldn't be! His father had never fought Louis and besides . . . he shook his head and gazed up at the wall. It was no good, he was too short! He whipped around. Trapped! Why had he run here? He had to hide. Desperately, he saw some cardboard boxes stacked against one of the walls thirty feet up the alley and ran to hide behind them.

It was then he discovered he still had his gun. He looked at it in disbelief. How had he gotten it? Of course, Curly must have stuck it in his hand as he lay on the floor. The rat had not only run away, he had framed him, for if the man really were dead, they'd say he'd done it. Damn it, why had he let Curly talk him into it? He looked for a place to throw the gun, but at that moment the policeman appeared at the head of the alley.

Jimmy crouched with his empty gun and watched him approach through a crack between the boxes. The policeman wore a blue uniform, and a nightstick hung brutally at his side. Worse yet, he had drawn his gun. Had he taken the time to check the shop and seen the owner's body? Was that why he was so cautious? Slowly he grew closer. Jimmy could see his badge and hear his shoes, which were so new they squeaked. He drew back into the shadows against the building.

The darkness behind the boxes reminded him of the broom closet and Eveline, the white girl he had loved when he was twelve. Evy had betrayed him too, acted like she cared and then locked him in that closet where she had lured him. *You ugly nigger, did you think I'd let you even* touch *me?* He closed his eyes, seeing her lovely face become horribly deformed with contempt and disgust just before she had slammed the door. And afterward he'd heard her girlfriends' faint laughter as he lay on the cool tile in the darkness, heard it for hours long after they'd left.

He opened his eyes. The squeaky footsteps were closer, and for the first time he saw his life with something like completeness. He had started off so well, enjoyed such a head start. All during his boyhood he had been on top, been the one who ran the fastest and threw the farthest. He had been the leader, and all the kids had looked up to him. When had it started to change? When the boys had grown taller and started beating him in sports? There was Johnny, for example, who after three weeks of being trained by his father was moving in the ring, headgear, gloves and all, like he had been born there. And Lee, who almost overnight seemed to have acquired an inability to drop a football. Wherever it was thrown, he'd catch it, a fact that big name schools were beginning to notice. He bit his lip. Or could it be that things had started to change when he'd entered a snobbish white school and found himself treated like scum? Or when his father's earlier promise, like his own, had crumbled and he had started to drink? Maybe it was all those things working together which had progressively pulled him down, but he knew now if he just had the good fortune to get out of this calamity, he'd climb on top again. There'd be no more Curlys. He'd run his own life.

The policeman was even with him now. If he glanced his way and searched just a little, he was finished. *Don't look, please. Just go back!* But the policeman continued forward. He was almost to the wall now, and when he turned, he was sure to spot him. Jimmy rose from his crouch. It was now or never.

He sprang out, and such was his luck that the policeman caught the faintest movement in the corner of his eye. If Jimmy had waited an instant longer, the policeman would have been closer to the wall and the angle would have prevented detection. As it was, he spun just in time to see light glint on the gun Jimmy had forgotten to put down.

"Hey!"

Jimmy sprinted toward the head of the alley, his heart pounding. If he only made it to the street, everything would be different. He was getting closer. Never had he run so fast. He was a winner again, the fastest runner around!

"Stop or I'll shoot!"

He heard two shots and for an instant considered stopping, but freedom was just steps away. He had won! Exultant, he reached the head of the alley, not knowing the policeman had lowered the gun and aiming for the pavement at his feet, had pulled the trigger one more time. This shot he didn't hear at all. Instead, he felt only a stunning blow at the base of his skull, and then, nothing at all.

# Chapter
## Sixteen

### The Manliest Art

In the locker room before the fight, Johnny clapped his hand to his mouth and rushed to a sink. He stood retching into the cold porcelain bowl, feeling his insides empty of the high protein meal his manager had bought him just hours before. After a minute he felt better and turned on the tap, letting the water run until it was ice cold. Then he stuck his head under it and shut his eyes tight, feeling sick and wanting only to go home.

"Hey, Champ."

He took a couple of gulps of the cold water and turned to see a sympathetic face. The face cracked into a smile and sent a towel floating through the air to him. He caught it and dried his face with shaking hands, trying to remember the guy's name.

"You O.K., Champ?"

He removed the towel. Odets, that was it. Fast hands but a glass jaw.

"Yeah."

Odets glanced around the almost empty locker room and moved closer. "Hey, what are you getting sick for? You've won four straight fights by knockouts, man."

He shrugged. "Just couldn't help it. Anyway, I feel fine now."

Odets nodded. "Sure, just a case of nerves. My dad says even the pros get it."

"Yeah? Well, I'm no pro."

"Don't sell yourself short. I've seen you. Four straight knockouts and three of them in the first round." He shook his head. "I wish *I* could bang 'em out. You know, I just can't take one on the chin. I bet Marciano could tap you there and you wouldn't feel a thing."

Johnny managed a smile. "Don't tell me The Rock's out there!"

"Don't worry. Two more stiffs and you'll be Mr. Golden Gloves, on your way to the Nationals. Say, who you fighting today, anyway?"

"Wardlow."

Odets' eyes widened like saucers. "Wardlow! Last year's National Champion?"

He nodded. "Know him?"

"Hell, yes!" He studied Johnny. "No *wonder* you're scared. Shit, man, I'd forgot you was a heavyweight. You look more like a light heavy to me. How old are you, anyway?"

"Sixteen."

"Sixteen, huh? And I bet you don't weigh no more than one ninety. Wardlow's got thirty pounds on you, and he's old enough to vote."

He swallowed. "Well, I've fought guys older and bigger before. Jackson—"

"Kinda different, son. Jackson was fat and green. Wardlow's *hard,* and he's got *experience.*" He stood sizing Johnny up. "Shit, you're a babe in the woods. Wardlow's had over a hundred and fifty amateur fights, and the word is he's already fought for money."

Johnny's mouth fell open. "According to the rules—"

"I know, if you fight for a nickel just once, you're as much a pro as Marciano. But Gunther, Wardlow's manager, is a big shot and knows how to hush things up."

"Why the hell doesn't he just have him turn pro?"

Odets shrugged. "Probably he just wants Wardlow to get some more seasoning first. And if he bumps off a few more palookas and repeats as national champ, it'll look *twice* as good on his record."

Johnny stared at him in amazement. "You mean they're just going to let them get away with it? They can break all the rules and nobody's going to stop them?"

Odets patted his shoulder. "Welcome to Fuck City, son. When you've been around as long as I have, you'll have seen a hell of a lot worse. Why, just last year—"

The door crashed open and Jimmy Wiggins' father entered carrying a bag. He glared at Odets.

"You got business here, boy?"

"Uh, no, sir."

"Then hightail it. I got business with my fighter."

After he left, Johnny looked at his manager. "Mr. Wiggins, where's Jimmy?"

"Aren't you ready yet? Boy, you'll be fighting in half an hour!"

He took Johnny's arm and directed him to his locker where he mechanically undressed. Tying his shoes, he looked at Mr. Wiggins' face, sensing his anger.

Mr. Wiggins pulled up a stool beside his and started to wrap his hands. Johnny watched him expertly crisscross his knuckles again and again with gauze, smelling the sweet cloying sting of urine and disinfectant and soiled clothes that belonged to locker rooms everywhere. When he was finished, he taped the gauze securely at the wrists. A thought struck Johnny. Should he tell Jimmy's father he'd thrown up? After all, the man had paid for his lunch. He studied the handsome, mustached face with the styled hair, sensing the other's power. Yes, maybe he'd better. After all, Mr. Wiggins didn't like him to keep anything back.

Mr. Wiggins looked up. "Johnny?"

"Y-yes?"

"I didn't want to tell you this before because I thought I could work it out. But I can't."

A boy entered the locker room and went to a urinal, whistling an Elvis Presley tune. Johnny stared at Mr. Wiggins, feeling sick.

"It's about Wardlow, isn't it?"

"How did you know? Well, it doesn't matter." He opened his bag and pulled out a pair of boxing gloves. "Johnny, Wardlow's a professional, not an amateur. He's had half a dozen fights down South for fair-sized purses."

"That's against—"

"I know. Damn it, I've tried everything, even went to the commission, but his owner has it in his hip pocket. Probably bribed them to look the other way."

He held out his hands, and Mr. Wiggins slipped on the gloves and tied them.

"How do they feel?"

"Great. Just tight enough. You sure know how to do it."

Mr. Wiggins nodded. "Let me put it to you straight, Johnny. The boy you're fighting is twenty-one and he'll come in at around two twenty. But most important, he's had *professional* experience."

He swallowed, finding his mouth cakey. "Has he ever been beaten?"

Mr. Wiggins took a deep breath. "Johnny, he's never even been knocked down, but apparently Gunther thinks he needs more time."

He nodded. "Well, I've . . . done all right so far."

Mr. Wiggins gazed at him. "Johnny, if you were a couple of years older, just a couple of years, you'd have a chance. You'd be bigger, stronger." He shook his head. "Eighteen is a man. Sixteen is a boy. It's just two years, but it might as well be ten, especially when you're going up against a professional. Johnny, you're a great prospect, maybe the best I've ever seen. In a couple of years, though, this Wardlow's going to be a contender. Do you understand? You'll see him ranked in *Ring Magazine*, striking poses and hawking Wheaties."

"Are you saying I don't have a chance?"

Mr. Wiggins stared at him for a moment and then exploded. "Damn it, it's not fair! You're not ready!" He rose and drove his fist into a metal locker, causing Johnny to wince. "I've seen this rotten game before, all my life. It's a dirty racket. Fixed fights, crooked referees, even buckshot in the gloves. I never expected to find it here, though, in the Golden Gloves. This ain't the pro's, it's supposed to be for amateurs!"

Johnny watched him, momentarily forgetting his fear in shock at his manager's loss of control. "Somebody told me his trainer wants him to win the national championship again," he said. "Thinks it will help his career when he turns pro."

Mr. Wiggins nodded reluctantly. "Gunther's sharp, all right. Owns a dozen fighters body and soul. Fight for him and you're just meat, man. Hell, all he cares about is winning. Start to lose and he'll send you in against better fighters you don't have a chance with, even bet *against* you, setting the odds himself and picking the round you fall." He shook his head. "But if there's one thing the maggot knows, it's horseflesh. He's got a *gift*, a God-given gift for knowing his boys. He can just *touch* them and sense what their weakness is, what they need to get better. So if he thinks one of them, like this Wardlow, needs a little extra polish before heading for the big time, then I guess he's probably right."

Johnny looked down at his gloves. "You make it sound hopeless."

Mr. Wiggins gazed at him. "I just wanted you to know the truth so you could change your mind. Johnny, you could get hurt in there." He paused. "As a matter of fact, I don't know if you'll last a round."

"Then why did you put these gloves on?" He bolted to his feet. "Damn it, if you think I'm going to get slaughtered, why didn't you tell me *before* you taped my hands and tied the laces?"

"Now, Johnny—"

"You know what I think? I think . . . I think . . . you want a second chance at Sailor Levy, and you don't care how you do it. You'll do it over my dead body if you have to, even if it . . ." He broke off, almost crying in his rage, which was half at Mr. Wiggins and half at himself for getting himself into this. What was he doing here? Why wasn't he painting a picture in the cellar where the worst thing that could happen would be his father catching him?

Mr. Wiggins shook him by the shoulders. "Johnny, you're getting yourself upset. You don't know what you're talking about!"

"Don't I?" He knocked his hand away. "Well, then you tell me. Why'd you wait until you put my gloves on before giving me the goods? No, I'll tell *you*. It's because you figured I wouldn't back out then, that I'd listen to your pious warning and climb into the ring anyway." He shook a glove beneath his nose. "What's wrong with you, anyway? You think you can get back at the man who buried your career by sending me in there to get killed?"

"You can't talk to me this way!"

"Yes, I can," he said, looking directly into Mr. Wiggins' eyes, which were three inches above his own. "And you know why? Because I've given up *everything* to let you train me, everything to enter this tournament. Do you know my father doesn't talk to me anymore? To him, I'm dead. No, I'm worse than dead, I'm nothing, I never even existed. If I was dead he'd at least say the Kaddish for me. But I'm not even worth *that*. I thought when I entered the Gloves he'd be angry, maybe even kick me out. Only it's worse. I eat at the table, and he doesn't see me. If I speak he doesn't hear. And if I need something, like for school, I have to tell my mother, who's suffering more than any of us." He paused, trembling. "Damn it, you're my manager. You should have told me first!"

Mr. Wiggins gazed back for a long moment. Then he looked down. "You're right, I should have. But it's not what you think. Johnny, I'm your trainer, and I'd *never* do anything that wasn't in your best interest."

"Wouldn't you? You know, I've heard you tell about that fight a dozen times, just aching for revenge."

Mr. Wiggins stiffened. "What you're saying is wrong. I admit I think about that fight. I think about it a lot. But Johnny, there's a *reason* I waited until after putting your gloves on to tell you."

"What is it?"

Mr. Wiggins took his gloves in his hands. Johnny could feel the power in the other's body. It coursed through him like a current.

"Johnny," he said, "a man has to make his *own* decisions. You can't make them for him. If I had told you first, before putting on the gloves, it would be like you were a boy and I was making it easy for you. But with the gloves on, it's *your* decision. Johnny, *you* have to decide, and I can't protect you. Do you think I wanted you to feel you weren't even man enough to wear gloves?"

Johnny stared back into his eyes, knowing it was true, sensing it in his strength. "How do we fight him?" he said.

Mr. Wiggins smiled. "You're going on?"

"Like you said, I've got 'em on. It seems a shame not to use them." He forced a grin. "Tell me, you think the smart thing is for me not to fight him, but you'd be a bit disappointed, wouldn't you? I mean, I'd be running out."

Mr. Wiggins nodded. "If only this fight were a matter of guts, Johnny." He paused. "White boy, I sure wish you were *my* son. Somebody ought to set your daddy straight."

Johnny looked away, embarrassed but pleased. "Thanks."

"That's all right, I meant it. Though I'm afraid I haven't been much of a father to my own son. I neglected him for years when I was drinking, and now that I'm off it, I just can't seem to get through to him." He checked his watch. "Which reminds me. Jimmy was supposed to be here fifteen minutes ago. We need him in your corner."

"Aw, he'll probably pop up in a minute."

"Sure. Still, I'm surprised. I thought this meant a lot to him." He shook his head and shrugged. "Well, come on, raise your gloves."

He brought them up and assumed the stance he'd been taught, being sure to keep his legs close together. When he had first started learning, he had been corrected on his wide stance, which weakened his maneuverability and lessened his punching power.

"Now this man you're fighting is taller and has a longer reach than you," Mr. Wiggins said. "So what you've got to do is work inside."

Johnny was in the East Side Boy's Club again, bobbing around in the ring while his manager coached him. He waited until Mr. Wiggins started a right and parried it with his left, slipping in and stopping his right cross just inches from impact.

"O.K.," he said, "I wait till he throws and slip in. Hey, do you think I can muscle him a little from the inside?"

Mr. Wiggins shook his head again. "No, Johnny, he's too big and strong. Do that and you'll get *yourself* into trouble. You've got to sneak attack, use your speed and get out *before* you get hit." He paused. "Look, your opponent's never even been knocked down, and regardless of what I think of his manager personally, he's been superbly trained. Other than his cockiness, Wardlow just doesn't have any weakness. He's dynamite with either hand and knows the ring. And he never telegraphs a punch!"

He let his gloves drop to his sides, feeling despondent again and overwhelmed by the hopelessness of it all. What was he doing stepping into the ring against a professional who was also a national champion? He looked at Jimmy's father, thinking how hard it had been for him to stop drinking. Well, if *he* could do *that* in order to teach him to fight, the least he could do was try.

Jimmy's father seemed to read his thoughts, for he smiled and patted his shoulder. "C'mon, Champ, let me give you a rubdown and get you loose."

"Sure."

They went over to a table, and he lay down on his stomach. He felt Mr. Wiggins' fingers start to knead his back, expertly dissolving knots of tension. To his surprise, he started to relax, even feel good. Just another minute and he'd even—

The door opened and footsteps entered the locker room. At the same time, the fingers on his back faltered. When they resumed, their rhythm was changed, subtly altered. Puzzled, he sat up and looked around.

Two men were standing by a locker thirty feet away. One was a gnarled little man. The other was a young black man well over six feet with muscles that rippled beneath his silk shirt. As he watched, the man turned and their eyes met.

Mr. Wiggins touched his shoulder. "Wardlow," he said.

"Jesus Christ." He sat staring at him, feeling the chill of the locker room on his chest and stomach, feeling his legs tremble. Now the other man turned, and he saw his eyes light up.

"Jimmy Wiggins!" He beamed with delight and marched over, one hand extended theatrically. "Jimmy! Can it be *you*?"

They shook hands, Mr. Wiggins, it seemed, reluctantly. The man pumped his hand and continued to greet him effusively. Johnny noticed, though, it was the little man who was doing most of the talking. Mr. Wiggins' contribution seemed to be single words which he uttered grudgingly, and as soon as he got the chance, he freed his hand and turned to him.

"Johnny, I'd like you to meet Mr. Gunther, the manager of your next opponent."

He got off the table and reached out to shake hands. Then he realized he was wearing gloves and blushed. Gunther wheezed in appreciation.

"This your boy, Jimmy?"

"Yes."

"Well, what do you know!" Gunther stepped back to size him up, and he found himself remembering what Mr. Wiggins had said about all fighters being "meat" and "horseflesh" to him. He felt instantly vulnerable, as if he were a slave at an auction. Why should he be so nervous, though? Gunther was just a tiny little man.

"Well well well." Inventory completed, Gunther nodded in delight. "I see you have yourself quite a fighter here, Jimmy," he said. "Yes. Four straight knockouts though I'm afraid I miss them all. And three in the first round, too." He stopped and ran his eyes over him again as if tallying a cargo. "Yes, I'm afraid I miss your boy, but . . . I don't miss him *this* time!"

At the word *this*, he spun to face Mr. Wiggins, reminding Johnny of a Nazi officer. Of course! The man had a German accent, faint but reminiscent of all the stories his father had told him about gas ovens and concentration camps.

"We have a *problem*," Mr. Wiggins said. "A serious one. Unlike my *boy*, and all the other *boys*, *your* fighter is a seasoned professional with nearly two hundred fights under his belt."

Gunther's eyebrows rose above his smile. "I beg your pardon?"

Mr. Wiggins moved forward. "This contest is supposed to be for *amateurs*, Gunther, not pro's you want to hone for the big time. Damn it, don't you know your fighter could hurt these boys?" He pointed at him. "Johnny, here, is sixteen, and it's only his fifth fight. He shouldn't even be in the ring with your man, yet you stand there smiling like it's a joke!"

He stood glaring down at Gunther, angrier than Johnny had ever seen him. There was a sheen of sweat on his skin, and even his neatly trimmed mustache glistened with moisture. Gunther simply shrugged and made a gesture of dismissal. "Aach! No need to talk of these things. You know as well as I do, anyone's eligible to fight in this tournament once he's turned sixteen. And what's a little experience between fighters? Once they climb into the ring, it's all the same, no? A mere matter of one fighter against another, and may the best man win."

"Yeah, the best man. And it helps a little, doesn't it, if you grease a few palms to get them to overlook the fact he's already fought for money!"

Gunther shrugged again. "A mere technicality," he said. "So what if he's fought for a few watches and some odd change? Besides, my boy's good for the sport. Have you seen the papers? It's not often a local tournament gets a national champ who's trying to repeat. First Cleveland, then the Nationals in Kansas City. I tell you, a little publicity is a tribute to the whole manly art of self-defense."

Mr. Wiggins sneered. "The manly art of self-defense, huh. You know, Gunther, you've been reading your boy's press clippings too much. You've gotten so you believe that swill."

Gunther simply smiled and turned to Johnny. "Kid, I hope you appreciate who's training you. Did you know Jimmy Wiggins was once ranked number five in the world?" He turned back to him, eyes flashing. "Yes, you were good, maybe the best all-round fighter I ever seen. You had fast hands and knew the ring. I remember some of us thought at the time if there was *anyone* who had a chance against Louis, it was you." He paused. "Only you never got to The

Brown Bomber, did you? Let's see, what happened? Oh, yes, you got taken out by some palooka and after that—"

"Gunther," Mr. Wiggins said, "get the hell out of here."

Gunther grinned and turned back to Johnny. "Good luck to you, kid," he said. "See you in the ring."

He turned and walked back to the locker, and Johnny was surprised to find he had forgotten all about Wardlow. Now he saw his opponent was dressed in a flashy silk dressing gown that contrasted jarringly with Johnny's faded terrycloth robe. Wardlow's feet moved like lightning and his gloves sliced the air in neat quick jabs. Then, just as quickly he stopped and turned to stare at him. There was no smile, nothing human in his face.

Standing, Johnny fought the urge to look away and met Wardlow's stare. Unconsciously he brought his gloves up in a defensive position.

"Come on, Jason," Mr. Gunther said, "it's time we got to work."

They watched them leave. As the door closed, Mr. Wiggins moved toward it, muscles flexing in his arms. He stopped before the door and kicked it shut.

"So much for the *manly* art of self-defense," he said.

# Chapter
# Seventeen

## Fathers and Sons

Johnny took a deep breath. Mr. Wiggins forced a smile.

"Well, I guess we better hit the trail."

Johnny nodded and went to get his robe, which now seemed tawdry next to Wardlow's. Mr. Wiggins held the door open, and he slipped through just as Odets entered.

"Hey, Johnny, knock 'im dead!"

Without replying, he headed down the half-lit corridor toward the gymnasium, which was located in downtown Cleveland. Though it was on the first floor, he had the sensation he moved through a tunnel miles beneath the earth. A figure moved toward them, instantly familiar.

"John."

He stopped, fighting the urge to run.

"Hello, Father."

In the dim light his father's features were lost in shadow, but there was no mistaking the rigid form. The commanding eyes bore right into his as if no one else existed.

"John, I want you to come home with me."

"I can't."

"The car's parked right outside. I'll wait while you change your clothes."

He swallowed, not knowing what to do. Mr. Wiggins stepped forward and held out his hand.

"Mr. Roth, I'm Mr. Wiggins, Jimmy's father."

His father ignored him. "John, please get dressed."

"I . . . I can't. I've got a fight."

"A fight?" His father stiffened and then whirled on Mr. Wiggins.

"You did this! *You* went behind my back without even asking for my permission and seduced my boy into this barbarity!"

Mr. Wiggins touched his father's shoulder. "Mr. Roth, there's no need to get upset. This is a clean sport. Thousands of fine boys have built character and learned discipline as a result of it. And your son has done just won—"

His father slapped his hand away, and for a moment Johnny thought he was actually going to strike the larger man. "Just wonderful? *Feh!* And will it be just wonderful if my son gets hurt out there? Or worse still, if he maims or kills some other child whose parents' hearts will be broken?"

Mr. Wiggins' face darkened. "How can you say that? How can you say it would be better if *Johnny* was hurt? He's your son!"

His father's beard trembled. "Yes, he's *my* son, Mr. Wiggins. Not yours. And I believe I know a little better than you do what's right for him."

"If you did, you wouldn't be here now doing this. Don't you realize Johnny has a bout in a few minutes? What are you trying to do, get him so upset he can't—?"

"He shouldn't be here in the *first* place!" his father screamed in the dim corridor. Johnny watched in amazement. Had his father actually screamed?

"I know what you feel," Mr. Wiggins said gently. "Johnny's told me how you want him to study and be a rabbi. But don't you see, you have to consider what *he* wants, what's right for him. Like his painting, for example. Only he knows—"

"Bah! He knows nothing. He's a child."

"Mr. Roth, please listen. Look, I have a son the same age as yours. As a matter of fact, your boy and mine are friends. They've played together, grown up together."

"And gotten into trouble together," his father snapped. "Yes, I know all about your fine son. I know how he's led John into all sorts of foolishness." He shook a finger beneath Mr. Wiggins' nose. "Mark my words, it would be wise if you tended to your own child rather than presumed to instruct me on mine. I've heard all about your drinking, Mr. Wiggins. It's no secret you've neglected your boy." He turned to Johnny. "Well, I'm not about to neglect *mine.*"

Mr. Wiggins paused. "Mr. Roth, what you say is true. But I hope it's not too late to rectify it, for me to be a . . . father again." He smiled tentatively, and Johnny felt a small shock of recognition. How many times had he himself struggled hopelessly to find a common ground with his father?

"If you only knew what a fine son you have," Mr. Wiggins said. "You should be very proud of Johnny. I can't tell you what it's meant—"

"Then don't tell me," his father said. "Go teach your own boy for a change. Assuming you know what alley he's hiding in."

Mr. Wiggins gasped and drew back. "Now wait a minute!"

"Father," he said softly, "I'll go home with you."

His father turned to him. "What did you say?"

He glanced at Jimmy's father who stood bristling, not wanting the situation to get any worse.

"I said, 'I'll go home with you.'"

"Johnny!" Mr. Wiggins said, while his father slowly smiled. Just at the point, though, where the smile threatened to engulf him, he spoke again.

"On one condition."

"Condition?" The smile disappeared. "What?"

Trembling, he raised his gloves so his father could see them. "I'll take these gloves off," he said, "and never put them on again if you'll do one thing, just one small thing for me."

"And what might it be?"

"Let me paint for six months."

His father stiffened. "No! Never!"

"I see," he said. "You'll cry and whine about me getting hurt, or worse still, about me hurting someone *else,* but you won't lift a finger to stop it."

"As long as you live under my roof, you'll do as I say," his father said. "As long as I buy your food, pay for the clothes on your back—"

"Mr. Roth," Mr. Wiggins said, "what can be so bad about letting Johnny paint for a few months?"

"Nothing's bad about it," Johnny said. "It just doesn't fit my father's narrow view of the universe." He smiled weakly. "Painting's for the *goyim,* isn't it, abba? It's that simple. But if you really don't want me to fight, for once you're going to have to make a small concession and give me back my paint, brushes, and art supplies for six short months."

He stopped, his eyes flooding with tears. Would his father hit him? Did it really matter?

"I'm going to Juvenile Court right now and have you declared an incorrigible," his father said.

"Fine!"

His father shook his head. "Fine," he says. "John, how can you do this? Do you know how hard I've struggled to give you the chance I *never* had?" He held out his hand to Mr. Wiggins as if beseeching him. "A mind like a star my son has, and you want to use him to break bones!"

"I know you've sacrificed a lot for me," Johnny said. His father was waiting, watching for the slightest sign of weakness. And he knew if his father saw it, he was lost. His father had a way of turning the smallest lack of resolve against you. He plunged on lest he surrender. "I know you've given me all you could" (*don't think of what he's done for you, don't!*) . . . "but I've got to live my own life, decide what's right for me." (His father's eyes were fastened like leeches to him; if he stopped, he was a goner.) "Damn it!" he shouted in anger that threatened to dissolve. "You never listen to a word I say! You don't give a damn about me!"

He stepped around him to go to the gymnasium. As he did, his father caught his arm.

"John, if you won't do it for me, at least do it for your mother. How can you do this to her? You can't hear her because she doesn't want you to know, but in the night she cries into her pillow. She weeps for you, John, she fears you'll be hurt and come home all broken. How can you do this? She's the finest mother in the world, and yet you put her through all this suffering."

He almost gagged. With the last of his strength, he tore his arm away and headed toward the gymnasium. His mother's face leaped into his thoughts. It was true. She *was* the finest mother in the world and made constant sacrifices for him, even sitting up all night with him whenever he'd been sick as a child. How *could* he do this to her? He felt Mr. Wiggins' hand on his arm and forced her brutally out of his mind, concentrating instead on the brightly lit square of the gymnasium that grew from the size of a child's block to a blazing battlefield he was about to enter. This was the real world, not the dark corridor behind him. In just one more second . . .

"John!"

Mr. Wiggins pushed him forward, but he turned anyway. From where he stood, the corridor was a long dark tunnel, and he couldn't even see his father.

"John!" his father shouted again out of the darkness, his voice almost sobbing. "How can you do this to me? How can you?" He broke off, then continued. "It's a tradition! *Honor thy father and thy mother!* I obeyed my father, and he obeyed his. It's always been this way! It's the *only* way!"

It was too much. He took a step forward and then stopped. What should he do?

"Maybe he's right," Mr. Wiggins said behind him. "My apologies, Johnny. I was wrong to interfere. After all, I'm not your father, and as he said, I didn't even show him the proper respect of asking his permission to train you."

*Now you tell me this.* Johnny peered back at him. "So I should leave with my father?"

Mr. Wiggins stood silent.

*Thanks for the guidance.* Stranded between the two men, Johnny gazed down the dark tunnel, sensing his father was still there. What the hell was he going to do?

With a sob, he raised his fists, fed the air a savage one-two-three combination and wheeled around. Mr. Wiggins took his arm again, and together they entered the gymnasium.

# Chapter
# Eighteen

## A Cinch for the Nationals

He was blinded at once by the bright light, for he had spent too long in the dim corridor. Mr. Wiggins, though, seemed to be born for dark places and steered him adroitly to one side of the gym.

"O.K., Johnny, let's warm you up a little."

Listlessly he moved his feet and jabbed at Mr. Wiggins' poised hands. Over his shoulder, as his eyes adjusted, he could see two middleweights in the ring pawing at each other. Both were leaving themselves wide open.

Mr. Wiggins grabbed him. "You're not even concentrating. Do that in the ring and you'll get yourself killed."

Killed. The word clanged in Johnny's head like the bell at ringside. *It's just what he wants,* he thought. *Didn't he say he'd rather I got killed than someone else? Well, maybe I'll give him his wish, get really hurt and come home all bloody.*

"Johnny, snap out of it! What's wrong with you?"

He shook his head, angry at his self-pity. Imagine thinking of getting hurt to spite his father. Still, he did not feel right. It was like he'd been gutted and had no heart.

"Look, Johnny," Mr. Wiggins said gently, "you've got to forget him."

He shook his head again. "You don't understand. What he said about tradition, about obeying your parents. It's all true. It's always been that way in our family. And I —"

"And *you,*" Mr. Wiggins said, "are entering that ring in just ten minutes against a national champion." He rubbed Johnny's shoulder. "Believe me, you can't afford to take your father in there with you."

"I know. You're right. It's just—"

"Hey, Johnny!"

They looked up to see Lee bounding down the wooden bleachers at the front of the gym. He took the steps three at a time, waving and grinning at them in his excitement. Johnny glanced away.

"Hey!" Lee said when he reached them. "I didn't see you guys come in. Where's Jimmy, anyway?"

"I don't know," Mr. Wiggins said. "If I find him, I'll shoot him. He was supposed to handle the sponge."

"Crimmey! You mean he didn't show?"

"That's right. I don't suppose *you'd* know anything about it?"

"*Me*? Far as I know he was supposed to be here at two. Say, you want me to sponge him up?"

Mr. Wiggins gave a despairing look around the gym. "Well, it doesn't appear he's going to show. Damn that kid." He considered Lee reluctantly. "O.K., but I don't want you goofing off like you usually do. All you have to do is sponge his back and neck between rounds, maybe rub his shoulders a little to relax him. Think you can handle it?"

"Sure!" Lee beamed with delight and Johnny glanced away again, troubled by his avid stare.

"O.K. Then why don't you grab one of those buckets near the judges table?"

"Sure, soon's I tell my girl. She's in the stands."

They watched him run off. "Seems like that kid always has a broad somewhere," Mr. Wiggins said.

Johnny didn't answer but scanned the gym, avoiding the ring where two light heavies were feeling each other out and where *he* was due to fight next. He remembered what Mr. Wiggins had said about his opponent fighting professionally. Was he actually expected to climb in there with Wardlow? He wanted to run; instead he gazed at the spectators who surrounded the ring on all four sides. Soon they'd be jumping in their seats, screaming for his blood. Beyond the section to his left, Lee's long legs climbed the wooden bleachers three steps at a time toward the blonde waiting for him. Or was it a redhead this time? Lately he had acquired an interest in redheads and was collecting them like trophies. He looked up at the vaulted roof and spotted a sign near one of the metal girders. What did it say? BRIGHT LEAF. WHEN YOU WANT THE FINEST. Ah no, that was Mr. Wiggins' sign, the one he'd seen just before . . .

"Johnny," Mr. Wiggins said, "it's time."

He turned and headed woodenly toward the ring. Lee was already there, clanking down a pail of water on the floor beside the steps which he was expected to climb. For an instant he considered running out of the gym and right back down the corridor where he'd met his father. His foot hit the first step and Mr. Wiggins sprang ahead to part the brightly colored ropes so he could slip through. If he was going to run, it had to be *now*! Lee was right behind, though, nudging him forward. He slipped through the ropes and stood up.

He didn't want to look but had to. In the opposite corner, Jason Wardlow was already dancing about in ruby red trunks and a glossy silk dressing gown. His shoes had red laces with decorative red tassels.

Lee whistled. "Fancy-Dancey!"

He removed his gown, feeling stiff and unreal as Mr. Wiggins slipped his mouthpiece in. He bit down on the tasteless rubber and watched as Wardlow removed his robe with a flourish. The man's muscular torso gleamed in the overhead lights.

This time Lee's whistle pierced his eardrum. "Man," he said with shining eyes, "look at the *build* on that coon!"

Mr. Wiggins shot him a sour glance. "Boy, you going to wet your pants gaping at him or you going to get that water pail ready?"

"Oh. Sure!" Lee tore his gaze away and climbed out of the ring.

"Now, Johnny." Mr. Wiggins was in front talking to him, but the words were dust in the wind. He stared at Jason Wardlow who stared at him from the opposite corner. The man looked unconcerned, confident, not even turning his head as Mr. Gunther spoke in his ear. Wardlow's own private cheering section shouted "Kansas City, Kansas City Here We Come!" referring to the city where the national championships would be held.

"Johnny, remember what I told you?"

"Huh?"

"About how to *fight* him," Mr. Wiggins said. "Remember, work in close and get out fast. Don't try to mix it at long range."

He nodded, not hearing a word. The warning buzzer shrieked, and Mr. Wiggins patted his flank and reluctantly left. He swallowed and raised his gloves, gazing across at Wardlow's magnificent torso, which looked like it was covered in armor plate. Johnny was sure his gloves would bounce off the man like ping-pong balls.

The bell rang.

He tottered out, gloves held up like a blind man's, and saw Wardlow come straight at him without even pausing and shoot the first jab. It caught him stinging on the side of the jaw. Wardlow danced away supremely confident and openly contemptuous, five inches taller and thirty pounds heavier and God knows how many hundreds of fights more experienced. Plus he was better, just so much Goddamned better. Wardlow feinted, slipped, outflanked him while he waded across the canvas like it was quicksand. He felt a playful cuff on his ear from behind and realized in shame he was being toyed with. He turned, hearing someone in the crowd laugh, and threw a right hand lead that landed on air. Wardlow danced, jabbed, hooked him with a left to the jaw, a right to the belly. He retreated confused, unable to tell the pinwheeling faces outside the ring from the ebony one inside it. He threw a left which managed to find an elbow, then a glove exploded in his face like a flash bulb.

He was on his knees, listening to someone chant "Kansas City!" He turned his head, trying to find the source, and saw two faces cheering in delight. Nearer by, just outside the ropes, Mr. Wiggins was saying something too, only he didn't seem so happy. What was *he* saying? He tried to catch it, but a voice thundered in his ear.

"Five!"

Five? He raised his eyes and saw the voice belonged to a white sleeved arm. The white was immaculate, the whitest white he had ever seen, and it was attached to a body, the immaculate white suited body of the referee, whose arm was coming down again . . .

"Six!"

He pushed at the canvas and rose. The referee came close and peered into his eyes.

"You O.K.?"

"Hell, yes."

The referee's head snapped back in surprise. He glanced at the judges outside the ring as if to say, "What do you think of that?" Then he wiped Johnny's gloves against his shirt.

"O.K., son. Box."

Wardlow rushed. Johnny retreated, knowing if he went down again, the referee would stop it. This was an amateur contest, not a pro bout or a brawl in a smoker with bets riding, and the officials tried to halt things at the first sign of trouble to avoid injury. Wardlow, not so compassionate, drove him back into the ropes. Johnny slipped a jab, half-blocked a right, then a glove exploded in his face again. His knees sagged.

"Kansas City! Kansas City here we come!"

His legs quivered and wanted to fold, but he fought them. Damn it, the bloody hyenas wanted to see him reduced to a senseless pulp just so their precious hero could return to Kansas City. And if he went down, his manager would be right. He *wouldn't* have lasted a round.

In desperation, he grabbed Wardlow and buried his face against the man's chest.

"Lemme go, white boy!"

Wardlow twisted him away from the referee and rabbit-punched him. In pain, Johnny shoved away and rose up on his toes. What was it Mr. Wiggins had said? Oh yes. *Work on him inside.* Wardlow charged, hungry to end it, and as he started a right, Johnny moved in with a combination to the man's ribs then away, avoiding a left hook. He danced, feinted, then shot a jab which caught Wardlow flush on the nose, jolting him.

Clang!

He returned to his corner where Mr. Wiggins took out his mouthpiece and eased him down onto the stool. Lee sponged him frantically with cool water and jabbered wildly until Mr. Wiggins silenced him.

"Johnny." He knelt before him and held up three fingers. "How many?"

"Five," he said. "But you've got three heads."

Lee laughed, the sponge slopping everywhere and raining water down the inside of Johnny's trunks. "Holy Toledo. Can that guy hit! Johnny, I thought you were done for! Wham! You hit the canvas—"

"Hey, watch it, will ya? You're getting water down my ass."

"Oh, sure, sorry. It's just—"

"You were wrong," Johnny said to Mr. Wiggins. "I did last a round."

Mr. Wiggins nodded. "You sure did. But how do you feel?"

He considered the question. In the opposite corner a handler was rubbing Wardlow's chest. Gunther looked on, lips pursed. Some more water dripped inside Johnny's trunks, drenching his buttocks.

"I feel fine," he said. "A little sore is all."

"I bet." Mr. Wiggins whistled softly. "You got in some good licks toward the end, Johnny, did just what I told you." He sniffed. "But you took a hell of a beating, too. If you want to stop—"

"No."

Mr. Wiggins smiled. "That's my boy. Just remember to work from the inside and watch him when he comes out. He expected to get you last round and he'll be hungry."

The warning buzzer sounded and he rose watching Wardlow, painfully conscious of the difference between them. Wardlow was a thoroughbred while he at 192, was clumsy with a roll of fat around his middle. Maybe he *should* have quit!

When the bell rang, he found his manager was right. Wardlow came for the kill, throwing leather like a hailstorm. He covered with his elbows and gloves, absorbing the flurry as best he could. He took one on the temple and his ears rang. Bulled into the ropes, he spun Wardlow around and drilled a right to his chest, darting back just out of reach.

He stood poised in mid ring, waiting for him. Wardlow came out stalking, his mouthpiece a savage snarl.

"White boy, I'm gonna smear you!"

Johnny caught him with a jab. "Hey, Fancy Pants, I'm gonna drop you on your shiny britches!"

The crowd roared. Wardlow blinked, and in that instant he nailed the man again and began to move. Now he concentrated on what his manager had taught him: feint, watch his opponent's hands so he could counter, focus on using the ring and staying out of the corner so he didn't get trapped. Wardlow threw a right cross which would have leveled him in the first round. It missed by inches. Johnny found himself doing what he would never have thought possible: moving as quickly as Wardlow and even beating him to the punch. Ever since childhood he had thought of himself as slow. Now his hand speed and maneuverability came as a revelation. He watched his opponent grow increasingly frustrated and waited for the right moment.

It came. He dropped his left, hoping to lure Wardlow into throwing a right. Wardlow bit. Shifting his legs, Johnny came over Wardlow's arm with his own right and then unleashed a flurry of punches that spun him into the ropes right above his fans. Something flashed in the air; Wardlow's mouthpiece went flying as he sagged backward, and for a moment Johnny was staring not at Wardlow but at his whole noisy entourage. He raised his glove and shook it in their startled faces.

"Ain't gonna be no Kansas City, boys! Not this year!"

"Break!" The referee shoved him back and retrieved the mouthpiece, which he slipped into Wardlow's mouth with a look of concern. He stepped back.

"Box!"

Johnny charged, and now it was his opponent who retreated, his face stamped in disbelief. Wardlow caught him twice with flashing jabs, and even as he rushed, Johnny admired the other's excellence. Still, it did not matter. Willing to get hit five times to land just once, he dug a left into Wardlow's sculpted belly and whipped a right to his jaw. Wardlow dropped his hands, threw back an astonished face as if to consult the God of Boxing, and sat down promptly on the seat of his pants.

Pandemonium. The crowd was on its feet screaming with Gunther yelling at his fighter to rise. The referee thrust his face at Johnny.

"Opposite corner!"

He obeyed. When he got there, he saw Wardlow was still sitting in his flashy trunks, having been given precious seconds of extra rest due to his stupidity. He watched as the referee began to count.

At three, Wardlow got a knee under him and struggled to rise, only to fall back. Johnny saw a look of disbelief cover his face. At six, his superbly molded thighs bulged with effort and he reached for the ropes. At eight he got one knee under him again and at nine, every muscle tensed as he prepared to rise.

And he was still there on one knee when the referee counted him out and turned to raise Johnny's arm in victory.

Whooping, Mr. Wiggins burst through the ropes, tripping in

his excitement. He grabbed him around the trunks and raised him aloft.

"Johnny! Johnny ya did it!"

Lee was there too, grinning from ear to ear and slapping his back as his manager spun him round and round. He felt drunk with conquest as shapes and colors swept by. Here was the crowd and Lee again, and over by the ropes, Wardlow was still kneeling, surrounded by others. Johnny raised his arms toward the vaulted ceiling and shouted, feeling dizzily alive. Beneath him Mr. Wiggins started to rattle again in that astonishing language of his for the first time since he'd met him in a moonlit parking lot.

"Man Oh Man! I seen it but I didn't believe it! Right 'fore my eyes the very first time I seen ya an' time an' time again durin' trainin'! Right 'fore my eyes bright as the sun an' still I didn't see! Johnny, ya made me a believah! *Nevah* will I doubt ya again. If they was to set ya up 'gainst Louis, Marciano, an' Dempsey all rolled togethah, I'd take ma sweet hard change and slap it down *right next to ya name!*"

At last his manager set him down. Wardlow had disappeared behind a wall of bodies in his corner. Johnny removed his mouthpiece and approached, finding he still couldn't see him. He watched as the ring doctor ministered to Wardlow from a bag held by a handler. Gunther looked on in concern, occasionally asking questions which the doctor answered with calm little nods of his head. A hypodermic appeared in his hand, then vanished from sight. He saw the doctor shake his head.

Johnny edged closer. Gunther turned and shot him a look of pure fury. The people around Wardlow contracted. To Johnny it felt as if they wanted to shield the boxer from his very touch and keep him outside.

He felt a hand on his shoulder. "We better go, Johnny," Mr. Wiggins said.

He nodded and turned, sorry he hadn't said something to Wardlow or at least shaken his hand.

"Wait!"

He stopped near the opposite corner and turned. In his corner, Wardlow was shaking off the restraints of attendants and struggling to rise. He succeeded and stumbled forward. With a shock, Johnny realized one of Wardlow's eyes was swollen shut. Wardlow reached out and pointed a trembling finger directly at him.

"How come I never heard of *you?*" he asked.

Johnny shook his head, aware of their stares. "I never knew myself—till now," he said.

As soon as he said it, he knew it was true. Leaving the ring, he felt his mind fill with a new awareness. His whole body sang with it, and for the first time he savored his immense and peerless gift. Beside him, Mr. Wiggins cleared the way as if he were royalty, but he wanted only to climb back into the ring and face a hundred Wardlows! Lee pinched his arm and he looked into his grinning face, remembering how years ago, after another fight, Lee had told him there wasn't anybody he couldn't lick. Now, for the first time ever, with his fists thrumming with limitless power, he knew it was completely and gloriously true.

A girl appeared—Lee's girl. In a glance he saw this one *was* a redhead, like others Lee had been seeing lately. But more important, he saw that for the first time ever, a girl was looking at *him*, not Lee. Giddy with the moment, he hoisted her and hugged her to his sweaty chest, kissing her while bystanders howled. He felt her body stiffen and then cling to his.

With a laugh he set her down and marched past her flushed face, down the corridor which so recently had been his gallows walk and which now marked his triumphant return. Gone was his father, his guilt, and all his uncertainties. For the first time in his life, he felt complete and certain about what he was meant for.

The locker room door loomed. He straight-armed it and strode through to find the place was packed. To his amazement, all kinds of people were there. A reporter arrived and took his picture. Afterward, some fighters said, "Nice fight, Johnny!" and he grinned, knowing he could lick them all. He proceeded like a king to his locker. They watched him undress, their eyes hot and envious, and for once he was not embarrassed by his plump nakedness. He basked in their reverence, winking at Lee who fired cracks at the room in general.

"Yah! Thought Johnny didn't have a chance, didn't ya! Big mighty Wardlow, Kaboom! National Champ, Tim-ber! Hey, *Johnny's* going to be the champ, and we're going all the way to Kansas City!"

Mr. Wiggins was laughing too and trying to restrain him. For a moment, Johnny wondered where Jimmy was and why he hadn't been in his corner. Then he was stepping into the shower room and turning on the water as hot as he could stand it and just the way he liked it.

"Johnny!"

He turned his head. Mr. Wiggins tossed him a bar of soap and then just stood there grinning as he lathered himself up, feeling like the lord of the realm, like he had just reached the top of the mountain and could see the other side. Too bad Jimmy wasn't here to see him!

Afterwards he dressed and combed his hair. The room had mostly emptied, but there were still five or six stragglers, all of them here, it seemed, because *he* was here. He shook his head in surprise. What did they think he could give them?

In the mirror, the door opened and Mr. Gunther came in.

Johnny slipped the comb into his pocket and turned. Conversation ceased as if chopped by a blade. They all watched Gunther. Gunther and him.

"Ah, *there* you are!" The little man's fingers did a spidery dance as he approached. Mr. Wiggins quickly joined them. Gunther halted before him and smiled pleasantly. "Jimmy!" he said, his merry eyes riveted to Johnny's, "this is quite a contender you've got!"

"How's Jason?" Mr. Wiggins asked.

Gunther's eyes continued to hold him. "Jason? Fine. Fine. Course, he won't be able to fight again for six months. Your boy saw to that." He reached out and patted Johnny's arm. Something about the man made him step back, only to find his progress halted by the sink. Gunther maneuvered closer, the bright chips of his eyes like drills as he took his arm. "Yes, your boy managed things quite well. According to the doctor, Jason's jaw is busted in two places and he's got a bruised rib." For the first time, he looked at Mr. Wiggins. "You know what he told me just before they took him to the hospital to wire his jaw shut? He said he wouldn't have believed anyone could hit so hard, especially a sixteen-year-old boy. He said he'd never felt anything like it."

Mr. Wiggins shrugged. "Well, Johnny does have a punch."

"A punch? A *punch,* he calls it!" Wardlow's manager seemed to double up in merriment, but Johnny noticed the goblin-like creature hadn't removed his hand. If anything, his grip tightened. A heartbeat later, it became *very* quiet in the locker room. He was vaguely aware of faces watching them, of the room holding its breath.

"Golden Boy," Gunther purred, stroking his arm. "Golden Boy." He peered at Mr. Wiggins. "You know what you got here?"

Jimmy's father raised his hand and placed it on Johnny's shoulder. Johnny had the feeling they were fighting for him.

"I do now," he said.

"Do you? I wonder." Gunther turned his gaze back to him, and his touch seemed to go deeper. "Golden Boy," he intoned for the third time, and for an instant Johnny was reminded of a holy man's laying on of hands. Only this man's touch was not benign or meant to cure. It was as if Gunther could see all the way through him, down into his mind and his very bones. With an effort he raised his hand and removed Gunther's, broke the contact.

Gunther's smile died and burst into flame again. Something appeared in his hand.

"Son, here's my card. If you ever want to make some *real* money, just call me. The number's right on the card."

Reluctantly he took it. "Thanks, but—"

"Don't say anything now. Just think it over." He patted his arm again. "Tell you what. I'll give you five hundred dollars just to come and talk to me. Do you hear? Just to talk. No strings or commitments."

Lee's mouth fell open. "Wow, Johnny!"

Gunther glanced at Lee. "See? *He'd* listen." He winked. "Be smart, son. Come and see me. Just to talk."

"The hell he will," Mr. Wiggins snapped. "It's because he's smart, he *won't* get mixed up with you." He looked at him. "Johnny, give him back his card."

Gunther was already leaving. "Think it over, son. *Five hundred dollars.* And that's just for openers. You can have your own car, too." He jerked his head at Mr. Wiggins. "What can *he* give you?"

"Get your grimy little ass out of here!" Mr. Wiggins said.

Gunther smiled and opened the door. "You know, you were wrong, Jimmy. It wasn't *your* boy who shouldn't have been in the ring with mine. It was the other way around." He looked at Johnny. "Get yourself a manager who knows what he's doing, son. Sign with me and I'll take you all the way to the top and make you rich. Hell, you'll be *rolling* in it!"

The door closed. They stared at each other.

"Johnny," Lee said. "What are you going to do?"

He studied the card, no longer feeling so elated. His whole victory felt marred. Though he'd wanted to win, he'd never wanted to hurt anyone or to be troubled by other complications.

"Johnny, don't listen to that devil," Mr. Wiggins said. "I've seen a hundred boys like you destroyed by false promises of quick glory and easy money. Believe me, he doesn't give a damn about you. You're all a meat market to him."

"Yeah," Lee said. "But it's five hundred clams just to talk. And a car!"

"You did say he knew about fighting," Johnny said. He turned the card over, examining it.

Mr. Wiggins put his hand on his shoulder. "So do *I*, Johnny. In a couple of years you can turn pro. Then we'll get you *all* the money you want."

He turned the card back over, reading Gunther's number. "Maybe I want it now," he said.

Mr. Wiggins released his breath in frustration. "What are you going to do, Johnny?" Lee repeated.

He looked up. Lee was staring at the card like it was the Hope diamond. Johnny glanced at it again and then walked past them to one of the toilets. He dropped it in and flushed it, watching the card spin around and around until it was gone.

"You did the right thing," Mr. Wiggins said.

He nodded, feeling strangely somber. Lee picked up his bag, and they left the locker room and walked down the corridor to the parking lot. On the way Jimmy's father talked excitedly about the finals in which Johnny would be fighting in two days. After that, there was the national competition in Kansas City. He barely listened.

"Hey, where's Jimmy, anyhow?" Lee asked when they reached the parking lot.

"Who knows?" Mr. Wiggins said. He pulled out his keys to open his car. "All I know is he'd better damn well have—"

"Mr. Wiggins."

They all turned to find a policeman in a starched blue uniform. Mr. Wiggins stiffened.

"Yes?"

The policeman cleared his throat, apparently ill at ease. "Mr. Wiggins, I'm sorry to tell you this. But your son was shot and wounded today after attempting to rob a store." He paused, his gaze brushing each of them. "They've taken him to Mount Sinai."

Mr. Wiggins braced himself against the car. "Is he all right?" he asked.

The wind blew. The policeman opened his lips.

"He's in intensive care," he said.

# Chapter
# Nineteen

## The Catchers

**H**it one! Hit two! Hit three!"

When Slater snapped the ball, he was off like a shot. Then like he'd lost interest, he seemed to take himself out of the play, to slow down and drift, indifferent to the action and the drive toward the goal. Though the boy guarding him knew Lee's treachery and explosive speed, he still lagged back, so when Lee took off, he was embarrassingly outdistanced. The quarterback saw Lee was in the clear and started to throw, and such was Lee's lead that the result would have been an easy touchdown. But at the last moment a tackler deflected the ball, causing a wobbly pass which was almost intercepted.

Lean and lanky, Lee returned to the huddle, his cleats puncturing golden leaves which increasingly covered the field.

"Sorry," said Furillo, "prick got my arm."

"Let's try it again," Lee said.

Furillo looked around at the others. "O.K. Same play. On three."

Lee felt mildly disappointed the play had failed. He'd been all alone and in the clear. Even a half-assed pass would have done it. Still, it was only practice, and he was about to get another chance.

He returned to his position opposite the boy he'd just faked out, a rich kid named Wilson who was always rubbing Lee's nose in his father's money.

"You're not gonna lose me this time," Wilson sneered.

"Wanna bet?"

"Gonna suck your ass all the way down the field." He spat on the grass. "Stick to it like glue, pretty boy."

"Then you better get wheels, fat stuff. You're so slow you couldn't catch a cold."

A couple of his teammates laughed. Wilson scowled.

"Think you're hot stuff just 'cause you can run fast and get all the girls, don't you?"

"You bet. What's the matter, you jealous, Wilson?"

Wilson's scowl deepened. "Bet you five bucks you don't get away from me this time!"

"Aw, keep your daddy's allowance. It'd be like taking money from a baby."

A malevolent grin replaced the scowl. "What's the matter, poor boy? Can't you afford it?"

*Poor boy.* More members of the team were watching now, wondering if he would take up the challenge or back off. He waited a few seconds for effect and then smiled.

"O.K., rich boy, but it's your funeral."

"Hey," Furillo shouted, "did you guys come to play football or to socialize? I mean, if it's conversation ya want—"

"O.K., O.K.," Wilson said, crouching at the line of scrimmage. "Fuckin' wop," he whispered under his breath, fixing eyes on Lee that were flat as glass.

*Rat's eyes,* Lee thought, heart thumping as he considered Wilson's father, a wheeler dealer who owned an armada of car dealerships. *Poor boy. The bastard's always rubbing my nose in it, always cruising the streets around school in that shiny red sports car his daddy bought him. God, I'm going to have one just like it someday, and someday I'm going to be so rich my mother won't even have to work anymore. And as for our bet, well, fat little rich boy, I'll show YOU!*

Knowing he didn't have five dollars to his name, he crouched in anticipation before Wilson and smiled into his marble eyes. Then he glanced up and discovered the lonely figure of Johnny Roth watching them from a hill in the warm autumn sun. He remembered the fights Johnny had had so far in the Golden Gloves tournament. There had been five of them, and they'd lasted a grand total of fourteen minutes and ten seconds. The last one had been especially brutal. Watching from ringside, he had seen Johnny with a little bulge of fat showing above his trunks, hit his opponent so hard he had fallen ass over teapot halfway through the ropes, looking no longer like a fighter but a broken rag doll. His mouthpiece had gone flying and bounced on the canvas like a raw bone. What was especially impressive about Johnny's win was that his opponent had been the national champion the year before.

He frowned. Johnny might be fighting for the title tomorrow, but he still struck him as a loser. It was almost as if there were a hex on him. Poor Johnny with his doomed, damned face. That was how he thought of him, doomed and damned because Johnny's interest in art seemed to be a constant source of pain to him. Then, too, Johnny's father only made things worse, for he violently opposed not only his painting but his training and fighting in the Golden Gloves. Why did people make life so hard? Maybe it was because they were too deep for their own good and thought too much. Take Johnny, for instance. He'd been offered five hundred dollars just to *talk* about fighting and had turned it down flat. Why'd he do it? Bet if someone offered *him* that kind of bread, he wouldn't break his brains thinking about it. He'd leap at the chance! Hell, what was the point in pondering everything? He himself wasn't interested in analyzing moral fine points or in figuring people out and thinking about their problems. Life was too good. It was meant to be lived. Thinking, he was convinced, just caused problems.

Take Wiggins. Something must have really screwed up his head to make him rob a delicatessen. Some people just didn't seem to have any luck. The guy who does it with him gets away scot-free with all the loot while Jimmy . . . He frowned again as a persistent image returned: full-of-life Jimmy lying stone still in a snow white hospital bed, Jimmy neither alive nor dead with fragments from a cop's bullet still lodged in the occipital something of his brain. Above him plastic sacks hung down heavy with liquid. Tubes ran into his arms, occasionally moving ever so slightly in the faint air current while Jimmy slept on in a coma beneath the oxygen tent.

Oddly, though, the worst part had not been what had happened to Jimmy but Mr. and Mrs. Wiggins' tormented expressions. Jimmy's father had actually collapsed beside the bed and buried his bleak face in his hands, acting as if he could not bear to live. Jimmy's mother had tearfully embraced both him and Johnny and stood by her son's bedside clutching a Bible, looking like someone struggling to keep her faith.

"Hit one!"

Furillo's voice snapped him back. He dropped his gaze.

"Hit two!"

Raised his butt.

"Hit three!"

Again he was off, propelled by a hair trigger. This time Wilson did not make the mistake of lagging back when Lee briefly slowed. Still, it did not make any difference. Changing directions like a jack rabbit he poured it on, leaving his pursuer with the insulting view of flashing cleats and pumping elbows. Then at the proper moment, he turned his head.

And there it was! High, like a brown star in the blue sky. Five yards ahead of his man, his union with the football was a given fact. Nothing could prevent it.

Except one thing: the ball was hopelessly overthrown. Here he was, all alone by himself once again, and Furillo had thrown a pass it would take the Jolly Green Giant to haul down. Might as well just wave bye-bye.

But he didn't. Digging his cleats in, he poured on all his juice. The ball was maddeningly high, thrown so far it would land in the end zone. Still, it hung up there, and when he launched his 6'3" frame, the tips of his long fingers grazed the ball in a miracle of timing so precise, the football scout in the stands swore in awe. Like glue, Lee's fingers adhered to the leather, rode with it and gathered it in as he descended to earth, the whole act reminding the scout not so much of a completed pass but of aerial ballet executed with stunning grace and fluidity.

Touchdown!

All over the field shouts went up. Cunningham, a stocky guard, and several others ran up and pounded his back and shoulders. A couple of them belonged to the defense and forgot their competitiveness in admiration of the catch. Basking in the glow, he exuberantly launched the football high in the air, just as he had *The Cleveland Press* when he had delivered papers.

Smack!

Trotting back down the leaf-littered field, he let a small smile tug at his lips. Hail the conquering hero! He felt good. Poor little rich boy! Boy, had he ever sucked him in. He saw Wilson's glum, dough-like face and laughed. Yes sir, he could sure use his daddy's money. He laughed again, regretting only that his father had not been here to see his catch.

A small bead of sweat salted his lips, providing a pleasant tang to his thoughts. What a catch! And everyone had seen it. Wonder if a scout had? His eyes covertly swept the sidelines, but all he saw was a group of cheerleaders practicing their razzle-dazzle. Leaps and yells. Knee high skirts rising over pink panties. Red, white, and blue pompons. At least two of the prettiest he had deflowered just this year, one in the back seat of Coach Banky's car while Fats Domino sang "I'm Gonna Be a Wheel Someday" on the radio.

No, he didn't see any scouts, but that didn't mean anything. Sometimes, from what he'd heard, the most ordinary looking guys could be sharpshooters for the Big Ten. School had buzzed with rumors for months. Half the colleges in the country were after Leaping Lee, the fabulous junior who was going to be All-Conference end this year. It was just a matter of time before Ohio State or Notre Dame made their pitch.

Before he got back to mid-field, Coach Banky intercepted him.

"Great catch, Lee."

"Thanks, Coach."

"Uh, someone wants to see you." The coach slapped his back and jerked his thumb over at the stands, where a man he'd missed sat watching. "You better hustle over there."

"Practice isn't over, Coach."

Banky winked and slapped his butt. "You go on. This is more important."

Aware of his teammates' curious stares, he trotted over with a pounding heart. When he got close, the man rose and stuck out his hand.

"Lee Esner?"

"Yes."

"I'm Carter Dickson, talent scout for Masterson State. That was a humdinger of a catch you just made."

"Thanks. It wasn't nothing." So this was what a scout looked like! he thought nervously, removing his helmet. The man smoked an impressively large cigar and wore a bright plaid sports jacket.

"Wasn't nothing?" He smiled expansively. "Looked pretty as a picture from where I sat." He slapped Lee's shoulder pad. "C'mon, let's go for a ride."

In the parking lot, a brand new, sleek, 1958 red convertible with its top down awaited them. The man opened the door for him and he got in, careful not to scar the sporty interior with his cleats.

"Thought we'd go for a spin," the man said, getting in from the other side and turning the ignition on. "Give us a chance to chat."

They left the lot and surged onto the road. Dazzled, Lee gulped at the car's power and smoothness. He couldn't even hear the engine!

"Let's see now, Lee," Mr. Dickson said, tapping a half inch of ash into the ashtray. "You're a junior this year, aren't you?"

"Yes, Mr. Dickson."

"Make it Smokey, Lee. All my friends do on account I smoke so much." He laughed. "Some even say I came into this world asking for a light."

Call an adult by a nickname? He wrestled with the notion, remembering his mother's admonitions to treat adults always with respect. But he'd been asked to.

"All right, Smokey," he said, experimenting with the word on his tongue.

"That's better." "Smokey" slapped Lee's kneepad and jutted his cigar in his direction. "Now, like I said, that was one humdinger of a catch you made. Yessir, one sweet honey of a catch. Plus you was tailed by one pretty fair bird dog of an end, and you left him munchin' your dust. Know what it all says to me, Lee?"

"No sir, Mr. Dick—uh, Smokey. I sure don't."

"Means you got talent," Smokey said, slapping his kneepad again. "God-given, sure-as-shootin', natural talent. And we've known about you for some time. Yes sirree, we've had our eyes on you for quite a while now."

"You mean this wasn't—"

"The first time? Naw." He tapped off some ash, and then his tone became more subdued. "Fact is, Lee, we got a great organization at Masterson State. Lets us locate solid prospects early and follow 'em up, so to speak. I could have approached you sooner, but we generally wait till a boy is at least a junior."

"I see." So he *had* been watched. And if Masterson State had its man out, how many other schools did too? Pleased, he relaxed against the rich leather of his seat, beginning to enjoy the ride.

"Tell me, Lee," said Mr. Dickson, his tone changing slightly from serious to confidential, "have you given any thought to what you'll be doing after graduation?"

"Not much."

"Well, you should. Never too soon to start, especially these days when a college education is getting to be more and more important. Now in my day you could take it or leave it, but today you just gotta have a sheepskin to get anywhere. Know what I mean?"

"Sort of."

"Good. Which brings me to the point, Lee. You know what one of the best ways is for a talented youngster like you to get a sheepskin these days? Well, it's to be good with a *pig*skin."

"Meaning a football."

"Exactly!" he said, seeming to be impressed with Lee's perspicacity. "And the way you pulled down that last pass just confirms our judgment. In fact, if your progress continues, and I think it will, we may be prepared to offer you a full athletic scholarship for four years at Masterson State, plus certain fringe benefits."

Wow. He'd been expecting something, only nothing quite like this. He started to speak, but Mr. Dickson—Smokey—was addressing him again.

"Tell me, Lee, have any uh, other schools communicated with you?"

"About playing with them? No."

"Well, that's good," he said, seeming to be relieved. "However, I can assure you they will. Yes sirree, they sure will. And I wouldn't be a bit surprised if some of their offers won't sound, well, attractive. Just remember, though, it was me who came to you first, and Masterson State has one of the best football teams in the country. What's more, I think we can top any package any other school can offer. Will you remember that?"

"Sure, Smokey." For some reason, "Smokey" now seemed comfortable to him, and he remembered another adult who had once asked him to address her informally, without the Mrs. and last name. In her case, there had been benefits attached as well. He dismissed the memory and stretched luxuriously, feeling as if *he* were in the driver's seat.

"Good," Smokey said. A card snapped into the scout's fingers. "Now here's my card. If at any time you have any questions, just call the number printed here. Reverse the charges. Will you do that? Especially if you have any doubts or somebody offers you something which seems good? Because some of the folks who may be talking to you, well, it hurts me to say this about those in my own profession, but they may bend the truth a little, and I don't want you to be led astray by their promises. So will you promise to give me a call first? I mean, before you do anything."

He took the card, turned it over.

"Sure."

"Great. And I'll be checking back with you every couple months. Just remember, Lee. Whatever happens, I came to you first."

A light turned red and the sleek powerful car slid soundlessly to a stop. A couple of beautiful girls, wearing shorts and flashing long, tantalizing legs in the sun crossed before them, causing Mr. Dickson to launch into praise of the "humdingers" to be found at Masterson State and their automatic appreciation of football heroes. As excellent as Masterson State's academic program was, it seemed the school's greatest accomplishment was the stunning array of female pulchritude the star of the gridiron had only to crook his finger at to enjoy. Plus there were good times and endless parties. And for a good-looking boy like himself, Mr. Dickson suggested, slipping him a wink, "it'll be like you was locked up in a candy store."

"Candy costs money," Lee said.

"Whad ya say?"

"It's just you gotta have money to do things," he said, figuring the angles and surprised to find a new part of him was opening up. "Look, Smokey, after graduation I need a job. My uh, father left us years ago and what my mother makes as a secretary doesn't stretch very far. So I can't afford to spend four years just chucking a pigskin around."

Mr. Dickson grunted. "No problem, Lee. The people I represent are progressive in their thinking. They know a boy like you needs real folding money to spread around while he pursues an education and plays for us. As 'Bull' Ryan our coach himself says, 'They've got to earn while they learn, and you've got to make it pay for them to play!' Like I said before, there are certain fringe benefits involved, including employment opportunities. I think you'll really like Mr. Ryan and playing for us at Masterson State. We look after all our boys, and you'll find it just like being a member of a family."

Lee let the sentiment of joining a close-knit family slide in favor of a more practical consideration. "What kind of job would it be?"

Mr. Dickson winked. "Oh, let's just say something which pays well and doesn't require much work, if you know what I mean."

Lee found he understood perfectly. He tapped the dashboard and cast a covetous gaze over the bounteous instrument panel. In addition to the usual attractions, it contained a tachometer plus other gauges he could only guess at.

"Sure is a nice car."

"Ain't it, though?" Smokey grinned with pride. "It's custom-made. You wouldn't believe what I've put in this baby. "Dual carbs, fuel injection—"

"Yes sir, it sure is nice. Wouldn't mind having a car like this now and then at Masterson State to take a girl to a party in. Make your offer seem just about impossible to turn down."

Surprised at his audacity, he watched a new look enter the scout's eyes. Mr. Dickson removed his cigar, and Lee could almost hear him switch mental gears as he realized he was dealing not so much with a green kid as a young hustler.

"Matter of fact, I think that can be arranged too. We've got a fleet of fine cars and lend them out regularly for worthwhile purposes." He winked again. "Go with us and you go in style, Lee."

Lee grinned and glancing out the window, was surprised to find they were cruising past the apartment buildings which had been on his old newspaper route. Mrs. Futch. She had been the first, just four years ago. Yep, he had come a long way since he was bar mitzvahed at thirteen. Then it had cost just a couple of bowls of pistachio ice cream to buy his virginity. Now the number of buyers was growing, and they would soon be offering full athletic scholarships, sexy girls, and sleek convertibles. Not to mention money. He was a hot item and would get hotter. Ice cream wouldn't snag him this time, though he had no regrets about Mrs. Futch, who had taught him all the moves, including a few which weren't even in the book. Whatever had happened to Mrs. Futch, anyway? Oh, yeah, she'd met a guy with a pile of dough and moved down South. Mobile, maybe.

"Say, Smokey."

"Huh?" Mr. Dickson stopped in the midst of lauding the glamor and glory contingent upon attending Masterson State.

"You wouldn't happen to have another of those wicked looking cigars, would you? I could sure go for one about now."

Mr. Dickson looked at him a bit irritably and then grinned. Removing a cigar from his pocket, he stripped off the cellophane. Lee put it in his mouth and waited as Mr. Dickson touched the end of his cigar to it. At the right moment, with timing as perfect as he had displayed in catching the football, he winked.

Yep, he thought, settling back, he was in the driver's seat now. Or what was the story they'd just read in Mrs. Murdstone's English class? "The Catbird Seat." Yeah, that's where he was, he thought, remembering how Furillo, the team captain, joked about how he'd like to play Hide The Salami with her and thinking also how pretty Mrs. Murdstone was and how much he liked her, how much he wanted her too if he was honest about it. (Well, someday, somehow, he would have her, it was just a matter of time.) Yeah, that's where he was all right, riding high in Mrs. Murdstone's catbird seat, in control of everything and with his whole life mapped out before him fully for the first time. He would go to Masterson State or to whoever was the highest bidder. The sky alone was the limit, and with a little luck he'd run forever. He wouldn't turn out like his friend Johnny who painted things his father hated and who would probably end up getting his brains bashed open in the ring. And he certainly wouldn't do anything stupid like Jimmy and get his head half blown off while robbing a delicatessen. No, he'd ride the glory and gravy train all the way out of poverty to the golden payday that was waiting for him and his mother. Life was a snap if you didn't think about it so much and just took it easy.

Only sometimes it seemed things came just a little too easy and simply fell into place. Oh, sure, he didn't have much money and kids like Wilson reminded him of it. Still, he felt even that problem would work out eventually. It had been smooth sailing for a long time now.

Girls. Grades. Now this. It was as if his life weren't quite real, as if he were a fake in some way. Puzzled, he puffed on the cigar, and briefly the faint disappointment returned which had brushed him while he'd trotted back after making his victorious catch. His father. If only he hadn't left his mother when he was small. If only he had been there to see his catch.

He took another puff, trying to remember what his father had looked like. But all he could ever remember was waking as a child in the night to find a figure standing over him in the darkness. There had been crying, and for a moment in his confusion he had thought *he* was crying. Then he had realized it was his father. Why, though, was his father crying? The figure had stood there softly crying for a long time, and no matter how hard Lee had tried, he couldn't see its face. Then he must have fallen asleep because when he woke up the figure was gone, if indeed it had ever been there to start with. He had often wondered if he hadn't simply imagined it, created a father in a dream. Whatever the case, one thing was for sure. He had never seen his father again.

*His father.* If he had one, he thought, maybe he'd have had someone to play catch with and come to scout meetings on Father's Night. Not that he minded only having a mother, of course. After all, she tried as hard as she could, and they did *everything* together. Still, if he had a father, maybe he himself would be different. Maybe he'd be better. But different from what? How better? He was being ridiculous, he knew. Well, maybe he wouldn't feel at times like he . . . lacked something. Maybe his father would protect him. *Lacked what? Protect him from what? What could there possibly be which he needed to be protected from?* He shook his head and tried to put it aside, aware that Jimmy and Johnny at least had fathers, even if one drank and the other kept after him all the time. All he'd ever had was a face in the darkness which never would come into focus. And as nice as his mother was, it would have been even better to have a father too who could help him and show him things . . .

"Lee."

They were back in the parking lot, and his spirits instantly brightened into harmony with Mr. Dickson's jacket. Placing his cigar in the ashtray, Lee opened the door and got out.

"Thanks for everything, Smokey."

"Sure thing, Lee. Just remember what I told you. And don't forget: I'll be in touch."

Mr. Dickson shifted gears and started to drive off. Then he stopped. For a moment he looked right at him through the bullshit which was his stock in trade.

"You know, kid, I admire your style. You got class. Keep it up and you'll go a long way."

Some students, among them Wilson and other members of the football team, were watching them at the doors leading to the gymnasium. Glancing casually in their direction, Lee sensed their awe and admiration and could almost hear their excited speculation. *Look who Lee's talking to! Bet he's a big-time scout.*

He turned back. His handsome face broke into an easy smile, displaying even white teeth. He rapped the car lightly as if to signal the end of his childhood.

"Thanks, Smokey. That's exactly what I plan to do."

# Part
## Three
### 1963

# Chapter
# Twenty

## The Funhouse

The trouble with using charcoal on a hot day, Johnny thought, is that it gets too muddy and sticky. You've got to have a real feel for it or your work will develop a gummy texture destroying all efforts at nuance and form.

The Kansas farmer posing for his portrait couldn't have cared less about the properties of charcoal on hot days. Sunburned and impatient, he had grumbled ever since his wife had browbeaten him into opening his ancient, misshapen wallet and parting with three dollars. The bills had looked as ancient and misshapen as the wallet, worn smooth, he'd bet, from all those days the damn miser had sat on them while riding a tractor.

"Finished yet?"

Ignoring the question, Johnny resisted the urge to add a wart and an extra half inch to the farmer's nose, and picked up the mouth atomizer he'd made. Delicately he applied the fixative, used a thumb to soften a contour, and added a few last touches.

"There."

The wife gummed. "Paw, it looks just like you!"

"Paw" gazed impassively at the fruits of his forbearance while his wife gushed about the sketch. After a moment he reached into his pocket and yanked out a plug of chewing tobacco, which he bit into and then replaced. Only then did he deliver an assessment of his investment.

"Whole lot to pay for a durn picture."

Johnny slipped the sketch into a cheap cardboard frame and handed it over, careful not to say "Thank you" as they left.

The carnival lay sweltering in the noonday heat. Despite the riot and excitement it possessed during its peak hours, it reminded him of a drop scene from a play, as if it and the world itself were not quite palpable, not quite real. Who knows, perhaps he himself was an illusion, a pale fantasy. He shook his head, spurning such nihilism, and concentrated on seeing the trappings about him as concrete forms with reality and weight. Yes, they were real, and he existed too, no matter how different he was from others and no matter how perverse the ideas that drifted through his head. Yes, but for all his corporeality, you could bet life would go on just as merrily with or without him, though in a few hours another rube or redneck might be dragged his way to fidget reluctantly on a stool and bemoan the loss of three dollars which could have been spent for something useful, like chewing tobacco. Wiping the sweat from his glasses, he started to gather his instruments and then sat back, letting his eyes rise tiredly to the sign he had drawn when he had first hitched up with this operation and turned "carnie."

JOHN ROTH, ARTIST
PORTRAITS PAINTED
Charcoal $3.00
Pastel Profile $7.00
Pastel Full Face $10.00

Beyond the sign some of the booths were closing for lunch. Across from him, Benny's setup, DUMP BOBO IN THE WATER! MAKE BOBO SPLASH! was unattended, probably because BOBO was sleeping it off or having a bit of the hair of the dog. But drunk or sober, BOBO could sure blow one mean horn, he thought, hearing the sweet snarl of BOBO's trumpet in his mind. Well, however liquid BOBO's condition, it would be an hour at least before he climbed back up on his collapsible chair to insult hayseeds willing to spend a quarter for three baseballs so they could impress the crowd with their marksmanship and manhood.

He replaced his instruments and headed down the midway, passing attractions that had been new to him just a few weeks before. A carrousel, endlessly playing the Waltz from *Faust*, a Ferris wheel and Tilt-a-Whirl, a funhouse, freak show, fortuneteller, faith healer, shooting galleries and booths with balls, rings, teddy bears to be won, Exotic Dancers, Guess Your Weight, hot dog stands, ice cream stands, candy apples, cotton candy . . .

Before him, placed so it commanded the midway, rose the carnival owner's shining inspiration and central attraction, a towering high-striker that bore his name: Bunyan's Banger. At night it was the chief jewel on the diamond-bright midway, drawing marks like moths to its flame. Since joining the carnie six weeks ago, he had seen it billed and advertised in the towns they had gone to as a Supreme Test of Strength because it was supposedly twice as high as any to be found elsewhere. *$100.00 To Anyone Who Can Ring The Bell On Bunyan's Banger! Test Your Strength On The Highest Ring-The-Bell In The World!* In the beginning, the constant flow of country boys who had matched their homegrown muscles against this Mount Everest of Challenges had fascinated him. One by one they had parted with their fifty cents, lifted the huge mallet which reminded Johnny of Paul Bunyan's legendary ax, and in Herculean swings had competed for immortality and the smiles and awe of sweethearts and farm boys like themselves. All had failed, though a few had pounded the metal disk as high as POPEYE, which at 2400 was just one notch below the bell itself.

Now, though, Bunyan's Banger had ceased to amuse him. It had become just another fixture in this land of flat corn fields and endless sun between fairgrounds where they set up and folded tents and booths and moved on, moved on, moved on. After just six weeks, he was already tired of making cheap charcoal sketches of yokels who couldn't tell art from fertilizer. Unless they hit a major city soon where things were less boring and where you didn't think you'd slide right off the map if you weren't tied down, he'd have to move on once again and try something else.

Bad as it was, though, he had to admit there had been worse jobs. For example, there'd been that timber camp in Oregon a couple years back where he had almost fallen a hundred and thirty feet from the top of a fir tree. Then there had been the time in South Carolina when he had stupidly tried to be an actor. Yes, there had been worse jobs and sadder places, but no matter how you figured it, they still came up to the same depressing total, which was an apt reward for his transgressions. Against his will, he heard the voice of the rabbi who had instructed him as a child.

"For our sins we were exiled from our land."

"Hi, Johnny!"

Turning, he saw Belinda Myers waving to him before a poster of Super Himalaya, The Monster Man, and his stomach flipped over like a pancake. There was one thing about working here he did like: Blonde Belinda with her white shorts and swirling hair. Maybe she was the reason he hung on.

Shyly, smelling the burnt caramel from a popcorn stand, he walked over. At twenty-one he had reached six feet three, weighed two thirty, and had acquired a muscular leanness he had lacked when he'd been a plump teenager. Still, a little of the timidity or shyness remained which had caused him so much trouble while growing up, when boys had picked on him.

"Hi, Lin," he said. "What's up?"

"Artist's treat. I'm holding you to the promise you made the other day."

"Promise?"

"Have you forgotten already? You made a solemn vow to take me to the funhouse."

Lump in throat, he played along (he hadn't promised) and accepted the delightful cargo of her arm through his own as they started down the midway. On the way they passed the Wheel of Fortune, where a barker named Trapp tipped his hat at Belinda while working the marks with a concealed foot gaff and the gift of tongues. Johnny noticed he sported a cigarillo and pointy shoes (not to mention a friendly shill among the crowd), and that even though his eyes followed her like radar, he didn't drop a stitch of his spiel.

> "The Wheel of Fortune goes round and round,
> And where she stops, nobody knows!"

Before he knew it, they were standing in front of the funhouse next to some heavy duty extension cords which ran along the ground from one of the thrill rides. Not ten feet away a sign offered questionable advice: LAFF YOURSELF TO DEATH.

"Well, how about it?" she said.

"I don't know," he replied, eyeing the huge clown's face that adorned the front and was capable of a grisly laugh which pulled the marks in like crazy. Right now, though, the thing was silent. All the mechanical monsters were asleep; even the clown's leering grin seemed less sinister.

She nudged him. "What's wrong, Johnny, you're not afraid of a little old funhouse, are you, a big boy like you?"

"No, of course not."

"Well?"

He contemplated the front of the funhouse with a feeling not far short of trepidation. Funny. In Oregon he had learned to climb Douglas firs fearlessly. But funhouses were different. Somehow they had always frightened him. Inside them was a booby-trapped universe, an eternal Halloween, a cosmos gone mad. Outside, things hewed to laws of logic and order; inside, gravity itself was turned topsy-turvy. It was pitch black in there, a maze of passages leading straight to hell, and God Knows what horrors were likely to pop out at you on the way. Gruesome Ax Murderers Drenched With Blood. Zombies and Blood-Thirsty Pirates. Frankenstein Ghouls and Giant Spiders. Not to mention Banshees and Vampires and Werewolves. Why in the hell did people insist on calling it a FUNHOUSE, anyway? There was nothing fun about it. It was a place where laughter was perverted into shrieks and screams, the laughter of fear and death.

She was watching him with surprise. He turned to her.

"Anyway, we can't go in there now."

"Why not?"

"It's lunchtime. Nobody's around." Which was true. During peak hours, Chillman was usually up on his pitchman's roost, ballying the marks with a polished spiel, playing on the boys' fears to make them take their girls inside. GHOSTS AND GOBLINS AND GHOULS, ALL THE COMFORTS OF HOME! STEP RIGHT UP AND ENTER THE MOST HORRIBLE HOUSE OF HORRORS IN NINE CONTINENTS, GUARANTEED TO MAKE YOU FAINT AND YOUR HAIR TURN WHITE OR YOUR MONEY CHEERFULLY REFUNDED! COME ON, ARE YOU MAN ENOUGH FOR IT? WHAT'S THE MATTER, SON, YOU'RE NOT SCARED, ARE YOU? BET YOUR *GIRLFRIEND* ISN'T.

Well, he was! This funhouse didn't look as bad as some he'd seen. One had been as big as Xanadu with a boarding platform and gondolas that rode along sunken tracks and crashed into massive wooden doors shaped like dragons' mouths. And God knows where you were in *that* one. The cars turned and twisted and wound back upon themselves in the darkness of eternal night, and demons of all descriptions leaped out at you when you least expected.

"Of course we can go in there," she said. "Why can't we?"

He pointed at the platform. "There's no one there. We can buy some tickets at the booth, but we'll have to wait till after lunch."

"Fiddle-faddle." She took his hand and towed him to the platform. "Mr. Chillman?" she called. "Mr. Chillman?"

He appeared almost at once, or more accurately, seemed to materialize out of nowhere. Chillman had a room back there, a tiny closet of sorts where he ate and slept and for all Johnny knew, made love. But his living accommodations were of less interest to him than Chillman's appearance, which was not the kind to inspire confidence in the tour ahead. For Chillman was an albino, and a peculiarly stunted one with gnarled, twisted limbs which were chalk white. Only his eyes seemed to have any color, and they managed only a sickly pink. His hair itself was a ghostly white, bleached, he'd bet, by the terrors of his unenviable kingdom.

Chillman's equally ghostly features broke into a broad smile.

"Belinda! How are you?"

"Just fine, Mr. Chillman. And you?"

"Tiptop, my dear, absolutely splendid. But tell me, how's your father?"

"He's doing much better, thank you, Mr. Chillman," Belinda said. "He's following the diet you recommended."

"Good. Good!" Chillman bounced and nodded, hugging his deformed arms to his chest like trophies while Johnny watched the albino's concern in surprise. He acted like he was her father, not a freak. But of course, in the carnie, adults often looked after others' children, and there were no freaks. Freaks and monsters were for the outside world, the marks. In the carnie you were judged by your job and how well you did it. Nothing else mattered.

Still, Chillman's solicitude felt subtly different, perhaps because even among these gypsies, who were outcasts themselves, Johnny sensed there was something different about Chillman, a quality he couldn't define. Though friendly, the man did not quite seem to fit in,

was not with it and for it as the carnie folks said. So it was probably
only a matter of time before he would move on. Frowning, Johnny
started to ask Chillman a question, but he was already speaking.

"Tell me, Belinda, would you like to go in the funhouse?"

"Oh, don't go to any trouble, Mr. Chillman."

"Trouble, Smouble. It's no trouble at all. Wouldn't lift a finger if it
was." Chillman actually seemed to dote on her. He flapped a white
hand at the entrance. "You children go on. I'll start things up."

"Oh, thank you, Mr. Chillman!" She seized Johnny's hand.
"Come on!"

Reluctantly, he climbed the steps and followed her to the
entrance. Everything was dark as a tomb in there.

"Hey," he said, "I was meaning to ask him. Is his name *really*
Chillman?"

"So far as I know, why?"

"It just sounds odd. Like he made it up on purpose."

She smiled. "Well, maybe he did. Does it give you the *chills?*" She
mock-shivered. "Want to turn back, big boy?"

He gazed with foreboding into the dark tunnel, penetrating as
far as five feet. Music started—eerie, haunting chords that reminded
him of open graves and the wails of the damned.

"'Abandon all hope, ye who enter here,'" he said.

"What?"

"Oh, nothing. I was just anticipating the future. Tell me, do you
think Roderick Usher is at home?"

"Roderick *who?*"

"He's a character in a story. As I recall, he came to a sad end in a
house much like this one."

"I see. Well, what's it going to be? Do you want to turn back?"

He shook his head, eyes riveted to the dark entrance, remembering
tales of a funhouse which kids had entered and then never been
seen again, not even a stitch of their clothing.

"Do you want to turn back?" Belinda repeated.

Johnny swallowed. "Not on your life," he said, aware of the irony.

"O.K., then let's go."

Since the tunnel was narrow, they had to go in single file, and
since he was the man, he had to go first. Gingerly he ventured
forward, feeling his way an inch at a time along the floor like it was

made of thin ice. He blinked, seeing a little light, and waited for his eyes to adjust.

The floor! Suddenly it moved! Startled, he struggled for balance on boards which rocked back and forth. He reached out, groping, and grabbed the railings on both sides.

"Watch out!"

"I am," she laughed, skipping onto the boards. She seemed to trip and threw her arms around him from behind. "Whoopsy-daisy!"

"You all right?" he said, aware of her body against his.

"Sure. Soon as I catch my balance."

"Good. Try the rails."

Carefully, he came to the end of the rocking boards and stepped off. He turned and extended his hand. Her slender fingers closed over his. With a hop, she joined him.

"Any more surprises up ahead?" he asked.

A mocking whistle. "Why should I tell *you*?"

"It's your funhouse, that's why. Come on, give."

He heard her laugh and realized she was close again. Too close. What if Len Dalton found out? He stepped back, bumping against the wall and finding he could barely see her.

"I'm not going to tell you anything," she teased. "Everyone's got to go through the funhouse for the first time and find out for himself. I wouldn't want to spoil it for you."

"You won't spoil it."

"Well, if you're chicken, I'll go first."

He straightened. "What, a big, brave man like me *scared*? Why, I don't know the meaning of the word. I'm just shaking because I like it!"

She giggled and pressed his hand. "Oh, Johnny, you're so different from other boys I've known! Come on, we've got a long way to go."

He peered ahead. It was as black as the devil's pocket in there, and for all he knew, there was a sheer cliff or a nest of rattlesnakes just ahead. That was the worst part of it, not knowing. Ahead of him the funhouse waited, malignant and evil, its unseen jaws grinning with infinite patience. If he could only *see* what awaited him! But that of course, was the *idea* of a funhouse: Suspense, the Unknown, the Unexpected. It was the reason for darkness, so you couldn't see what lurked just before you, or could see just enough to scare yourself nearly to death with half-glimpsed horrors. If only Chillman would turn off the witch music. It gave him the creeps. His mouth twisted with a wry thought. If Chillman himself were to jump out of the shadows, it would be the supreme horror!

He took a step. Peered ahead. Listened. Perked up his ears like antennae. Took another step . . .

A chill blast of air goosed him, and he jumped a foot. An air hole!

"What is it?" he heard Belinda ask.

He grinned in the darkness. "Oh, nothing, dear."

"Then why did you scream?"

"Did I scream?"

"You know you—EEEK!"

He laughed. "What's the matter?"

"You bum! You didn't tell me about the air hole!"

"Why, I thought it was *your* funhouse!"

"It is, I just forgot about it. Oh, Johnny, it almost scared me to death!"

He felt pleased, then wondered if she had just acted frightened. After all, it was her funhouse, and maybe she was trying to make him feel brave. Maybe she was cleverer than she looked and hadn't forgotten the wind machine. He considered the possibility and then conjured up an image of her in the darkness. No, such a pretty girl couldn't be so deceptive. But didn't he feel braver now? A real hero? Yes, he did. He looked ahead, no longer peering. Illusions, that's all it was, cheap, shabby tricks which gave boys a chance to cop a quick feel from their frantic girlfriends in the dark. It was make-believe and papier-mâché, and like the carnival, it was only a place where people left their laughs and screams when they were through with them. He was the one who was real, not the funhouse. It could hurt him only if he let it. He took Belinda's hand and squeezed it, and there flashed upon him another time, another place when he had crept through the darkness with a girl. Only then the girl had been Theresa and the spook house had been a woods, and the terrors had been real terrors, like a gang that could kill you. This was a mere toy by comparison, a plaything, an elaborate but harmless masquerade.

He took a breath and proceeded. They crept deeper into the

bowels of the funhouse, turned sharp bends, twisted and doubled back through serpentine passageways. He thought of subterranean labyrinths and Minotaurs that devoured you alive, quick-springing Medusas who froze you forever into stone. But now there was pleasure in anticipating what lay ahead and in sharing it with her. Sometimes monsters jumped out at them with prerecorded screams, and he thumbed his nose at them. A witch in a pointed black hat pitched forward, knife coated in red paint that glowed in the dark. A rope caught her in time. Then just beyond a grinning human skeleton which flashed out of the darkness, he found they were in a room wrenched all out of shape like a mad painting. Tables and chairs hung down from the ceiling, and chandeliers poked up from the floor. The ceiling slanted down as he entered, so to leave, he had to stoop through a little doorway. Beyond it, he found a brilliantly lit room filled with mirrors, and they weren't the wavy distorting ones which made you look like everything from a peanut to an elephant. These were large ones without a flaw bordered by dazzling light bulbs.

"Hey!"

She laughed. "Didn't know there were so many of you, huh?"

He felt stunned. Never before had he seen so many mirrors. There had to be a thousand of them, and a thousand of *him*. He raised his hand. Simultaneously a thousand Johnny Roths imitated the gesture. He lowered it; too slow, though, to beat them.

She came and stood beside him. "Which one is the real Johnny?"

"Beats me. I've been trying to figure *that* one out for a long time."

"Have you succeeded?"

"Not yet. But at least I know who the real Belinda is."

"Oh, you do, do you?" She cocked her head at him, and he thought how good it was to be somewhere where he could see her clearly. The place was bathed in brilliant light.

"Close your eyes, Johnny."

"Huh?"

"Close your eyes."

"Why?"

"Just *do* it."

"O.K. But it sounds funny." He closed them. Counted to five. "Now?"

"Yes."

He opened them and found she was no longer beside him. She was farther away, delivered back to him by a thousand gleaming mirrors. He blinked. Wheeled around.

"Lin, where are you?"

A thousand Lins giggled. "Johnny, I thought you knew who the real Belinda was!"

"I do."

"Then come and get me."

He moved forward, blinking against the brightness, and approached her image. No, not that one. He turned to another. There she was, he was sure of it. He reached out.

And struck a mirror.

He stood watching her wobbling image, seeing a thousand of her laugh. Well, at least this one wasn't her. That left only 999 more. He reached out, dazzled by the light, and almost stumbled over another mirror.

"Lin, where are you?"

"Right over here, smarty."

He spun around. The mirrors reflected each other, so of course she could be *anywhere!*

"Belinda?"

"Find me!"

He had to use his head, but how? How could he find her in this shining madhouse when he couldn't even . . . her voice! He could track her by it. Let's see, where had it come from? Seemed to him it had come from his left, over there by the little door they'd come in by. He stalked forward.

"Lin?"

He heard giggles. More to the right. Over there. Closer. Closer.

Ah, one of the Lins moved, only not in a mirror, and he charged after her, hearing her laughter tinkle like water as they raced down another dark tunnel.

"I'm going to spank you!"

"Gotta catch me first!"

Just another step and he'd have her! He reached out, touched her arm, and . . .

Burst out into the blinding sunlight.

They stood just outside the exit, shielding their eyes from the sun while Mr. Chillman laughed. Johnny was surprised it was a rich laugh, deep and hearty, the laugh of a man. It sounded as if it came from vast depths and unsuspected dimensions inside him. "Ho, ho, ho," Chillman continued. "Did you enjoy yourselves in there, children? I heard someone scream."

"It was Johnny, Mr. Chillman."

"Oh, no, it wasn't," he laughed. "We both did."

"Well, I'm glad you enjoyed it, children. Come back anytime." He smiled at Johnny. "You too, son. Come back and I'll show you how to run the funhouse."

"Thank you, sir." He looked at Belinda. "Maybe I will."

"I mean it, *any*time."

"Good-by, Mr. Chillman," Belinda said, taking Johnny's hand. They went to the stairs and descended to the midway.

"Well, what now?" he said, looking up at the clown's now prosaic grin.

"How about some lunch?"

"Same as before, artist's treat? You know, he let us in for free."

"Yes, only this time it'll cost you. You haven't forgotten you also promised to *buy* me lunch."

He hadn't, of course, but nodded as if he'd just remembered. "Of course, my dear," he said, magnanimously waving a hand at hot dog and hamburger stands. "Then what'll it be? Heartburn? Ptomaine poisoning? Your wish is my bellyache."

She laughed. "Let's play it safe. A thick gooey milkshake will do nicely."

# Chapter
# Twenty-One

## Tale of the Palm

**M**inutes later he sat watching her sip a strawberry shake on the
other side of a picnic table while his root beer in its frosty mug
sat untouched. He hadn't paid for them either. Apparently, when
you were with Belinda, your money was no good. Everyone loved
her and gave her things for free. And could you blame them? Just
look at her. Corn ripe hair. Delicate sunlit features. White shorts and
long golden legs. Stunning. He even liked the strawberry rim above
her lip.

Seeing her this way made him want to do something for her,
like win her a teddy bear or kewpie doll at one of the pitch or shoot
sideshows along the midway. Or maybe take her on the carrousel
for a ride. He turned his gaze to it, watching the galloping horses
and rhythmically flashing brass poles while the calliope played in
lilting blasts he was long since tired of.

"Sometimes people get married on it," she said.

"What?"

"It's an old carnie tradition. When a boy and a girl want to get
hitched, they ride the carrousel together."

"Really?"

She nodded. "Or it used to be. It's fading out, now, though the
old ways die hard. Last year Madame Zenina got married on it."

Madame Zenina was the exotic gypsy fortuneteller from a
"far countree" (born in Trenton, New Jersey) who conned marks
with a crystal ball and so much hocus-pocus you almost believed
she could tell your future. When he had first joined up, she had
dragged him into her dim candlelit tent and forced him to sit while
she had hunched over a ball which she had probably ordered out

of the magician's catalogue and whispered prophecies concerning his fate. *I see all, know all. Pick your pants if I get a chance.* What had she predicted, anyway? Well, it didn't matter; it was all a bunch of malarkey. *Double, double toil and trouble; Fire burn and cauldron bubble.* She reminded him of one of the witches in *Macbeth*. And a married witch at that, though it seemed to him...

"Wait a minute," he said. "Madame Zenina isn't married."

"No, that's true. But she used to be. You see, she did something you're never supposed to do."

"What?"

"She married a straight, an outsider. It worked for a while, but then he wanted to take her away to Philadelphia. She wanted to stay here. After all, the carnie was her life. Since the age of five, it was the only thing she knew."

"So what happened?"

She shrugged. "Finally he told her she had to make a choice between him and us. And she did."

"I see." Gloom washed over him and Belinda, sensing it, covered his hand with her own. "It's the old ways, Johnny, and like I said, they're changing. Besides, you don't have to remain an outsider, not if you don't want to."

"I don't?"

"No. You can join us, I mean *really* join us, not just work here. There are people here who like you, such as my parents and Mr. Chillman."

"Chillman?" Surprised, he thought of the albino, who he sensed didn't even like the carnie. "He likes *me*?"

"Yes. Why do you think he offered to show you how to run the machinery at the funhouse? He's never done that with anyone else, Johnny. I think he's really fond of you, and it would be your chance to really fit in here, assuming you want to."

He pulled his hand away. Despite her kindness, the gloom was descending, darker even than in the funhouse. He couldn't prevent it. Yet he couldn't ignore her either, for she was quite possibly the prettiest girl he had ever seen. And he didn't have a snowball's chance in hell with her.

"How's your work going, Johnny?"

He frowned, eyes caught on the swell of her breasts.

"It goes."

"That bad, huh?"

He shrugged. God, he wanted her.

"Tell me what's happened," she said, taking his hand.

He felt a shivery weakness in his legs as if he'd just been guillotined at the knees. Damn it, he didn't want to talk about his art. He wanted *her*. His art was dead, the end of an adolescent dream. His canvases had long since drained whatever inspiration he had started with. What had some poet written? "The painter's brush consumes his dreams." All painting had ever done for him was to cost him the love and support of a Jewish father, to whom all art was foolish, immoral, and sacrilegious. What had painting, especially the abstract kind he had once felt compelled to create, ever done for him except bore, confuse, amuse, or enrage others? In Ohio his more erotic work had plunged him into trouble at school, and now, after five years of wandering from job to job, he had finally hit bottom here on a Kansas prairie, grinding out cheap sketches.

To change the subject, he mentioned his paltry take of $52.00 for the week, of which Miles Bunyan, the carnival owner and supreme boss man would get half, and pointed out that if it weren't for the free food and charity, he would have had to quit the carnival weeks ago.

"Don't call it 'charity,'" she said, "it's what we do for each other when we need help."

"Sure."

"No, I mean it," she said, squeezing his hand. "You weren't born into it so you don't know yet. When you're 'carnie,' Johnny, you stick together. You're part of something bigger: a family. And when you join it, I mean really join it, in *here*," she said, touching her heart, "you know that 'charity' is just another word for love."

Sentimental crap. Yet the words, coming so unexpectedly from a seventeen-year-old girl, had a quality that briefly stirred him. Still, there was no place in *his* heart for such sentiments. The only thing that rang a bell in that particular void was his desire for her, which made absolutely no sense. She was Len Dalton's girl, signed, sealed, delivered. And she knew it, too. Knew it and wanted it that way.

So why was she sitting here holding his hand? Friendship? Curiosity? As if in answer, she turned it over.

"Funny."

"What?"

"Your hand. It doesn't look like an artist's." She turned it this way and that, examining the heavy palm and crude fingers. "It looks more like—"

"I didn't know you read palms."

"I take over now and then for Madame Zenina."

"Madame *Belinda*?"

"Laugh if you like, but I have some regulars who swear by me. Now lay your hand flat. Hmm. You know, each palm is different and has a tale to tell. Sometimes it's just a little thing, not even noticeable to most people. You have to know what to look for. Yes, this is very interesting. *Very interesting* indeed."

She bent close over his palm, seemingly in intense scrutiny. A soft breeze stirred the pale down on her arm, and her hair was filled with country sunlight.

"Well, what is it?" he said, his voice thickening.

"Nothing. It's just you're a mystery like Mr. Chillman. There's something different about both of you I can't fathom."

Johnny shrugged, remembering his impression of Chillman. "We don't fit in, even here in gypsy oddball heaven."

"It's not so simple." Her finger traced his life line. "As I was saying, your palm doesn't seem to belong to an artist. It looks more like a—"

"Pickpocket's?"

"No."

"Lover's?"

She laughed. "No!"

"Safecracker's?"

"No, your hand's too strong for a thief. I'd say it looks more . . . like a farmer's."

"Hey!"

"No, that's not it either," she teased. Turning his hand over again, she laced her fingers through his, causing a tidal wave inside him.

"I'd say it looks more like a . . . butcher's!"

His face froze. He pulled his hand away.

"Oh, come on, don't be so sensitive. I was only kidding. Johnny, I don't know much about art, but I do know you're good. Awfully good. Some of the stuff you do, well, I don't hardly understand it. I mean I haven't seen anything like it before, but I can tell you've got talent."

"Sure, that's why they laugh."

"Not all of them laugh, Johnny. Only those who don't know any better."

"Like Len?"

She smiled. "Len's just being Len. He doesn't mean anything."

"No, of course not. Anyway, maybe he's right. Maybe it takes showbiz to drag these yokels in. Maybe I should become an entertainer and open up my own funhouse." He leaned forward, finding he was talking about painting against his will. "You know what I saw last year when I was in New Orleans during the Mardi Gras?"

"No, what?"

"I saw artists with blindfolds blast away with spray guns at a giant canvas. Machine gun art. The crowds on the street loved it."

"You're kidding!"

"No, it's the rage these days. Any nut with a mop and a bucket of paint can be the next Picasso. You know, I even saw one sharpshooter sling bullets into paint-filled balloons stuck to a mural. Made a great hit with customers. Maybe I should try it."

Belinda laughed and raised her hands to her pink cheeks. "I don't believe it. You mean he actually used a gun?"

"Yeah."

"Oh Johnny, that's not art is it?"

He shrugged. "Some people think it is."

"What do *you* think?"

"Me? I think it's a mess, a bloody accident. If there's one truth about art, it's that it has to have a design. Without a conscious purpose in the mind of the creator, it's a cheat, a Technicolor lie."

She squeezed his hand warmly. "You're something, Johnny."

"What do you mean?"

"The way you talk. The things you think. I've never met anyone quite like you."

He glanced away, pleased but embarrassed. "Yeah, but would Len approve?" he said, wondering why he had mentioned *him* again.

"Don't worry about him," she said. "As I said before, what he says doesn't mean anything."

He thought of Dalton, the shady operator of Bunyan's Banger who was full of piss and vinegar and constantly snickered at his work. For the life of him, he couldn't see what Belinda saw in such a lout, who wasn't fit to be used as paper at the bottom of a birdcage. Bullies. Wherever he had found them, they seemed to belie man's richness and complexity, to refute and reduce it irrevocably by their base thoughts and boring predictability.

According to the lore of this place, Gentle Len had put a couple of the more presumptuous hayseeds in traction for even smiling at Belinda. Looking at his hand, he remembered things he wanted to forget and rose to leave.

But whatever it was that had made her seek him out now caused her to skip after him and take his arm again. If Dalton saw . . .

"C'mon, Johnny, let's spin the wheel."

# Chapter
# Twenty-Two

## The Spinning of the Wheel

Wheel. Wheels within wheels. Circles within circles. Her scrap of carnie jargon, which meant to "ride the Ferris wheel," made him see the whole carnival as an artist and probe beneath its chaotic, meaningless surface for significant patterns. Yes, a carnival was wheels. Wheels and circles. Merry-go-rounds with horses in an endless race to nowhere, none of them winning. Wheels of Fortune. Hoops and rings you threw to encircle bottles and pegs and other targets. Round peas inside walnut shells. Circular tracks for stock car races. Even the Ferris wheel. What was it but a vertical merry-go-round? Not to mention—

"Buenos días, Señor Gomez," Belinda said to the man who sat reading a Spanish newspaper before the Ferris wheel. "How is la Señora Gomez today?"

The man raised a swarthy face which instantly brightened. "Ah, Belinda! La señora? She's fine, just fine, rides me like a burro." He winked. "And what can I do for my charming señorita?"

Belinda fluttered her eyes and demurely looked away, playing the shy, devious little coquette with such delightful naturalness that Johnny was almost fooled. Obviously, it was a daily game with them, and he'd just bet it wouldn't cost him a dime.

"I was just wondering, Señor Gomez, if you would . . ."

"Sí?"

". . . give me a ride."

Gomez looked at him and winked. "For the handsome hombre too?"

Belinda blushed. Was that also part of her act? His heart skipped. "If it's no trouble."

"Trouble? Trouble? For my pretty little señorita with the eyes like blue ponds, it is no trouble at all!" Like Chillman's, his eyes lingered fondly on her and then seemed to discover him again. "Amigo, how you find it here with us? You like it, yes?"

He nodded. "Yeah, it's fine."

"And Kansas? You like Kansas too?"

"Sure, it's a great place to get buried in."

Gomez threw his head back and laughed. "Ha ha ha ha ha. Yes, that is very good. I like your friend, Belinda. He is right. *"Semejante los buitres no tienen gordo en este distrito execrable!"*

He looked at Belinda. She laughed.

"He says 'Even the vultures are skinny in this lousy land!'"

Johnny frowned. "But there aren't any vultures in Kansas."

Gomez laughed again. "You see, it is even worse than I thought. In Kansas there aren't even any vultures!"

Belinda laughed, and he found himself laughing too and liking this Gomez, who he'd seen only a few times before. Usually Johnny kept to himself and made it a point not to get involved in things.

"Amigo," Gomez said. "You are from this land? The South, maybe?"

"No. Ohio."

"Ah, a what you call it, Yankee. Then you are a pilgrim, like me. It has been many years now since Mexico," he said, pronouncing it "Me-hi-ho." "Someday maybe I go back. Someday I see the bullfights again. ¿Quién sabe? Perhaps it is not written. Anyway, enough with my talk. Excuse me, it is a weakness of mine, and I do it all the time. Come."

Getting up, he escorted them to one of the cars. Johnny got in with her and watched nervously as Gomez shut the bar, locking them in. What had she gotten him into this time? Now he could see what was coming but didn't want to. He wished he were back in the funhouse, or better yet, at the top of a tree in Oregon where things were comparatively still.

He turned to her. "Tell me, don't you pay for anything around here?"

She wriggled her nose. "I have muchos amigos."

"I bet you do," he said, finding himself a little angry. "And as for your artist's treat–"

Gomez started the engine, and the car rocked forward. Then he pulled a lever, and the engine's sound was joined by creaking and cranking as the whole wheel turned. The earth fell away as they rolled up—going backwards!

"Ummphf!"

She giggled. "Scared?"

"I'm not hot on riding these things." They reached the top and started down.

"Unnnh!"

"Hold my hand."

He obeyed. The wheel rolled up and backwards again and then fell. By the third cycle he felt better and even laughed.

"Hey, this is great!"

"Haven't you ever been on one?"

"No," he admitted, looking at her. She was so close, and she did have eyes like blue ponds, eyes that danced and sparkled. For a moment he wondered again if she wasn't cleverer than he thought and was playing some kind of game. Well, this *was* a carnie, and you couldn't stray ten feet without stumbling over a game of some kind designed to part you from your money. If only he understood girls better. Though he'd met and bedded his share in the past five years, they continued to perplex and confuse him. Many guys read girls easily and found them obvious whereas he was a babe in the woods and often got lost after the first few minutes of meeting them. The experience resembled wandering in a funhouse maze, only sometimes there was no way out and he had no business being there in the first place. Take Belinda. She seemed fresh and home-spun, but did he really know her? Maybe she had some sneaky motive and wanted something from him. Ah no, he was being ridiculous. Still, she did seem to be acting a bit strange. Her cheeks were bright as blossoms and carried a fragrance—

She squeezed his hand.

Dalton! What would he do if he came back after lunch and found him "spinning the wheel" with his girl? What if he picked a fight with him? He glanced down at the earth, trying to see if Gentle Len had reopened Bunyan's Banger yet. He had never seen the carnival from the air before with the sky pressed against his head, and it looked different. He located the Dodgem, where tiny cars bashed against each other and spat electricity overhead, and from there traced a path past the Loop-the-Loop to the hootchie-kootchie, where for the price of six tickets you could see Princess Tania and her erotic court bump and grind and strip down (but not too far, after all this was Kansas). Beyond the strip joint, his eyes rose from the funhouse and carrousel to the Wild Mouse, a miniature roller coaster he had watched being assembled and dismantled in three different states. He even heard the clatter of cars on its tracks as they rounded a bend before plunging in a crescendo of screams, and looking still farther, he found the trailer park in the distance where some people in the carnie lived. Why hadn't Bunyan's Banger opened for business yet? More important, where was Len? What if he found out and picked a fight with him? His knuckles whitened on the crossbar as he remembered again that time in Cleveland . . .

"What were you looking for?"

He tried to sound casual. "Your boyfriend."

"Len? What for?"

He met her blue eyes. "Well, you know what folks say."

"About what?"

"About his being . . . jealous. I heard he redesigned the features of a couple guys just for looking at you."

She glanced pointedly at his muscular body. "Scared?"

"Well, you are his girl."

She squeezed his hand. "Am I?"

The car rose and he rose with it, only now it wasn't the Ferris wheel making him dizzy.

"Everyone says you are."

She shook her head, blonde hair billowing. "That's what Len says. He tends to make up his mind by himself."

"And you're not?"

"If I was, would I be up here with you?"

His heart fell through his body. Slowly, he lifted his hand and stroked her cheek. Her eyes softened.

"Johnny, know what carnie folks say?"

"Tell me."

"They say it's bad luck to 'spin the wheel' with a girl who likes you and not kiss her."

"You're making that up."

"Yes."

Leaning forward, the whole universe spinning now, he kissed her.

He felt her embrace him and stroked her swirling hair, which was silk smooth and wild in the wind. Her lips tasted like honey and blossoms, and he drank their fragrance hungrily as he held her. Then breathless, he started to pull back but she clung to him. When she finally released him, he sat back and gazed up at the sky.

Neither of them said anything. The emptiness inside him had filled to overflowing. He felt he would burst.

Too soon the ride was over. Gomez grinned at the looks on their faces as he pulled back the bar so they could get out, but they didn't even notice. Belinda took his arm.

"Come on, Johnny, let's get this settled!"

Her words skimmed over his head, and he didn't even hear Gomez's cheerful farewell. "Adiós, amigo, don't take any wooden pesos!"

Belinda squeezed his hand. "He's a real character, but one of the best. Poor Mr. Gomez, he misses his country so. Says it's been years since he's seen a cactus or a mesquite bush."

Floating, a million miles from Mexico and oblivious to danger, he let her lead him to Bunyan's Banger, which had opened again after lunch.

# Chapter
# Twenty-Three

## Artist's Treat

**W**hen they reached it, he found a crowd had already gathered. Johnny watched one abnormally well-muscled farm boy drive the metal disk as high as HE MAN, which at 2300 was two notches below the summit. BANG! BANG! 2500. How many had striven for immortality and the $100.00 prize promised to anyone who could reach the top? How long had the procession been of the bold and the greedy? Though many had tried, all had been found wanting and fallen short of glory.

The country colossus who now possessed the mallet refused to accept the Judgment of the Gods. Muscles bulging, teeth clenched, again and again he lifted the ponderous mallet and slammed it down on the round platform. And again and again the result was the same: HE MAN, 2300. Finally, he handed over two more quarters and stripped off his shirt in frustration, revealing immense bronze muscles that seemed capable of anything.

Belinda nudged him. He looked down at her and winked.

The boy now assumed a posture reminiscent of such mythic figures as Atlas and Hercules. He ached to paint him like that, a young Titan poised in superhuman confrontation with the Gods, striving to reshape his own destiny and reach the peak of Mount Olympus, there to abide forever. If he only had his brush! His canvas! His fingers ached.

Down came the mallet. Crash! The disk shot up. But whether due to fatigue or fate, it now soared no higher than TOP DOG, which was pegged at 2200. Two more swings brought the same result, and in ultimate disgust the boy snatched his shirt from a friend and left.

"Why don't you try it, Johnny?" Belinda asked.

"Aw, that's kid stuff."

"Go on, it'll be fun!"

He looked nervously at the mallet. "I just remembered, I'm broke," he lied.

"Well, we'll just have to fix that!" she laughed, digging into her pocket. She gave him two quarters as he protested and poked him forward.

Others were ahead of him, however, and he waited tensely as a couple of wiry aspirants slammed the disk up to BIG BOY, 1800, and MUSCLE MAN, 1900. Then came a succession of pretenders who drew hoots and remarks questioning their manhood. SAD SACK, GOOD GIRL, SICK DUCK. One in particular launched the disk no higher than MILK MAID, 700, and slunk from the stage in disgrace.

It was now his turn. He was at the front of the crowd.

Then Dalton saw him. As their eyes met, Belinda took his arm, and he realized three things.

The first was that she had brought him here to make clear her choice and have it boldly out with Dalton, which meant she had manipulated and played with him from the beginning and was far more complicated than she looked. Like Chillman, she had deceived and misled him by her appearance, which he had accepted as everything. Or maybe he had deceived himself, been blinded by surface realities. The second thing he realized came like a bolt of déjà vu. Somewhere he had seen someone like Dalton before, but who was it? His mind swept the past, only he couldn't remember. The third thing he realized was that he knew exactly what would happen. Strange, he thought, how some things in life are not complex and profound at all but simple, mundane, and boring. He felt weary as he recognized the banal beginning of the old drama. Bullies. No matter where you found them, they all lacked imagination. Inevitably they sensed in him a weakness and an easy conquest.

But why did they always pick on him? Could it be just because he was different? He had often wondered about it. Why must some Arabs always hate Jews? Why must some whites hate Negros and Germans, Poles? He had never been able to understand it. How could you hate someone just for being different? Was it because man was basically a bastard, rotten, no good, innately depraved as the Christians believed? It did not make any sense, and the only explanation he had ever been able to find was that people hated others because they hated and were ashamed of something in themselves and were frightened in their great loneliness, their sense of inferiority and insecurity driving them to persecute and commit atrocities against their own kind. Still, he did not understand even that. It was a mystery which confounded the mind. Evil. The word itself had a sharp sound, like the slice of a knife. The Hebrew word was even more foreboding. *Rasha*. It also meant a wicked and ungodly man, a moral criminal. But was Dalton an evil man or only a hollow one, a creator of discord not because he was wicked but only because he was sick and empty?

"Take over, Jack," Dalton said and came over.

Tattooed arms. Eyes you could smash diamonds on. Removing a small sack from the breast pocket of his blue denim jacket, he began rolling a Bull Durham cigarette with hands that had a genius for palming fares and cheating at poker.

"Hi, Lin," Dalton said, not taking his eyes from Johnny's face.

"Hi, Len."

"Hi, fairy."

"Len!"

"You surprise me, Roth," Dalton said, thumbing his straw hat back. "Thought you played with your crayons so much you didn't have time for girls."

"I get around."

"Yeah, I bet you do, but not with my girl. Come here."

He followed him reluctantly to a totem pole twenty feet away staked in front of a shanty-like affair which sold cheap Indian trinkets and knickknacks. The stand was run by a full-blooded Choctaw Indian who Dalton in his ignorance insisted on calling Geronimo, after the chief of the Apaches. Dalton casually leaned his hand against one of the carved faces, smoke curling from the cigarette in his mouth. Over his shoulder Johnny could see Belinda watching them anxiously.

"I'm gonna be real nice to you, paint boy," Dalton said. "Stay away from her or I'll clean your ass."

"I'd say it's up to her, wouldn't you?"

"No, it ain't. Look, pal, maybe you ain't heard, but the last guy who even sniffed at her got his face rearranged."

He smiled and placed his hand on a green Indian face with a grotesque scowl.

"What's the matter, Dalton? Having trouble keeping her?"

"Not from you, I ain't. You're not gonna give me no trouble at all. No fairy's gonna prance in and waltz off with my girl. Not when *I'm* around."

"Oh yes, I've heard you're a regular terror. You're a real big shot, aren't you?"

"Fuckin' right."

"Yeah, you're aces, Dalton, especially when it comes to cheating kids and little old ladies. I hear you're strictly Big Time, palming twenty cent fares and selling yesterday's tickets. You ought to be real proud of yourself. Not everybody's got a reputation as a short-change artist and has half the company's spotters watching him to see he doesn't start picking pockets or rolling drunks next."

Dalton removed his hand from the totem pole and gripped Johnny's shirt. "Listen, I've had enough of your smart yap. Open it once more and I'll . . ."

Sam Duckett! That was who he reminded him of. Even their names were similar. For a moment he saw not Dalton's face but the first bully he had ever stood up to. There had been a couple of his friends there the first time. What had become of them? After the . . . accident five years ago, he had fled Ohio and never found out. Lee Esner, he knew, had all those colleges hot on his butt with football scholarships, and Jimmy Wiggins, poor bastard, had tried to rob a delicatessen for some stupid reason and got a bullet in the brain. Last time he saw him, he had still been in a coma. Hope he came out of it. Damn it, Jimmy was his friend. Why hadn't he stopped running long ago and gone home to find out?

Success, he thought, to some it comes easily, while others are losers from the beginning. Yet maybe it wasn't so simple. Maybe we can shape our lives. If he, for example, could just break the pattern of his life once and not have to resort to his fists or run away when pushed to the wall by someone like Dalton, then maybe he could change everything. Do it once and maybe he'd never have to fight or run away again and would be able to change other things, too. Only how could he do it? How could he break the pattern? It simply couldn't be done. He couldn't change. No, that wasn't true.

If tough guys like Dalton were boring in their predictability, other things, like how we turn out, are uncertain and can be repainted like a flawed self-portrait if we can overcome the darkness within ourselves.

Maybe it *was* time to go home. See about Jimmy and make peace with his father. Hug and kiss his mother again. He needed to exorcise or at least lighten the cancerous guilt he felt regarding both of them. Whether his father was right or wrong, Johnny knew the man loved him in his own way. Both of his parents did. He was their only child, the most important thing in the world to them, and the dozen or so postcards he'd sent home in the past five years were a poor substitute for his presence.

"Hey, Roth, I'm *talk*in' to you!"

Lin was still watching them, her face strained. Just seeing her made him feel good. He no longer felt empty and burned out, an aimless drifter trying to forget. He took his hand from the pole to remove Dalton's fist. Then he remembered what his fist had done.

"I hear you," he said.

"Good. That's the trouble with you four-eyed punks who read books and draw them pictures, you don't listen so good. Your head's always off in the clouds somewhere. You know, Roth, you really got some folks here fooled. They think you're a regular genius when it comes to drawin' pictures of ratty old men. But I got you figured out. You may have the size for it, but underneath you're yellow."

"At least I don't need my fists to keep *my* girl."

"Hey, listen! Shut your face or I'll make it so even your mother don't recognize ya. How'd you like that?" He nodded toward Belinda. "Want her to see ya get it? Big yellow fairy like you? The only reason I haven't kicked your face in is I don't want to look unfriendly in front of her."

"You're all heart, Dalton."

"Yeah, and I'll tell you what you're gonna do. You're gonna go back to your crayons right now without blinkin' an eye or saying boo to her. Get me, Roth? You're gonna walk right past her and if you so much as say 'Howdy,' I'm gonna bust ya permanent. Understand?"

"Perfectly."

"O.K., then take a hike."

He removed his hand from the pole and squeezed it into a fist, memory an old enemy inside him. How many faces like Dalton's had he seen? How many bullies had shoved their chests like insolent walls against his own?

Stepping around him, he walked toward his stand.

As he passed Belinda, she caught his arm.

"Johnny! Why are you doing this? I know you're not afraid of him."

He gazed at her.

"Johnny—why?" Tears broke out in her eyes. "Why don't you stand up to him?"

He turned and walked away.

Back at his stand he found a customer waiting. Like most, she considered the pastel rates too high and chose charcoal. Mechanically, he posed her and went to work, blew on the fixative and slipped the end product into a cardboard frame. The three dollars he pocketed without thinking.

After she left, he lifted the lid of a battered red box studded with travel stickers. Reaching under the lid which he had used for countless games of solitaire, he drew out a warm bottle of Pabst Blue Ribbon and twisted off the cap with his fingers.

Ah. So good. Leaning back on one of Belinda's Cane back chairs, he let the liquid pour down his throat and fill him with imagined frost, trying to blot out everything but its taste. If he concentrated hard enough . . .

He jerked upright in the chair. Belinda was standing in the sun, just ten feet away.

"Why, Johnny?" she said. "Why did you do it?"

"Go away," he said. He raised the bottle and drank.

"Not till you tell me why you left that way. I know you're not afraid of him."

He gazed up at her. Even from here he could see her blue eyes looked darker, as if filled with tears. Fighting the desire to rise and hold her, he took another drink.

"Oh yes, I am. I'm a coward."

"I don't believe it."

"Well, it's true. I've been one for a long time."

He tossed the empty bottle away and flipped open the lid of the box.

Twisting the cap off another bottle, he saluted her with a mock toast.

"Artist's treat!"

He drank deeply in long swallows. When he lowered the bottle, she was looking at him in surprise.

"Do you always do it like that?"

"What?"

"Open bottles with just your fingers. I've never seen anyone do it before."

He shrugged. "It's a little knack I picked up. A man named Wiggins showed it to me." He paused. "He showed me a lot of things."

"He sounds like someone special."

"He was, but he drank too much," he said, taking another pull from the bottle. "Anyway, this isn't the only one I'm going to open." He patted the box. "I've got a whole regiment here of brave little soldiers just dying for combat, plus a jug of Bust-head from the hills of West Virginia I've been saving up for just the right occasion."

She shook her head. "So you're going to get drunk, just as Benny does when he can't face his problems."

He thought of Benny splashing in the water as a result of a well thrown baseball and managed to imitate a laugh. "Bull's eye, honey. You're dead right. I'm going to get *stinko*. Bury a few soldiers and wade in some mountain dew. And when I get high enough, I'm going to fly right over and blow BOBO's golden horn."

Now her eyes *were* filled with tears. "Johnny, didn't what happened on the Ferris wheel mean anything to you? Didn't you care? Didn't you—"

He raised the bottle and drank, hating what he was doing to her. *Please leave, Lin. Please leave me alone.*

When he lowered it, she was gone. He could see her long golden legs moving like heartbreak back up the midway, out of his life and back to Len. *Johnny, didn't what happened on the Ferris wheel mean anything to you?* He forced down the pain and looked away. Well, it was better this way. Besides, it was time to move on again. He'd been here long enough.

# Chapter
# Twenty-Four

## The Bell Ringer

The thought of moving on again hit him like a truck, and for a moment he couldn't even think. He didn't even hear BOBO's screeching taunt of a plump farmer at the pitch-and-dunk. "HEY FATSO, YOU COULDN'T HIT THE BROAD SIDE OF A BARN IF YOU WAS STANDING IN IT!"

Where could he go? For the first time ever he seemed to have reached a dead end. He had run out of places to run to. After this there was noth . . .

"OINK OINK PIGGY! GO ON BACK TO THE FARM! YOU COULDN'T HIT—"

Crash! He heard the laughter and didn't need to look to know BOBO had been dunked. He had seen it all a thousand times before. The mark would be standing, probably tossing the ball proudly up and down in a calloused hand while he basked in the crowd's mirth. And BOBO, their common enemy who would one day go too far and get himself killed because he outrageously punctured all their delusions and self-images and made them feel foolish, would be climbing back up on his perch as feisty and unsinkable as ever.

"HEY HEY! WHADDAYA KNOW! TWO-TON TONY JUST GOT LUCKY! THAT'S ONE IN A ROW NOW, CHAMP, TIME TO GO HOME AND SLOP THE HOGS! YOU COULDN'T DO IT AGAIN IF YOU WAS STANDING WITH YOUR FAT NOSE ON IT!"

Look what he had done to Lin. How could he have done it? She was so sweet, so . . . no, he was no better than Len. If anything, he was worse. At least Len didn't treat her this way. It took someone proud of his moral superiority to do it.

So what could he do? he asked himself. Fight Len for her? Resort to his fists once again? The thought triggered memories, and in pain he leaned forward and put his hand on the table before him.

Lin was right. It wasn't the hand of an artist, and though she'd been teasing him, maybe she had just about hit the nail on the head when she had suggested it was more like a butcher's. Crude and endowed with artistic skills which were at best dubious, its main virtue from the beginning seemed to be the ease with which it could open beer bottles without an opener and break things that got in its way.

He took another drink, then returned to his hand.

His father had hated the things he had done with it and tried everything to stop him, he thought, examining its unlovely features from a variety of angles. The drawing and painting had been bad enough, God knows, especially when the works had been abstract or explored the naked human form. *Narrishkeit* and sin! To his father's Orthodox mind, his efforts had been at best childish, at worst deadly slime from the sitra achra, the other side, which threatened and waged war with his religious and moral training.

But there had been the other thing too, the gift which he had never wanted and which no one could question because there was no room for opinion or interpretation. A sketch or painting was good or it was trash. Beauty, after all, was in the eye of the beholder. But a broken jaw was as irrefutable as a clap of thunder, as Jimmy Wiggins' father knew when he had persuaded him to use his crushing talent by entering the Golden Gloves, a pursuit which his father had also found objectionable. A fighter in his family? Unthinkable! If anything, it was more debased and perverted than the art.

His father's bearded face filled his vision, rigid and intolerant. How Johnny had loved him and hated him, wanted to embrace him and at the same time smash him until . . .

*God, don't make me remember. Please!*

The occasion: The Finals for Cleveland's Heavyweight Championship, with him riding a streak of knockouts that had stunned the crowds. His opponent: a sixteen-year- old boy like himself whose pleasant face bore no resemblance to bullies he had known.

He had expected an easy time. A little feinting, dancing around, and then *whop! whop!* and Collins would go the way of the others. But Collins had proved unexpectedly difficult. A southpaw, he had circled to his right instead of his left and repelled his attack with elbows, gloves, and a bobbing head he couldn't reach. And always there had been the odd angle punches and mosquito-like jabs in his face. Far from commanding the fight, he had felt foolish.

Then midway through the third and last round, he had solved Collins. Following the instructions Jimmy Wiggins' father had given him between rounds, he had slipped to his right and managed to land a glancing hook and then a straight right. As it connected, he sensed it differed from all punches he had ever thrown. Collins' jaw seemed to dissolve. After the referee had counted Collins out, he had continued to lie there. He had never gotten up.

For a long moment, Johnny kept his eyes shut. When he opened them, his hand was clenched, a painful, inescapable mystery.

To create or destroy: from the beginning it had been that way. Were these fingers meant to hold a brush or to be sealed in a boxing glove? Who or what was he? Would he ever know? For all he knew, he should have studied harder to become a rabbi as his father wanted. Guiltily he remembered the Bible which his father had given him when he was thirteen for his bar mitzvah, the ceremony in which he had supposedly become a man. Now that Bible was sealed in back with his other few possessions. He had tried a hundred times in the past five years to read it and to throw it away. In both he had failed. He remembered reading from the scroll at his bar mitzvah about Noah and his ark, reading about the flood that had purged the world of evil and wickedness and corruption and brought rebirth. He remembered reading about the flood that made one new again with cleansing rain.

The myriad sounds of the carnival returned to his consciousness. Looking up, he saw the Ferris wheel he had ridden with Lin. *When you're 'carnie,'* she'd said, *you're part of something bigger.* Well, she had been born into it and belonged to something from the beginning. The shoot-the-ducks gallery she and her parents ran was all she needed to feel she fit into the vast design of things. It was her birthright. She was a carnie brat. *He* was a wandering Jew, forever searching, at home nowhere. He didn't even know what he was meant to be.

He listened to the sounds of the carnival, watched its ebb and flow. Circles within circles. Wheels within wheels.

Rising, he entered the tent he had pitched behind his display of sketches and emerged with a large canvas which he secured on an easel. Then he chose and prepared his oils, thinning them with turpentine on a palette.

He began slowly, searching. Tentatively he drew a circle, then another, and joined them with a line. The brush groped, looking for a purpose, a plan, a theme it could warm to and seize. Before him the carnival waited, not a "carnie" yet but a mishmash of forms wanting a miracle. He struggled to awake, then counseled himself. *Easy, let it come by itself, don't force it.*

The sun lanced down. He began to sweat. The brush moved back and forth between the palette and the canvas, warming and probing. The carnival. See. It is not sound and fury. It signifies. It is raw and violently alive. Crude and passionate and yet suffused with a significance that will explain half of existence if you can just touch it and not let go.

There was no hesitancy or tentativeness now in the brush, no furtive or fumbling search. He stabbed with a broad bristle, letting the paint twist and scream. Once, in a moment of meekness, he started to cool it with blues and greens more in keeping with a lawn party for children, but recovered his courage. Ever more alive, ever more knowing, he attacked it again with reds and yellows, gashes of vermillion, oblivious to the footsteps behind him and the accumulation of witnesses. He did not hear them, for he was with it and for it now all the way as the carnie folks said, and his brush loved the funhouse with its cheap illusions and the towering Ferris wheel where he had kissed her, loved even the Fat Lady with her countless chins and volcano-like laughter. It loved Chillman and Gomez, the rigged games and the bright lights, and most of all, it loved Belinda, who in some nameless way was the force that drove his brush. Soon, though, he reached a point where his sweat was a fire in his eyes and his shirt a cotton cage. Reluctantly, hating the need for it, he turned around, started to remove his shirt.

And saw them.

Thirty faces, silently watching the forms that moved and grew on the canvas. Country faces. Faces burned by Kansas sun. Carnie faces.

He paused, embraced them with one look and then ripped his shirt off. Naked to his waist, he attacked the canvas again, sometimes darting, sometimes crouched, sometimes poised on his feet, like a fighter.

At last he sensed a hiatus, a necessary breathing space in the torture of inspiration and stepped back to survey his work. Enough. It was good. Very very good. He would finish it later.

Around him the carnie breathed, an animal of countless dimensions. Wheels within wheels. Circles within circles.

When he left, he did not know his destination. One moment he was studying his painting before an audience, the next he was walking down the midway with the sun burning the hard naked muscles of his chest, arms, and back.

The sun burned too on the sunglasses of the stunted ghost who stood waiting for him far down the midway. When he reached him, Mr. Chillman touched the protective brim of his hat in greeting.

"Johnny, your painting of the carnie is glorious. You've captured our spirit as no one else has."

"Thank you, Mr. Chillman." *How could you possibly know what I painted? You weren't in the crowd when I turned with the brush and ripped my shirt off. I could never have missed you! Even if you were there, you couldn't have gotten all the way here so quickly.*

Chillman moved closer, his deformed, chalk-white form barely reaching Johnny's chest. "Your painting has changed me, son. It's opened my eyes and made me see. Like you, I'm beginning to feel closer to the people here, no longer so alone."

It took a few moments for all the man's words to sink in. When they did, Johnny realized he'd just received the greatest compliment in his life about his painting. He felt stunned, proud, and humbled. His painting had actually changed a man.

"Thank you," he managed.

"I'll miss you when you return home," Chillman said, embracing him.

*When I return home? How can you know such things?* Overwhelmed by the man's prescience, Johnny reached down and embraced him in return, feeling a strange bond ripen between them. He remembered feeling the funhouse operator was somehow different and Belinda herself saying Chillman was a mystery beyond her understanding just as he was. As Chillman pulled back from him, Johnny tried to speak, to give the man something of equal value. Before he could, Chillman patted his cheek. "We'll meet again, son," he said and waddled off.

Remembering his mission, he struggled to collect himself and continued down the midway. Wheels within wheels, the carnie turned. Circles within circles.

High in the air, the bell waited: another circle.

Dalton was collecting four bits from another hopeful when Johnny stepped in and dropped Belinda's quarters into his hand. Going to the mallet, he picked it up and returned.

"A while ago you did me a favor," he said. "Remember? You were kind enough not to beat me up. Now it's my turn to return the courtesy."

He tapped the round platform dented by thousands of failed swings. "See that, Dalton?" he said. "I want you to imagine it's your head down there." He jabbed his finger at the bell on top of the vertical tower. "Or up there, near the clouds."

As the crowd watched, he lifted the heavy mallet and gazed again at the bell on Bunyan's Banger. *BANG! BANG! 2500. $100.00 To Anyone Who Can Ring The Bell On Bunyan's Banger! Test Your Strength On The Highest Ring-The-Bell In The World! The Mount Everest Of Challenges.*

He set his feet and prepared himself, feeling the wood which was worn smooth by countless hands which had failed before him. The mallet reminded him of the hammer he had once used to smash a glass-faced fire alarm in school. *In Case Of Fire Break Glass.* He laughed and glanced at Dalton whose mouth hung open like a hooked fish.

The mallet rose in his hands, reached its apex, came down. Behind it was all his strength, all the fury of his years of searching and being lost.

*Bang!* The disk rose, a streak in the sun, and struck the bell sharply. Even as it fell he was resetting his feet, lifting the mallet again.

*Bang!* Again the disk shot up, ringing the bell and sending out reverberations that caused heads all over the carnival to turn in his direction. Again the disk fell, again he swung, his muscles gleaming. Again and again the bell rang, pumping forth ripples of sound as if it were the vibrant red heart of the carnie itself.

At last he stopped and returned to Dalton, whose face was undergoing an interesting variety of color changes. He swallowed, started to say something, stopped. Johnny gazed into his eyes and then forgetting his resolve not to hit him, drew his fist back. Dalton saw it and retreated, but Johnny was already moving forward, anticipating the feel of his fists against his body.

*Break the pattern.*

Do it once, and maybe you'll never have to run again.

Do it once, and maybe you can change *everything.*

The fist came down and he was still, for the first time in his life neither running nor fighting. Then he raised his other arm and with more force than strictly necessary, he delivered the mallet's head directly into Dalton's stomach, making him grunt and double over.

"Forget the prize," he said. "I'll take the girl."

He turned and headed down the midway to find her.

# Chapter
# Twenty-Five

## Reunion

On the good days there was only a little pain and a slight rim around the sun. If he was especially lucky, and his medication was working, the numbness in his left side virtually disappeared and he could dispense with his cane.

Today was one of those days. He awoke feeling young again, ready to race the world from here to the corner. The stiffness and blurred vision resulting from the bullet fragments in his brain seemed more of an incentive than a handicap, his faint headache less of an old enemy than a merciful reprieve from days of agony when he would lie in bed all day wishing only he could die.

On such good days it did not hurt him so much to watch the children play, to see their young bodies engaged in eternal games where physical excellence was worshipped as the only thing of value, conferring a semi-divine, not-to-be-questioned grace upon those whose only achievement was that they had been blessed by birth with a gift and doubly blessed in not having it taken away by bad luck or a policeman's bullet. And on such days too, he could almost forget that infirmity of any kind was the one unforgivable sin, a crime against the principles of existence whose only appropriate punishment was scorn and ridicule.

At the moment he was watching swarms of school kids play a game on a concrete playground a few streets from where he worked. The game was a jumble of activity involving a volleyball they ceaselessly chased and kicked. It was clear there were two teams and the object was to kick the ball past the other team's goal line, but who belonged to what team and what the score was, were matters which seemed to be treated with cavalier disregard.

There *was* a leader, however. Taller than the others, he waited like a prince for them to bring the ball to *him*. "Give it to Gary," they shouted, the little girls jumping up and down in excitement. "Give it to Gary!" Again and again he watched their little hero receive his just tribute and kick the ball harder and truer than the rest, scoring points which made the boys slap his back and the girls go wild.

Though it was only October, winter seemed to crouch in the gray sky like a giant cat ready to spring. Feeling his spirits darken, he turned from it and opening a small paper bag, set the contents on the bench beside him. With his penknife he sliced the bagel and applied a little cream cheese. Then he put the lox between the slices and began eating, enjoying the salty taste of the salmon and the chewy texture of the bread.

He remembered playing such games when he was a boy. Sometimes they left the doors open at school during the summer, and he and a lot of other kids would play in the gym all day. One game had consisted of nothing more than throwing a volleyball or basketball at others to hit them or make them drop the ball. The last one left won the game. It had been wild and savage, and some boys had fired the ball so fast it could really hurt you. That had been the best game. As often as any of the others, he had won because of his cannon-like arm and quickness in dodging the ball.

A bird swooped at the edge of his vision, and his eyes fluttered uncontrollably. Carefully, he set his sandwich down and closed his eyes. In the early days, just after it had been determined he would see again, it had taken little more than a particle of dust to cause attacks which lasted for hours and made him nauseated. Such were the mysteries of the human brain. A few bits of lead scattered here and there . . . Master of the Universe, who could fathom it? Even the doctors with their degrees and Latin jargon couldn't explain precisely why his body acted the ways it did or predict his chances of recovery.

"Give it to Gary!"

He waited patiently behind his closed lids. Patience: it was a quality he had never possessed when growing up. Now he had a high regard for it. More important than his medicine or babble about "pressure points" and how to apply them to gain relief, was this homely virtue which he had come to see as distinctly Jewish. One endures, as he had been told often enough. One suffers in silence and does not bewail his fate.

Slowly, breathing an inner prayer, he reopened his eyes.

His eyes were steady, the fluttering gone.

Grateful, he rose and dropped the paper bag into a container. He had to get back to work fast. The new Assistant Manager was unreliable and disrespectful, and Groucho was dying and wouldn't be there today to help keep him in line. Damn it, he should have listened to the old man and never hired the kid in the first place.

Thinking of Groucho's approaching death stung him with grief too deep to bear. The old man had done so much for him out of love, especially at the store where an affectionate Yiddish word or two and an arm around his shoulders had gradually made customers accept a crippled black kid's growing role and accumulation of power. What's more, *he* was beginning to accept it himself.

Back at the shop, he found the assistant manager leaning idly against the counter and joking with cronies with an easy smile, ignoring him as he entered and got the broom and apron. As he swept the floor, he listened to their laughter. Once the assistant manager told a joke which made them erupt into guffaws.

He worked fast to get the place ready for afternoon customers. When he remembered to look for the assistant manager again, he found the shop empty. *Probably sitting in the office behind* my *desk,* he thought nervously, *just taking things easy and reading one of those "girly" magazines again.*

Replacing the broom and apron, he summoned his courage and entered his office. The assistant manager was leaning back in the swivel chair, feet up on the desk and his face hidden behind an issue of *Men's Life* which bore on its cover a blonde with a staggering mammary development. He did not look up as Jimmy entered.

"Do you mind?" he said.

The assistant manager turned a page.

"I said, *'Do you mind?'*"

Sensing a presence, the assistant manager lowered the magazine and gazed up at him with a look that stopped just short of insolence. A sneer breezed across his face. On days when Groucho, the original white owner, was too sick to keep Jimmy company, he was far more likely to face such contempt and disobedience.

*You bastard*, he thought, *you'd like to call me a sawed-off, crippled little nigger, wouldn't you? If Groucho was here, you wouldn't dare treat me this way.*

Though he'd won his attention, the assistant manager still didn't move. "Do you mind?" Jimmy repeated, raising his voice. "The *desk*."

The assistant manager considered the matter. Then his feet left the desk, and he rose in stages. Moving around Jimmy, he slumped into the chair before the desk and continued reading.

Quietly, Jimmy sat behind the desk and faced him.

"Mr. Whitehead."

The blonde's breasts came down. "Yeah?"

"I think it's about time we had a talk."

"Yeah, what about?"

"You."

"I don't—"

"It's really quite simple," he said, steeling himself to the arrogant contempt in the other's eyes. "Ever since I hired you two weeks ago, you've been nothing but trouble. On days when Groucho" (a *white* man) "is here, you're barely adequate. When he's *not* here, you show me no respect at all, and I have to watch you like a hawk. If I don't, you'll rob me blind and give half the food away to your friends."

"I don't steal no food."

"Yes, you do."

"Well . . . maybe a little. But mostly it's the kids around here, especially the ones in that gang. They're so quick you can't even catch them."

Jimmy stared back, determined not even to blink.

"But you do steal *some* food, don't you?"

The assistant manager started to protest then apparently sensed that replying from a slumped position was somehow improper. He sat up. The blonde in his lap crinkled a paper nose and slid to the floor.

"Now look, a couple of snacks ain't no big deal."

"No, *you* look. I'm not a philanthropist, I'm a businessman. I can't afford to feed you and your friends. Anything you eat comes out of profits." He paused. "Besides the fact that you're a thief and don't follow orders, you're also lazy. Instead of sweeping the place out at noon like I told you, you loaf and talk to friends. I've talked to you before about this. This is a delicatessen, not a social club. When I tell you to do something, I expect it to be done."

"Look, it's my lunch hour," the other answered, "and besides, the joint doesn't need cleaning up. What do you think you got here—Bloomingdale's? It's just a place for selling sandwiches."

The assistant manager stared back, surly, defiant, and capable of stamping him flat. Fear surged through him, which had the effect of upsetting the precious balance of his metabolism and causing his left arm to throb. That's all he needed right now, a neuromuscular attack which would leave him half-paralyzed. Well, this time he couldn't afford to be patient. He'd have to risk it.

"Listen, you *gonif,* you *bulvon,* you *schlemiel,*" he said, using words the old man had taught him. "I'm going to say this just once. You answered my advertisement, and *you* work for *me.* Either follow orders or get out."

"Well, you don't have to get mad about it," the assistant manager said, his body a good deal straighter now.

"It seems I do," he answered. "Besides everything else, you crack dirty jokes that offend customers and treat me with contempt. Today you ignored me when I returned from lunch." He shook a cigarette from a pack on the desk and tried lighting it with his *left* hand. Three times his thumb failed to turn the notched metal wheel of the lighter. He concentrated on his thumb, aware of the assistant manager's stare. On his fourth attempt, the little ball turned, and he was rewarded with a bright orange flame. Lighting up, he settled back in the swivel chair, pleased at his small victory.

"Tell me, George," he said, "how old are you?"

"Twenty-one. Why?"

"I'm twenty-one, too. Is that why you resent working for me, because we're the same age? Or is it because I'm a little nigger who half the time needs a cane just to stand up?"

"I never said that."

"No? Well, you've hinted at it often enough, and I've heard you joke with your pals about me being a spastic little shine who should be selling pencils out of a tin cup."

"Aw, I didn't *mean* anything," the other said. "I was just joking."

He took a puff, noticing the other's shame and finding it easy now to meet his eyes. "Well, I'm not going to put up with it any longer, George, neither your jokes nor your attitude nor your friends. Look, work with me and do your job and we'll get along fine. Continue what you've been doing, and you can hit the street. Understand?"

The assistant manager looked at him with respect. "Yes, sir."

"All right, now why don't you go out there and clean up like I told you?"

The assistant manager rose and left the office. Jimmy leaned back in his chair and took a deep drag from the cigarette, his thumb playing with the ball of the lighter.

After a minute he rose and left the shop, passing the assistant manager who was now hard at work and the Yiddish proverb that faced him from the wall.

*Mit mazel ken men alles.*
With luck, everything is possible.

Opening the door, which caused the bell above it to ring, he continued on across the street, stopping only when he reached the field he had played in as a kid. There he turned and gazed back at the sign he had personally re-lettered just a month before.

*Jimmy's Delicatessen*
*Bagels Kosher Meats Orders To Go*

For a while he gazed at it, feeling an upheaval in his chest as he recalled how difficult it had been for him to stir the paint and handle the brush, to keep within the lines of the letters he had drawn. Painting it had been hard, but he had regarded it as something necessary, a task, a self-imposed test he had to pass if he was going to accept the challenge of a dying old man without family and both run *and* own the store. After all, if he couldn't change the delicatessen's name himself, how could he make the business work?

Now, facing the sign, he felt he had finally earned the old man's trust, for by standing up to the assistant manager, he had taken an important step in a journey he had begun five years ago from a hospital bed. True, there would be hard days ahead, plenty of them. But along with the days of fever, pain, and semi-paralysis, there would also be new stores, all with his name personally painted upon them.

He turned his head. Someone was approaching from a long way off, yet even at a distance, he could tell there was something familiar about him. Only he couldn't quite place the person. As a kid he'd had eyes like a cat. Now they misted over whenever he had headaches.

He didn't have a headache *now*, however. Touching his eyes, he found they were wet and he'd been crying because of the sign and all it meant to him. He wiped his eyes. Instantly he grinned and resisted the urge to run, recognizing the figure at once long before it drew near and resolved into the face and form of Johnny Roth. Johnny reached him and stopped, grinning back at him.

"Well, Jimmy," he said.

"Johnny!"

They gazed at each other for a long moment. Then they ran into each other's arms. Jimmy felt Johnny embrace him like he was a doll and his feet leave the earth before being returned hastily to it.

"Hey, I'm sorry! I forgot."

"It's O.K., I'm fine. God, it's good—"

"Same here! I've missed you. So many times I wondered if you were all right, if you'd—"

"Heck, you can see I'm good as . . . Gee, Johnny, you've changed! No belly at all and tall as—"

Abruptly he stopped, and like friends everywhere who meet after a long absence, they stood nodding their heads idiotically at each other, shy and unable to think of a thing to say.

Jimmy broke the silence first.

"Like I said, you sure look good. Big and tall, and no one's going to call you 'buttergut' now!"

"Well, look at *you*. You haven't changed a bit. How are you really?"

"I'm fine, mountains of bad times but . . ." He stopped to consider. Yes, things *were* fine now. "Anyway, everything's working out all right."

"That's good."

They stood grinning at each other.

"So how do you like my place?" Jimmy asked, waving with a

proud flourish at the delicatessen.

Johnny turned his head and read the sign. "'Jimmy's Delicatessen,'" he said. "You know, I just don't believe it. I didn't believe it when I arrived home yesterday and my father told me, and now that I'm here I still don't. How—"

"You're living at home?"

Johnny nodded, still incredulous. "Yes." His eyes welled up. "My parents were both so glad to see me. And they keep crying and hugging and kissing me, even my father. I don't know how long it'll last."

"Maybe your father's changed, Johnny," Jimmy said. "People can, you know."

"I hope so, Jimmy. I know I have." Johnny dried his eyes and blinked at the store. "'Jimmy's Delicatessen,'" he repeated. "'Bagels. Kosher Meats. Orders To Go.'" He slapped his knee and laughed. "God damn it, Jimmy, I can remember when you didn't know kosher from knishes or bagels from borsch. Now you're selling the damn things! God, I can't believe it! Next thing I know, you'll be telling me you're a convert to Hasidism and your favorite tzaddik lives right up the street."

"Hardly," he smiled, pointing to his head, "can you imagine me growing earlocks with *this* hair?"

Johnny's eyes widened. "You *know* about such things?"

Jimmy laughed, delighted at his surprise. It sure was good to see his old friend again.

"Sure do. Matter of fact, I know about a *lot* of things." He punched Johnny's shoulder playfully, remembering a day long gone. "Bet this 'black sheep' of the family is a better Jew than you are any day."

"I still don't get it. How did this happen?"

"C'mon," Jimmy said, taking his arm. "We'll have a glass of tea and I'll tell you."

He led him across the street and into his shop, the bell ringing above their heads as they entered. In his office he plugged in the samovar and brought out two cups.

"Something I picked up from the old man," he said.

"Groucho?"

"Yeah. Like a lot of Russian Jews, he sure likes his tea, especially when sipped through a cube of sugar."

"I know," Johnny said. "My father and I used to drink it that way all the time." He puffed out his cheeks. "Sometimes we'd study Talmud for hours, and the only thing which kept me going was those 'tea breaks.' I used to sip the stuff real slow."

When the tea was ready, Jimmy poured them both a cup.

"L'chaim," he said with a wink.

"Shalom."

They each took a cube of sugar and held it between their teeth as they sipped to sweeten the liquid.

"So good," Johnny said, savoring its clean sharp taste. Looking up, he was surprised to find Bellows' *Stag at Sharkey's* thumbtacked to the wall. "Hey, I didn't know you liked paintings."

Jimmy nodded. "I put it up years ago, I guess because it reminded me of you."

In the painting the two club fighters strained and bashed each other like exhausted gladiators while cigar-smoking men outside the ring which imprisoned them shouted and worried about their bets. Johnny gazed at it uneasily. He had always liked its realism but was bothered by the way Bellows made the boxers look like puppets who were controlled by others and forced to fight against their will. Then, too, the artist had blurred the details of their bodies, depriving them of individuality and reducing them to mindless forms bent only on destruction.

There was a shout. "Mr. Wiggins, come out here!"

Johnny forgot the painting and looked at Jimmy.

"For Chrissakes, come out here! I've got him. Help!"

Jimmy heaved himself up. "What is it this time?" he grunted. "Jesus H. Christ, it sounds like the bloody store's on fire!"

# Chapter
# Twenty-Six

## Teamwork

The first thing they saw when they left the office was the assistant manager clinging desperately to a boy by the display counter at the front of the shop while an older boy tried to tear him loose.

"I've got him, Mr. Wiggins! I told you I wasn't the one stealing the stuff. Here's the proof!"

"O.K.," Jimmy said, reaching them. "I believe you. Now let him go."

"But he'll—"

"Let him go!"

Whitehead reluctantly dropped his arms and stepped back. Jimmy considered the boy.

"Why did you do it, son?"

"I didn't—"

"Don't lie to me." He moved quickly and pulled the boy's hand out from behind his back. "What you got here?" He pried open his fingers, exposing a handful of crushed doughnuts. "Is this all? Or is there more?"

"Leave him alone," the older boy said. "He wasn't doing nothin.'"

When he spoke, they noticed him more clearly. Johnny felt a shock as he recognized the greased-back hair and stiletto shoes. And on the glossy shirt, reminiscent of a night of terror, blazed the words he would never forget, not in a hundred years.

*The Cossacks.*

"Wasn't doing anything?" Jimmy said. "I suppose he was just taking those doughnuts for the fun of it."

"Aw, he was gonna pay for 'em. Don't make such a—"

"No, I wasn't," the boy said.

They turned to him. "You weren't what?" Jimmy asked.

The boy swallowed. Jimmy watched the eyes dart here and there like trapped birds, thinking if the boy had been black, it could have been him just five years ago.

"I wasn't gonna . . . pay."

"Shut up, ya punk," the older boy said. "Before ya—"

"Go on," Jimmy cut in. "What?"

"I . . ."

"Go on, tell me. If you don't tell me, I'll have to call the police. This is serious business, son. You can go to jail for this. And if you do, it'll be on your record for the rest of your life."

The boy's throat gurgled. "I—"

"Shut up! Fuck it, I'm splittin'!"

"No, you're not," Johnny said, speaking for the first time. He slid between the boys and the door. "You're not going anywhere."

"Why'd you do it?" Jimmy said, his eyes still riveted to the boy's face.

The boy glanced nervously at his partner. "It was *his* idea."

"His?"

"Yeah, Francis said if I wanted to get into the gang, I had to rob a store. And he had to be here to see me do it."

"Francis?" Whitehead burst out laughing. "That's a *girl's* name!"

"Shut up!" the older boy snarled.

"Francis? It's a talking mule! They made a movie—"

"My name's *Frank*, y'hear me? *Frank*. Call me that again and I'll slit your gizzard!"

"Nobody's going to slit *anything*," Jimmy said, "at least not in *my* store." He studied the boy. There were freckles on his face and not even a trace of beard. He didn't even look sixteen.

"Let me get this straight," he said. "You mean you let him *talk* you into it?"

The boy glanced at Francis and nodded.

"You let him *talk* you into it?" Jimmy repeated. "Don't you know you can get hurt that way?" He rubbed his forehead and then grabbed the boy's shoulders with both hands, ignoring the pain. "Don't you know it's stupid?" he yelled, shaking him. "All it takes is one mistake, just one person doing your thinking just once in your life to ruin it." He shook the boy harder, trying to make him understand, trying to put so much fear in his eyes he'd never forget. His voice went still higher. "Don't you know all a boy has to do is make one mistake? It doesn't take two, just one. All he has to do is make *one* goddamn mistake and his whole life's ruined. He's a cripple for the rest of his life and he can't even move for the pain—"

"Let 'im go, ya crazy bastard!" The older boy moved forward.

Johnny intercepted him. "I wouldn't."

The boy sneered. "Buzz off."

"No."

"Get out a my way or I'll kill you."

"Uh, I wouldn't," said Jimmy.

"Stay out of—"

"I mean it," he said. "You don't want any trouble from my friend Roth. Believe me, you don't want any trouble from him at all."

Uncertainty swept the boy's face, and then his hand went to his pocket. When it came up, there was a knife in it. He pressed the button and the blade flashed open.

Johnny froze, blinking at the superimposition of another face on Francis'. It was a double exposure that curdled his senses. Then the intruding face took possession and he was in the parking lot again, surrounded by The Cossacks and watching the moonlight glitter on George's blade. George sneered and flaunted the knife before his face.

"Johnny, watch out!"

The knife moved again, not a warning this time but the strike of a snake. He pulled his belly in, just saving it from the flashing steel.

The knife withdrew, poised to strike again.

Aware of the risk, he closed his eyes to exorcise George's image. When he opened them, he found he was back in the shop.

"Put the knife away, punk, or I'll make you *eat* it."

The boy hesitated, wet his lips.

"Put it away, you bloody Cossack, or your name won't even be Francis. It'll be mud!"

The boy grunted, seeing something in his face that stopped him cold. After a moment, he folded the knife carefully and returned it to his pocket.

"Are you going to have me arrested, mister?" To the young boy, it was as if nothing else had happened.

"It depends," Jimmy said.

"On what?"

"On whether or not you're going to do this again."

"Oh, no." The boy shook his head violently back and forth. "Never."

"And it also depends on whether you're going to let someone else do your thinking for you again and talk you into something or whether you're going to do your *own* thinking and to *hell* with the gang."

The boy hesitated. "I'm going to do my own thinking."

"Promise?"

He glanced at Francis, then nodded.

"O.K.," Jimmy said. "You can both go."

"Hey," said Whitehead, "you're not gonna—"

"Shut up."

"But—"

"I said, shut up." He jerked his head at the counter. "We're short on chopped liver. Make some up."

Whitehead started to protest but reconsidered. He disappeared into the back, where they could hear him open the freezer and rummage around inside it.

"O.K.," Jimmy said. "Now scram, and from now on make your own decisions."

The boy smiled with relief and then almost ran to the door, followed closely by Francis. Jimmy gazed after them, hearing the door slam and the bell ring.

"Damn kid."

They returned to his office where Jimmy poured them both a fresh cup. He raised his with trembling fingers and then lowered it, slopping half the contents on his desk.

"Damn kid, he could have been me just five years ago. He did the same thing I did, only not with a gun."

"Hey," Johnny said. "Take it easy."

Jimmy looked at him and grinned. "We made a good team out there, didn't we?"

"You bet. Batman and Robin."

Jimmy laughed. "As a matter of fact, that was Curly's favorite comic book." He nodded toward the front of the store. "You think he learned something?"

"Maybe. Let's hope he did. That's all we can do." He paused. "Let's just hope he doesn't make some of the same mistakes we did."

"As Groucho would say, 'From your lips to God's ears.'"

"That's exactly what my father used to say," Johnny said, and then inhaled as the aroma of baked challah reached him, making his mouth water. How long had it been since he'd had a piece of his mother's bread? Five years. Five years, two months and nine days, though he expected some tonight. Taking another deep sniff, he went and closed the door for privacy.

"O.K.," he said, "now tell me."

"Tell you what?"

"Everything." He waved about at the store. "I want to know how you got this and why you've changed so much. You know, you don't even *sound* the same. You used to murder English. What did you do, take diction lessons?"

Jimmy settled back in his chair. "As a matter of fact, I did, plus I studied the Torah and Talmud and a few other things you wouldn't believe. All thanks to the old man." He motioned at a chair. "Sit down, Johnny. I think we've both got a lot to tell."

# Chapter
# Twenty-Seven

## The Sounding of the Shofar

Johnny sat down, thinking of the old man and not wanting to come out too directly when he asked.

"Wasn't he . . . hurt too? That is, he was an old man, and I heard he was on the critical list."

"Yes, he was," Jimmy answered. "Curly, the boy who was with me, really hurt him with his gun. But Groucho's tough. He was up in no time, cracked cranium and all."

"Bet you were relieved."

"Actually, I never had a chance to be. I was in a coma nearly a month. When I came out of it, the first thing I saw was the old man sitting there in a blur beside my bed, wearing a skullcap and prayer shawl and rocking back and forth. And you know what he was doing?"

"No."

"He was chanting, reading out of a prayer book and praying for me."

"For *you?* But if it hadn't been—"

"I know." He shook his head. "But the old man didn't look at it that way. As soon as he found out I was hurt and unconscious, he made me his own personal crusade. You know, he arranged for me to have a private room, and whenever I awoke, which was always in pain and sometimes in the middle of the night, he was always there. It was like he was keeping a vigil." He shook his head again. "That old man. He was amazing. You know, sometimes when he didn't know I was conscious, he'd pause in his praying, look up at the ceiling, and say, 'Master of the Universe, what do you want of this boy, he should suffer so much?'"

Johnny put his cup down, moved by the tone of respect which entered Jimmy's voice whenever he said "that old man."

"Must have cost him a mint."

"It did." He laughed. "Groucho used to joke about it and blame me. He kept saying he'd have to go back to being a 'bagel man' again and sell them on the street to make ends meet. 'Darling,' he'd say, 'you're my cross to bear, my little holdupnik.' But he was always happy when he said it."

"I don't believe it. Why did he help you so much?"

"I guess because he never married, though he often joked about his nagging wife, and didn't have any family left. Besides being alone, he saw my coming to his shop as somehow forging a link between us. I know it's incredible, but he sort of adopted me even though I already had a father. I became Groucho's son. And what happened to me became an affront he just wasn't going to tolerate." He waved his hands in the air, chuckling as he considered again how implausible it sounded. "Imagine, a white Jew adopting a black kid from the ghetto!"

Johnny laughed. "You're making all this up!"

"It almost sounds as if I am, doesn't it? Especially when you consider what a tough mean nut he was when Curly and I robbed his store. He almost killed me! But there's something else, too."

"What?"

"I think it had something to do with my pain. If there's one thing I've learned over the years from being with him and listening to him and studying with him, it's how much the Jews, like black people, have suffered throughout history. He used to tell me stories, such as how the Cossacks attacked his village in Russia and killed everyone in his family except him. I think . . . my sickness somehow made me a Jew to him, a member of his people, which in a way I now am. Anyway, it swept away everything I did to him and made him pull a few strings to get me placed on probation and released into his care. Curly, by the way, robbed two more stores and went to prison."

Johnny rose to pour himself another cup.

"And this shop?"

Jimmy shrugged. "He gave it to me—lock, stock, and barrel. All in my name, though I continue to split the proceeds with him right down the middle." He sipped his tea. "There's one last reason Groucho gave me this place. He's dying, Johnny."

Outside the office, the bell rang as someone entered. "I'm sorry," Johnny said. "I like Groucho. I used to pick up corned beef for my father and listen to his corny jokes. He gave free gumballs to us kids."

Jimmy sat forward and put his hands on the desk. "You know, I owe everything to that old man. If it hadn't been for him, I don't know what would have happened to me. He kept me going, hired the specialists and therapists and wouldn't let me give up. He used to bring books to me all the time and read to me from the Torah and the *Narrative of the Life of Frederick Douglass*. Imagine! An ignorant slave learns to read and escapes all the way to freedom. I learned a lot from Groucho, learned what love really is. And when I was well enough, he took me into this place and brought me along until . . . well, you can see for yourself."

"I sure can," Johnny said, looking around at the office. Outside, the cash register rang as the assistant manager made a sale.

"Tell me," he said, "why did you . . ."

"Do something so stupid as rob this store?"

"Yes."

"It's hard to explain." Even now, after all this time, he found it difficult to think about, much less discuss. "I guess I just kind of lost my way, felt like a failure." He closed his eyes and was locked in the broom closet again, listening to Evy's faint laughter. Even after all this time, the closet was as dark as ever.

"I often wondered," he heard Johnny say, "Lee and I never talked about it, but I think we both felt something happened to you, something you wouldn't tell us, which soured you on things. One day you were jumpin' Jimmy. The next you just started to go downhill."

He opened his eyes, finding for once he saw clearly. There was not even the ghost of a blur.

"Yes, well, I guess you were both right." He smiled. "Anyway, now that you're home, I guess we'll have plenty of time to talk about things. Right now, there's you. Where have *you* been? After . . ."

"The fight."

Jimmy nodded, realizing for the first time they shared an

experience that had twisted their lives. With him it was a betrayal in a broom closet and all that came after; with Johnny, it was a dead boy in a ring. In a way they were the same.

"Well," Johnny said. "I—"

"You don't have to talk about it," he said quickly.

Johnny clenched his fists. Jimmy watched them. *God, they're like meat choppers,* he thought, remembering how Johnny had knocked him out when they were boys. *No wonder he killed that boxer. No wonder my father wanted Johnny to fight.*

Jimmy's face twisted with memories. He forced a smile.

"Say, Johnny, you got a girl?"

Johnny brightened. "You bet!"

"Is it serious?"

"I think it is. I met her at a carnie in Kansas. She and her folks run a shooting gallery, and I was drawing pictures."

"Pictures?"

"Yeah, you know, sketches of farm boys and their Daisy Mae's. That sort of thing."

Jimmy laughed. "Wow, Kansas! Sounds like you've moved around."

"I have," Johnny said, recognizing with emotion his friend's deep throaty laugh, which had filled his childhood. "Been from coast to coast and back again," he said. "Froze my ass in Saskatoon and burned it in Yuma. Hopped the freight in Detroit and rode it to the Pacific. Hitched my way across deserts where I had only cactus and Gila monsters for company."

"Come on, you didn't do all those things, did you?"

"Sure did, plus a lot you wouldn't believe. I've been a cook, a waiter, a truck loader, a dock worker, and the worst lumberjack in Oregon." He laughed. "I think the worst job I ever had, though, and believe me, there've been some real nightmares, was in summer stock."

"Summer stock? You mean you acted?"

"Yeah. Believe it or not, I hit up a few years ago with this traveling troupe in South Carolina. Anyway, one of the members had run afoul of the law—floated some bad paper I think—and they needed someone to play the son Clarence in *Life With Father*." He flailed his arms, imitating a drowning swimmer. "*Glub, glub, glub,* can you imagine *me* as an actor? They even dyed my hair red for the role." He frowned and looked away, making Jimmy feel left behind. "Like a lot of people, they tried to make me something I wasn't."

Jimmy cleared his throat. "And your painting? You're still . . ."

"Yeah."

"Huh. You know, I never could get into that when we were kids. I knew it meant a lot to you and your father hated it." A thought occurred to him. "Now that you're home again, has he changed his mind about it? I mean, it's been a long time."

Johnny shook his head. "I haven't brought it up yet. I assume Picasso's still not his cup of tea."

"So what are you going to do?"

"Paint."

"Even though he—"

"Why not? Like you, I'm twenty-one, a man. And like you, I've read the Talmud. Know what it says there about what every person should do for himself?"

"What?"

"Says there are two things. One is to choose his own friend; the other is to choose his own teacher. Well, I've decided to choose my own teacher. Not a rabbi, as my father wants, but an art teacher, or more exactly, an art school." He stood up and put his cup down on the desk. "I've decided once and for all to be an artist, Jimmy. My father will just have to accept it. Oh, I'm going to study my religion again, only this time it's going to be on my own terms, and any meaning I get out of it will be *my* meaning. What I'm also going to do is try to work things out with my girlfriend. We love each other, but we come from different ways of life so it won't be easy. Whatever the case, I plan to finish high school and apply to the best art schools in the country."

"Why? I heard some folks say you were good."

Johnny gazed off into the distance, making him feel left behind again.

"Not nearly good enough. Oh, I've learned a lot on my own, but you can't teach yourself everything. You see, no one ever showed me *how*. No one ever showed me technique. No one ever told me how good I could be. I've got to find out. And right now I'm getting ready to make the first step. I've already wasted a lot of time, and I've got a long way to go."

But where was he going? He had often wondered where his art was taking him but had never found an answer. Now, for the first time, it occurred to him that he might, among other things, strive to capture the soul and vitality of his heritage. He saw the scrolls and his father's joyous face at Simchat Torah, where God was a living God. And then there was the shofar, the ram's horn, symbolic of devotion and renewal of faith, which was blown on such holy days as Rosh Hashanah, the Jewish New Year which commemorated the birthday of the world and Yom Kippur, the Day of Atonement. Yes, he would sound the shofar in his painting, perhaps not in the strictly realistic, representational way which was the only way his father would probably ever tolerate, but according to his own vision, whatever it might turn out to be. He would follow *his* road, wherever it might lead him. And he would do it at whatever cost to himself. At whatever cost to others.

He trembled and then looked down, his gaze returning from wherever it had been. Jimmy saw Johnny's powerful chest relax and his eyes find him again.

"You know, I've chosen only one teacher before in my life, a good one. Your father—how is he?"

Jimmy met his eyes.

"He's dead."

Outside, in the shop, the bell rang.

"Dead?"

"Cerebral hemorrhage. Happened a few months after you left. Too much drinking, plus other things." He lowered his eyes. "It was my fault in a way. After I got hurt he just . . . fell apart."

Johnny sighed. "God, I'm sorry. He was a good man."

"Thanks. He really cared about you." He paused. "He said you could have been champion."

Johnny found he was gazing at Bellows' fighters and looked away from their agony. "I'm sorry to hear. I really liked him." He waited a few seconds. "Your mother?"

He bit out the words. "Liver cancer, two years after my dad. She's buried next to him."

Johnny leaned forward and clutched his brow. "Good God."

"Not so good," Jimmy said. "My friend, even if they break your heart, appreciate your parents while you have them. Do everything you can not to make their life harder."

"I will, I swear it." Johnny wiped his eyes with a handkerchief. After a minute, he changed the subject. "Jimmy, how about Lee?"

"Esner?"

"Yeah. You know, now and then as I tramped about, I kept reading about him. In *Life* magazine they said he was up for the Heisman. Did he get it?"

"No, just missed out. But he sent me a postcard. He's expecting to get an offer with some pro team which could make him a millionaire before he's thirty."

"Wow. So he should come out on top just like he said he would."

"What do you mean?"

"Oh, come on, remember that day at the merry-go-round? We were in the sixth grade then."

"Oh, yeah. Some kind of game." Jimmy shut his eyes as a spasm sliced down his arm. "Seems so long ago. A lot of blood over the dam since then."

Johnny laughed. "Remember how we ran and scrambled over each other trying to get to the top, with the winner being on Easy Street for the rest of his life? What did Lee call it? The . . ."

He opened his eyes, beads of sweat glistening on his forehead.

"The merry-go-round man."

"Yeah, the merry-go-round man. Anyway, looks like he was right. Old love 'em and leave 'em Lee. Always had all the girls, and now he's going to be King Midas, too. Everything he touches turns to gold."

"Sometimes that's not so good."

"Why not?"

"I'm not sure," Jimmy said, taking out his handkerchief and blotting his face. "Maybe it's just you find out after a while you can't eat or drink what other people do, and you can't even . . . anyway, games like that are just bunk. People have such silly superstitions."

"It's sure worked out for Lee."

"Naw, it was just a kid's game. You know, I bet even the cavemen tried to hocus-pocus the gods. Old Lady Luck, roll of the dice. Bet it's old as time. Folks try to fix their future, flimflam their fate."

"Hey, you sound like a philosopher."

He shrugged, careful not to disturb his inner balance. "What else can you do, flat on your back for nearly a year, except wonder why it happened to you? I mean, why all this pain? Why didn't it happen to someone else? Did Yahweh have it in for me? Was it a cosmic decree? Or just bad luck or no luck at all? Does the universe even care? For a long time I wondered about such things."

"And what did you decide?"

"That it was a waste of time even thinking about it. Keep it up, you'll just drive yourself bats. I mean, damn it, things just happen, that's all. Sure, some of us are born hardier and better looking than others, with good luck seemingly camped on our doorstep, but existence is too complex for easy answers. I mean, no one's got it made, not really."

"You don't really believe that rot, do you?"

"Sure." He winked. "There's even a proverb that backs me up."

"What is it?"

*"Yeder mentsh hot zein peckel."*

Johnny shook his head in amazement. "You've come a long way, Jimmy."

"Know what it means?"

"I've got to confess my Yiddish is a bit rusty. It sounds like 'Every man has . . .'"

"'. . . his burden. *Every man has his burden.*' I've thought about it a lot, especially when I was in the hospital, and it happens to be true."

Johnny snorted. "I've heard my share of Yiddish proverbs, and that's one of the few which has always struck me as false. Worse, it's a lie, a democratic myth spawned by the desire to make all men equal. Well, they're not. Just look around you. Any fool can see that. Some people are better, richer, taller, healthier, luckier than others, and it's a naïve fiction to pretend otherwise. Some people are just born winners and sail through life without a cloud in the sky."

"Not true," Jimmy said. "I admit some have it easier than others, but no one really has it made."

"Oh, come off it. I've met some beautiful people without a brain in their heads who couldn't be happier. To quote you a proverb that *isn't* Yiddish: 'Ignorance is bliss.'"

Now it was Jimmy shaking his head. "Maybe their ignorance

is their burden, and what they don't know hurts them in more subtle ways, diminishes them without their knowing. Think of what they're missing, Johnny, all the things they can't appreciate or understand because everything comes too easily. In a deeper sense, do they ever really accomplish anything or know the satisfaction of triumphing over their limitations?" He paused. "'*Every man has his burden.*' It's an old proverb, and like a lot of them, a wise one."

"Maybe you're right. Maybe there are no easy answers and we all pay a price, one way or another."

"Sure, and some of the folks you'd never think would make it, turn out all right. As I said, there are no easy answers. I mean, look at *me*. I rob a store and damn near get crippled for life as a result. But because I did do something so stupid, I met a wonderful old man like Groucho who makes me see and think about things for the first time. Thanks to him I not only get my head squared around but have a fair chance of becoming a *mentsh* too. Plus I have my own delicatessen with the prospect of owning others in the future." He lifted his shoulders in a bemused shrug, reminding Johnny of the timeless Jewish gesture that was its model. "I mean, how can you figure it? You tell me."

"I guess you can't, not without a crystal ball or a Ouija board. Take the kid who just tried to steal from you, for instance. He could end up as President or . . ."

"Or he could end up with his face on a 'most wanted' poster in the post office. That's right, either way you just can't say, no more than you could have predicted the things *we've* done."

"Maybe you *are* right," Johnny said. "Anyway, whatever knocks you and I have taken, and God knows there's been a few, it looks like we both have an idea now where we're headed. Maybe it's not Lee's Easy Street, but it's sure not a dead end, either—that is, as long as our luck holds out."

Jimmy nodded. "And you can never be too sure it will, as Job found out. But you know, speaking of Lee, he always was different from us. I mean, we liked him, and it was great to have him around, but somehow he didn't quite fit."

"Sure, he was a winner!"

He looked at Johnny, seeing the crude hands that had killed

a boy and created art his father hated. In their own way, perhaps those hands had caused him as much pain as any he himself had known.

"I wonder," he said. "Master of the Universe, who knows the answer to anything?"

# Chapter
# Twenty-Eight

## Teacher's Pet

"Lee, honey, you look so good I could eat you!"

These words were not spoken by a girl but by his mother, who stood behind him in the mirror. Knotting his tie, he smoothed down the rust colored cardigan he wore over it.

"Aw, mom, sure you're not a little prejudiced?"

"Well, if I am, I have a right to be. If only your father hadn't left us. My, he'd be so proud to see you now, so tall and handsome!"

He frowned and parted his hair neatly to the right, careful that the brown blond wave fell forward just a little on his forehead. Why did she have to keep harping about his father, who'd abandoned them so long ago he could barely remember him? A shadow was all he was, a dark form he'd once seen above his bed. Maybe he hadn't even existed. Sometimes he'd actually wondered about that. And why did she have to bring him up *now* when the money was starting to roll in and he'd been able to buy her this house and arrange it so she'd never have to work again? After all, it had been *he* who had done it, not his father, who had just walked out of the house one day and never come back.

And why had his father left, anyway? It was odd his mother never wondered openly why he had gone but only expressed endless regret he had done so. Day in and day out she complained in her quiet insistent way, never letting him forget for a minute what his father had done. Could it be she knew why he had left, and his father had been trying to escape her? After all, his mother did cling to him at times, did somehow make him feel guilty about such things as what his father had done. Had his father been trying to save himself, keep himself from drowning? He studied his mother's sweet reflection in the mirror. No, he was being foolish, and even worse, disloyal. His mother was *wonderful,* and as for his father, who needed *him*? He certainly didn't. They could get along just fine without him, so why didn't his mother just forget him? Considering all he'd done for her, she almost acted ungrateful.

He flashed a smile at his image and thought of sunnier things. What ivories! *Lee, my boy, if Mrs. M. doesn't melt today, she ain't going to defrost for nobody!*

Giving his hair a final pat, he executed a neat about face and stood at attention.

"Sir, Seaman Esner requests leave to go on shore."

She laughed and removed an imaginary speck of lint from his sweater.

"You look fine, sailor, but liberty's going to cost you a kiss."

"Sir, that's the one thing I have plenty of."

He bent and kissed her, marveling again at how small she was and how she just seemed to dwindle year after year. Such a tiny woman, yet she held him so tight!

Affectionately, he gave her another kiss and went to the door.

"Lee?"

"Yes, mom?"

"Be sure to treat your teachers with respect, now. Don't give them any trouble."

"Yes, mom." (Twenty-two and she still treated him like a baby. Show respect to grownups, don't talk back.) He saluted her. "Don't wait up for me, Captain. Today's a new port, and I'm going to find a girl to show me around!"

Outside the sun was a golden disk shimmering on white sidewalks, the sky a blue lake decorated with cotton candy clouds. A picture book day, it seemed as perfect as the wicked beauty of the red Jaguar awaiting him at the curb.

Sailor slim, he walked to it and hopped in, sinking into the bucket seat with a sigh of contentment. Deep rich leather. A floor gearshift. An instrument panel as complex as an airplane's. Not to mention an engine that actually purred and could go a hundred and thirty into the wind. *Smokey, my man, I've finally got you beat!* he thought, touching the tachometer. Starting her up, he leaned back and gazed at the autumn leaves which sighed and rustled along the quiet suburban street where they lived and which served to prove just one thing.

The only thing you really needed in life was money.

Leaving the curb, he headed for the university. This was one part of the day he especially liked, the ten minute drive during which he could revel in his sleek silent sports car and feel it respond like a leopard to the slightest touch. Cornering was a breeze and it braked on a dime. At traffic lights his foot itched to floor the accelerator so he could lunge ahead of others and laugh in their faces. Twice he'd been stopped for speeding, but they had let him off with warnings when they had discovered who he was. One cop had even asked for his autograph to give his kid.

Seven thousand dollars for this speed monster and every penny paid. All he'd had to do was wait patiently for the highest bidder, who had topped Masterson State and all the others. In a complex under-the-table deal he hadn't even tried to understand, they had not only bought him this car, but supplied the down payment on the house. And with a pro contract practically in his pocket, all he had to do was sit pat and wait for the gravy.

A light turned red and he stopped reluctantly. *Easy now,* he reminded himself. *Don't go breaking any more sound barriers. There's no point in taking chances and besides, you don't want to miss Mrs. M's class.*

Thinking of *her* made his heart pound, and he thought of what a horny French major had called her. *La spécialité de la maison.* The specialty of the house. Another student had been less Gallic and more chilling in his praise. Mrs. M, he had said, was a "Killer." Nervously wishing the light would change, he checked his watch. Eight minutes and forty seconds. Speeding ticket or not, he'd better step on it!

By treating a red light and two stop signs as if they were starting flags dropped at Indianapolis, he reached the parking lot with four minutes to spare. Even his reserved parking space was a bend-the-rules bonus for being a football hero in a football town. There were full professors with yard-long credentials who had to walk farther to teach their classes than he did to attend his.

The campus stretched serene in the sun, a composite of other blue chip universities differing only in that its ivy was perhaps a little lusher, its green lawns perhaps a little better manicured, and the clock on the stately building that commanded the massive quadrangle perhaps a little more awesome by virtue of its tradition. One other quality set the school apart as well.

This year the university stood an excellent chance of winning the National Football Championship.

Tucking his book under his arm like a football, Lee broke into an anxious run. From a third floor dormitory window, a large poster of a Buddhist monk engulfed in flames fluttered in the wind, prophetic of the protests and unrest concerning Viet Nam and the war in Southeast Asia that were to sweep American campuses in the late sixties.

"Hey, white rabbit, don't rush. You're already late!"

He slowed as a short boy with glasses, beads, and shoulder length hair joined him on the sidewalk.

"What?"

"It's who you reminded me of just now, the rabbit with the watch in *Alice in Wonderland* who's worried about being late."

"Oh." Lee frowned at him. What a nowhere! To him there were two kinds of people: winners and "nowheres." This one would be King of the Nowheres if it weren't for the fact he was his only rival in Mrs. M's English class and always competed for her attention with his deep thinking and endless supply of literary allusions. What the hell was his name, anyway? Oh, yeah, Ulysses something, and he wouldn't even know that if he weren't the only other A in her class and always got in his way with his babble about Kafka and Kierkegaard when he wanted to talk to her. On campus, Ulysses had the distinction not only of being the poet, but a user of LSD who kept a pet python fourteen feet long.

"Hey, where'd the birds go?" Ulysses asked.

"What?"

"See that maple tree? The big one with all those leaves which have changed color? Yesterday there must have been a million birds in there, all of them chirping and singing their hearts out like Keats's nightingale. Now they're gone!"

"So what?"

"So what? Man, there must have been a million of them, all hidden by the leaves so you couldn't even see them. I tell you, that tree was alive!"

"Uh huh."

"And now they're gone, in just one day! Like they were . . . Hey, Esner, know what that tree reminded me of?"

"No I don't," he said, "and besides, it's getting late." He checked his watch. Two minutes to class. "If we don't hurry we'll be—"

"Remember those big jars we used to see in drugstore and barbershop windows when we were kids? You know, the absolutely *immense* ones filled with pennies or marbles that made you guess at the number to win a big prize? Well, that's what the tree looked like to me. A big huge leaf jar. Talk about time warps, I must have stood by that tree for hours just like a kid, trying to figure out how many birds there were in it. And you know what?"

"No."

He grabbed Lee's arm and moved close as if to reveal some secret, bringing with him the smell of unwashed flesh. His eyelids beat a frantic tattoo as if to some internal, hysterical rhythm. Lee backed off in distaste and started walking. What a nowhere! Probably queer as a three dollar bill and crazy to boot!

Ulysses hurried to keep up, babbling about karma and metempsychosis. Ahead were the steps. Looked like he was going to make it after all.

"Lee!"

Before he could start climbing, he was surrounded by admiring faces. A boy with a fiery crew cut beamed up at him.

"How does it look for the Rose Bowl this year?" the boy said. "The papers all say we got a real chance."

Ordinarily he'd be pleased by such attention, which was part of the reward for being a football hero and one of the best wide receivers in the country. Now, though, they were making him late! Ulysses had already disappeared through the doors at the top of the stairs.

"Looks real good," he said, turning to get around him.

The boy blocked him with a move that would have done him credit on the gridiron. "Do you hear?" he said. Lee saw a couple of nowheres nod their heads on cue. "Boy, it would be great if we had a shot at it this year." He raised his hand and patted Lee's sweater. "Too bad about the Heisman, though."

In the building, the bell rang.

"Huh?"

"I said, too bad about the Heisman. If anyone deserved it, you did. Man, you were robbed. With your stats I figured you a shoo-in for sure. It blew my mind when you finished third."

Being reminded brought back to him the mild disappointment he had known at the time.

"Yeah, well . . ."

"Hey, you'll get it this year. After all, now you're a senior."

Impatient, he started around him again, only to bump a girl he had barely noticed before.

"Lee, it must be awfully hard doing those exercises all the time."

The statement went nowhere but didn't have to. Anxious as he was to get to Mrs. M's class, which he was already late for, he still had time to recognize a come-on. This girl was frankly offering herself to him. All he had to do was reach out and grab. And she was pretty. Long blonde hair, bold breasts. Automatically, he smiled back and filed her away for future reference; then, detecting a weakness in their defensive line, he excused himself and slipped through.

Inside he was surprised to find the corridors empty. Where was everybody? He must really be late! If it hadn't been for those students . . . He started to run, then stopped. What was he running for? He didn't like being late to her class, but in a way it was a perquisite of athletes to skip their classes or to drift in nonchalantly whenever they wanted. It was a sign of status, and besides, some came late just to get attention or to irritate their teachers. Who knows, maybe if he came late often enough, she'd notice him more and prefer him to Ulysses. Then *he'd* be her favorite. Sure, it'd be easy to pull off. Hadn't he always had it easy with women teachers? Hadn't they always fallen all over him? Still, he didn't like to do such things, especially in her class, for as his mother pointed out, it showed a lack of class to come late and cause a disturbance.

Room 101. He paused at the door, heart pounding. The corridor was strangely silent. He entered.

Immediately he could tell attendance had already been recorded and his seat in the front row was taken. His entrance disrupted a discussion. The whole room turned to stare at him. Unaccustomedly embarrassed, he looked around and finally spotted one seat left at the far end of the back row. He moved awkwardly to it, excusing himself as he stepped on a foot, and sat down.

In front the professor turned around, and he gazed into the eyes of Mrs. Diana Murdstone.

# Chapter
# Twenty-Nine

## Diana in the Sun

He inhaled slowly and closed his eyes. She had come a long way from an Ohio high school and so had he. But more amazing than their climb was the fact they had turned up here together. The first time he had entered this class and seen her, it had been as if a fist had squeezed once upon his heart. At first he couldn't believe it, then it had seemed somehow right, as if fate were giving him a chance to complete what he had left unfinished half a continent away. For years he had sat in her classes in high school, becoming more and more enthralled by her long-haired, sleek-thighed beauty. At first she had been just another beautiful woman; then . . .

Mouth dry, he didn't even notice as Ulysses raised his hand and asked a question.

A card flipped in his efficient mind. Harvey Murdstone, her husband, had been found hanging at the wrong end of a rope. And hadn't there been talk he'd done it because she had played around so much he finally couldn't stand it? Come to think of it, someone had even suggested his old buddy Johnny Roth had been mixed up in that mess. Let's see. Oh, yes, Johnny had drawn a naughty picture of Diana which brought a lot of things out into the open. He'd heard Jimmy Wiggins and other kids talk about it at the time.

Right now there was a fervent discussion going on between her and Ulysses about Keats's "La Belle Dame sans Merci," a poem about a mortal destroyed by his love for a supernatural *femme fatale*. He himself didn't like the stuff much, though he usually had to read it only once to remember it verbatim.

*O, what can ail thee, knight-at-arms,*
*Alone and palely loitering?*
*The sedge has wither'd from the lake,*
*And no birds sing.*

And a few stanzas later, the poor knight has to start explaining about the lady who made him "so woe-begone."

*I met a lady in the meads,*
*Full beautiful, a fairy's child;*
*Her hair was long, her foot was light,*
*And her eyes were wild.*

Really, if a guy couldn't handle his broads, he ought to leave them alone! Yet she and Ulysses were going on about how *haunting* and *poignant* the poem was and what profound insights it offered into the romantic psyche. At that *last* comment, Lee switched off his mental recorder, preferring instead to focus on her long dark luxuriant hair, gorgeous body, and delectable thighs, which were encased in sleek black lace stockings.

After class he headed straight for her, only to run into Ulysses, who was gesturing excitedly.

"Man, Keats really trips out on agony. I mean, he really digs old Thanatos, ya know?"

"Well, some Romantics were fascinated by forbidden experience and even saw beauty in the Medusa. Others sought a preview of death by annihilating their senses through artificial means."

"Sure, Coleridge, De Quincey, all those drugs . . ."

So it went, out the door and down the hall, where Ulysses finally slapped off in his tennis shoes to another class. He followed her, only to get separated by some students. By the time he caught up, she was on the sidewalk.

"Professor Murdstone!"

She turned. "Yes, Lee?"

"I just want to apologize for being late."

"It's all right."

"Something held me up."

She touched his arm. "You don't have to explain. After all, you're always prompt. Even back in high school, I can't recall you being late once."

"That's because I liked your classes."

"Really?" she said brightly.

"Yes. I used to take all your English classes because I liked them so much."

"How odd, because you seldom said anything. Even Jimmy Wiggins spoke more than you."

For a moment, his mind went blank. "W-w-well, since you mention it, I got a letter from Jimmy just the other day."

"Did you?"

"Yes. He's all right now. Can you believe that after all his trouble, he even owns his own store?"

"Really."

"Yes, and you remember John Roth, don't you? Well, Jimmy mentioned him."

"Oh, yes." She shook her head, and he watched sun flecks play in her dark eyes. "The boy who ran away."

He had never seen her in the sun before, and he realized it accentuated her pale skin and made her look different. Faintly, she reminded him of someone, but who? He raised his eyes and scanned the vast green lawns of the campus, which now looked so ordinary and prosaic next to her, so inanely commonplace. At the other end of the immense quadrangle he could see the poster of the Buddhist monk rippling in the breeze. Miles above, a jet streaked across the blue sky, trailing a white furrow which gradually dissolved behind it.

He lowered his eyes to the poster and felt an instant jolt of recognition. For months he had noticed that poster as he walked back and forth to his classes, but he had never really seen it before. It portrayed a form swallowed by scarlet flames. Now, for the first time, he saw the form was a human torch, a monk in agony. *No,* he corrected himself, *not in agony.* Didn't such holy men practice some kind of mystical mind control or spiritual yoga and eliminate the pain? And didn't they set themselves on fire for a humanitarian ideal? Still, whether they did it voluntarily or not, they ended up as roast pork. And for those who didn't have any psychic protection, it must be very painful indeed. Hell on Earth.

Turning back, he looked at her and realized at once who she

reminded him of. Yes, it was someone in a fairy tale. Though it was nearly ninety in the sun, he shivered. Glossy black hair, pale ivory skin, red lips. Yes. A lovely but wicked witch.

He found he had to clear his throat to speak. "Maybe Johnny ran away, Professor, but he's come back. And according to Jimmy, he's going to complete his high school education." He wet his lips, which were dry. "Jimmy also said John plans to go on to art school."

She smiled. "As I recall, he did draw some interesting pictures." Her gaze ran like fingers up and down his body, and her smile widened. "Very interesting pictures indeed, I might add. One in particular really impressed my husband. He found it so *uplifting.*"

"I think I heard—"

"Yes, now that I think of it, he was fit to be tied by what your friend accomplished. It gave him a rise, you might say, made him look at things from a whole new perspective. However, despite its numerous merits, I just could not condone your friend's behavior. You see, John used to draw pictures in my English class when he thought I wasn't watching. But I knew. I *always* knew. One can always tell about such things."

"How?"

"There are ways, Lee. But you know, even though he was absorbed in his drawing, he still contributed more to class than you did. Some of his comments on *Heart of Darkness* and *The Picture of Dorian Gray*, for example, were profound, probing, full of insight. He seemed to be able to see beneath the bright surface where others just doted on appearances, to look beyond the face in the picture which the world worships as reality. A rare talent, indeed. I think he even understood me a little. But *you* just sat there."

"Well . . ."

"Though you always received A's, as I recall. You had all the facts."

"Because you were such a good teacher," he said, struggling to improve his standing, which he felt had suffered in some way. Should he plunge, take a chance? "Actually, the reason I took your courses wasn't the stories and stuff. It was *you.*"

"I know."

He felt grass beneath him. Without noticing it, they had moved off the sidewalk and into a nook sheltered from view. A couple of leaves drifted down, adding to the carpet beneath them. She leaned back against a wall of ivy.

"You knew?"

"Yes."

"All the time?"

"I know many things, Lee."

He swallowed and moved closer. Despite the bright sun, this leafy enclosure seemed to be cave-like, a place of shadows. He couldn't even see her clearly.

"What do you know?"

"I know how easily things come to you."

"I—"

"And I also know how superficial you are."

He started to protest, but her hand was stroking his cheek. "My little hollow man," she crooned, "I've known all along just how terribly you've wanted me."

"You have?"

"Oh, yes. Now, why don't you tell *me*?"

He felt dizzy. Still, habit prevailed and he put his arms around her, slipping her his best smile.

"Professor, sir, I'd rather show you."

"Gentleman Lee, ever the man for actions, not words." Slowly, she brought her knee up in its sleek black stocking and moved it between his thighs. He felt himself stiffen.

"Sometimes that's all I want," she whispered, pulling his head down. "Just actions, not words."

*She took me to her elfin grot,*
*And there she wept, and sigh'd full sore,*
*And there I shut her wild wild eyes*
*With kisses four.*

Her lips tasted like wild berries of a kind he had never tasted before. Something indefinable eluded him in them. The air pulsed with incense, and he was breathless when she finally released him, feeling as if he would swoon.

"Take me to your car," she said. "*Now.*"

# Chapter
# Thirty

## The Awakening

Lightheaded, he obeyed, scratching himself on a bush, and as he walked across campus beside her, the university's clock began to strike twelve, shattering the placid stillness. In the parking lot he recovered enough to wave a proud hand at his Jaguar.

"Nice, huh?"

"Is it as fast as it looks?"

"You better believe it. Hop in."

*I set her on my pacing steed,*
*And nothing else saw all day long . . .*

Why did that poem keep running through his head? Streaking down the highway he glanced at her, not quite believing it was she who sat beside him. She gazed silently ahead, a lovely, dark-eyed mystery.

"Professor Murd—"

"Diana."

"What?"

"Just call me Diana."

"Oh, sure. Anyway—Diana—I was always curious about something."

"Curiosity kills cats, Lee."

"Yeah, well, it was about your husband, Mr. Murdstone. By the way, I was sorry to hear . . ."

"Ask it, Lee."

He avoided a pothole. "Well, what I wanted to know . . ."

"Should I finish it for you?"

"You know what I was going to ask?"

"As I said before, I know many things, Lee. You were about to ask me why I married such an older man as Harvey Murdstone, especially since he didn't seem to have anything special to recommend him. Am I right?"

He stared out at the beautiful fall day. "Yes."

"You were also wondering," she said, "if it was because he was such a good lover. Under his blighted surface, did there burn the randy heart of a Byron? In other words, could he *swyve* all night? Isn't that what you really wanted to know?"

He nodded, troubled that she saw through him so easily.

She laughed brightly, "Don't let it bother you, Lee. It was what all the so-called men were asking at the time. You would have been different if you hadn't wondered, too."

"Well, I didn't want to—"

"No, I'm sure you didn't. Anyway, would you really like to know, Lee?" she asked, leaning toward him with glittering eyes. "Would you really like to know what I've never told anyone before?"

Hypnotized, he stared back.

"If you want to."

"The real reason I married Harvey," she said slowly, seeming to savor each syllable, "was not his intelligence or his kindness, but his pure and infinite capacity for *suffering.*"

He blinked, automatically applying the brake as the light changed.

"I don't understand."

"Don't you? Of course you don't, not my sweet, delicious little Lee with the lemon meringue mind."

"Don't say that!"

"Why not?"

He frowned, disturbed by the way her gaze kept chipping at him. Deep inside, a warning sounded.

"Diana—"

"Turn right, Lee."

"Oh, sure."

Obediently, the powerful car cornered and streaked down the street. A child's red beach ball bounced across a lawn. "I don't get it," he said. "Why would you want him to suffer?"

She laughed, her fingers weaving labyrinths of delight to trap his confusion.

"Harvey was so pure. He believed in all the traditional values. Love, truth, especially fidelity."

"And you?"

She winked. "All the men, and all the boys I wanted. Some women too, if the truth be told. And Harvey, well—"she stroked her thigh—"he just couldn't stand it. So one night he decided to anoint a sacred rope and dance on air. He danced so divinely, and I was privileged to watch him."

The words lingered for him to consider in horror.

"Why?" he whispered.

"Why?"

"Yes. *Why* would you want him to suffer and die? What did you have to gain?"

She laughed and then her face looked lost and uncertain. Watching, he glimpsed the faintest remaining innocence beneath the corruption. Why was she this way? Maybe even she didn't know, and the answer, if there was one, was lost somewhere in her past, lost beyond recovery. Maybe it had been just a little thing, hardly noticeable at the time. Or perhaps it was something terrible she didn't want to remember.

He swallowed, seeing her turn to him with a smile that tantalized and stirred memories. What were those rumors he'd heard about her? Those whispers hinting at strange things she had done? Let's see, some of the boys had been holding a bull session in the dormitory one night when he'd come in . . .

Before he could remember, she turned to the front again and directed him to their destination. Cutting the ignition, he opened the door of his car and walked around it to let her out.

Diana's apartment was completely different from what he'd imagined. There was no medieval castle, palace, or even a mansion with exotic battlements and a fairyland aura as dreamlike and unreal as their conversation. Instead he found an ordinary little townhouse bathed in harmless sunlight with kids squealing in a playground nearby. He stood looking up at it, half expecting to see gargoyles and a Gothic spire or two. Where were the towers and turrets, the "Banners yellow, glorious, golden"? Where were the secret chambers and passageways? Briefly, hearing the children's cries, he felt disappointed, as if she had cheated him.

Inside, though, her spell seized him without warning and even stronger than before. Her bedroom was twilight and wind chimes rang softly in a breeze, stirring subliminal echoes (where had he heard chimes before, where?) Before him, a mobile of dragons revolved as if his own breath were stirring it.

She loosened her blouse. Her skirt fell, rustling. He took a step toward her, ignoring the warning that now flared like wildfire through his veins. In the moment before he spoke, he thought of pentagrams and pacts with the Devil.

"I always knew this would happen," he said.

"Did you?"

"Yes. Somehow I always knew we'd be together some day. I just knew it. It was like . . ."

"Like what, Lee?"

He searched helplessly for a word.

"Like fate, Lee?" she said, her face a mere shadow. She laughed, her voice sinuous ripples on a lake at midnight, and came toward him. "Then embrace your destiny!"

His lips accepted her white shoulder and swallowed her moans while she buried her fingers in his hair and drew him slowly to the bed. Oblivious to everything but her, he let himself be led. Then he seemed to be falling a long way in slow motion as if in a dream, and sank heavily upon her, seeking her fragrance. He heard her laughter just ahead, around some corner in a maze. Then her teasing changed and by degrees he found her again. She became dark with sin and witchcraft. Enchanted, he descended into her sensual warmth while her head thrashed from side to side on the pillow.

"Now! *Now!*"

Her fingers took him—a fiery lance. He rose slightly and let her hurl him into her depths.

And she moved beneath him, bore him upward upon her waves. His heart surged with love unbridled. Too soon he exploded and throbbed madly into her, blending himself with her shadows. He slowed.

"Don't stop!"

He continued, and such was his ardor he needed only a brief period to warm again. Faster and faster he moved, helpless before her insistence, and in time his seed surged into golden sands where he now sought an oasis.

She tore at his back, her eyes brimming with tears. "Damn you, I told you not to stop!"

Wilting, he felt the beginnings of fear. Why couldn't she let him rest? How much could she want? She seemed insatiable, a well which could never be filled. He drove himself against her, pleasure dissolving into pain. His breathing turned ragged. Her sleek thighs rose and locked around him. She scratched. She ground. Straining above her, he realized that all his life he had not only used women but been devoured by them. First Rosemary, then Mrs. Futch, even his own mother. Now it was Diana. In a way he was just fruit to be eaten and discarded as seeds. And this woman, this demented creature from his past he had thought he knew . . . How many other men had she known, consumed as she was consuming him?

> I saw pale kings, and princes too,
> Pale warriors, death pale were they all;
> They cried—"La belle dame sans merci
> Hath thee in thrall!"

> I saw their starv'd lips in the gloom
> With horrid warning gaped wide,
> And I awoke and found me here
> On the cold hill's side.

No. Suddenly, Lee saw it didn't have to be this way. As Diana tried to pull him down into her emptiness, he experienced a unique moment. For the first time, he saw clearly the long line of beautiful girls he'd mechanically worked his way through and realized he had a choice. He could actually change the pattern of his life. He did not have to submit anymore to Diana Murdstone simply because it was his habit or nature and because she was the most irresistible and darkly delectable woman he had ever known. Why couldn't he change and have a normal life and relationship? Why couldn't he love somebody as other young men did?

His heart pounded with hope. He could be different. He could be better and deeper, not so superficial as Diana called him. He could leave right now. Leave *her*.

He rose from her body, and Diana's sharp red nails lashed out, slicing his cheek. "What are you doing?" she cried as he left the bed. "Don't go. I want more!"

He hesitated, feeling her hunger reel him in. He fought it with all his strength. She was so lovely and bewitching. For the first time, though, understanding dawned and he felt pity for her. Like the creature in the poem she taught, Diana was empty, and her need could never be fulfilled.

"No, Diana," he said. "Whatever you want, you'll have to get it from somebody else."

She stared at him and screamed an obscenity. He watched her rise and leave the room naked, taking whatever remained of her spell with her.

A thousand years seemed to have passed since he'd come here. Trembling, Lee felt pain and touched his cheek. Blood. He stared at it, remembering how Johnny Roth had beaten Jimmy Wiggins with just one punch many years ago.

He closed his eyes and was kneeling beside Jimmy again, who was strangely still. About him were the woods, starker and more intense than anything he had ever seen. Everything seemed preternaturally bright, stripped forever of the illusions of boyhood. He could see a dead tree swarming with insects and taste the smell of fear. He touched Jimmy.

"Hey, Jimmy, you O.K.? Wake up!"

A bird screeched somewhere. For a moment he saw not the woods but Jimmy's face on a snow white pillow beneath an oxygen tent, sleeping on in a seemingly endless coma. He started to scream, but before he could the woods returned, sprinkled with the mockery of buttercups and he whirled toward Johnny, whose face mirrored his own horror. He opened his mouth, almost choking on the words.

"Holy cow, Johnny, I think you killed him!"

Johnny and Jimmy. He came awake then. He remembered the letter he'd received from Jimmy and decided it was long past time he looked them up. Lee smiled with anticipation, surprised at how much he missed his old friends.

Before him, chimes rang softly. The mobile turned, its dragons chasing each other round and round, going nowhere. He watched them.

*("Round and round she goes,*
*And where she stops, nobody knows!")*

*Nobody knows.* But if nobody knew for sure where the merry-go-round stopped and where everybody ended up, maybe there was hope. Maybe he could change if he just tried hard enough and remembered what was important. Something had happened today. For the first time he had recognized the pattern in his life and realized he had a choice. He could actually change things if he was strong enough. What's more, he had done just that by rejecting Diana even though it had torn him up inside. It was only the beginning, and he knew he faced an uphill battle. Maybe it was like he was in a tough football game for the university, and he was trying to catch one of those hopelessly overthrown passes he didn't have a chance in the world of even touching.

But at least he had to try.

# About
# the Author

JOHN B. ROSENMAN, a retired English professor from Norfolk State University, has published over 300 stories in *The Speed of Dark, Weird Tales, Whitley Strieber's Aliens, Galaxy, The Age of Wonders*, and elsewhere. He's also published twenty books, including SF novels such as *Speaker of the Shakk* and *Beyond Those Distant Stars*, winner of AllBooks Review Editor's Choice Award (Mundania Press), and *Alien Dreams, A Senseless Act of Beauty*, and *The Merry-Go-Round Man* (Crossroad Press). MuseItUp Publishing has published four SF novels. They are *Dark Wizard, Dax Rigby, War Correspondent*, and two in the Inspector of the Cross series: *Inspector of the Cross* and *Kingdom of the Jax*, a sequel which appeared last year. MuseItUp also published *The Blue of Her Hair, The Gold of Her Eyes* (winner of Preditor's and Editor's 2011 Annual Readers Poll), *More Stately Mansions*, and the dark erotic thrillers *Steam Heat* and *Wet Dreams*. His time-travel tale *Killers* is an Editor's Top Pick at Musa Publishing. Some of John's books are available as audio books from Audible.com. Two of John's major themes are the endless, mind-stretching wonders of the universe and the limitless possibilities of transformation—sexual, cosmic, and otherwise. He is the former Chairman of the Board of the Horror Writers Association and the previous editor of *Horror Magazine*.

John welcomes comments from readers at jroseman@cox.net and invites them to visit his web site at www.johnrosenman.com and blog at www.johnrosenman.blogspot.com. His Facebook author page is https://www.facebook.com/JohnBRosenman?ref=hl/

Curious about other Crossroad Press books?
Stop by our site:
http://store.crossroadpress.com
We offer quality writing
in digital, audio, and print formats.

Enter the code FIRSTBOOK
to get 20% off your first order from our store!
Stop by today!